SUNLESS
SOLSTICE

SUNLESS SOLSTICE

Strange Christmas Tales for the Longest Nights

Edited by
LUCY EVANS & TANYA KIRK

This collection first published in 2021 by
The British Library
96 Euston Road
London NW1 2DB

Cataloguing in Publication Data
A catalogue record for this publication is available from the British Library

ISBN 978 0 7123 5410 3
e-ISBN 978 0 7123 6709 7

Frontispiece illustration features a detail by Cecil Aldin from Washington
Irving, *Christmas Day*, London: Hodder & Stoughton, 1910.

Cover design by Mauricio Villamayor with illustration by Sandra Gómez
Text design and typesetting by Tetragon, London
Printed in England by CPI Group (UK) Ltd, Croydon, CR0 4YY

CONTENTS

INTRODUCTION

How do you like your weird Christmas tales? Is gathering round the fire with delicious food in a country house a key component? Or do you require nothing more than snow and ice and chilling encounters? As a character in one of our featured stories says: 'Oh dear, here's Christmas again. Isn't it awful! I'm going to bed. I shall sleep, and I hope dream, until this dreadful thing is over'. Perhaps this character wouldn't enjoy some of the more conventional tales in this volume but with this third entry of festive ghost stories in the Tales of the Weird series we also bring together some less traditional tales with a wintry theme. The winter solstice, considered so significant in many cultures, brings the shortest day of the year and the extreme of winter. The symbolic death and rise of the sun and the hope that comes with longer days is a fitting time for a ghost story. The tales featured in this collection present the very height of the season, from a snowy mountain ascent to a chilling encounter on the ice.

The stories in this collection, presented in chronological order, were published from 1893 to 1974 and feature some writers who may be immediately familiar. Dames Daphne du Maurier and Muriel Spark are household names. However, of Lettice Galbraith and Frederick Manley we know very little. Bringing both the well-known and undiscovered authors together in this volume gives us a rich tapestry of winter stories.

In this selection we see some of the familiar tropes of the festive story. There are snowy London scenes, Christmas parties and 'plum puddings, mince pies and Yorkshire ham', which we encounter in

'A Fall of Snow'. There are cloven hooves and haunted rooms and a visit from a medium. But what less traditional themes do we find in these stories? Marriage and affairs of the heart are at the centre of many of these stories. From the unexpected reappearance of Ganthony's wife to the ghostly comeuppance in 'The Man Who Came Back', from the brutal conclusion of 'The Third Shadow' to the sinister apple tree that haunts du Maurier's story. Unhappy relationships provide the basis for ghostly goings on and shocking vengeance. The black cat, considered lucky or unlucky depending on your folklore, here appears in malevolent form and the story makes for a decidedly untraditional Christmas Eve fable. Those like our character in the opening paragraph, who appears in 'Mr Huffam', will be delighted to read a story based around the Society for the Abolition of Christmas which can be found in 'The Leaf-sweeper'.

This selection of stories was confirmed during the warmth of summer, perhaps a strange time to be reading such a wintry collection. But there is something about reading these stories on a warm day and still feeling the chill of a well told ghost story. We hope winter readers enjoy the shudders and strange scenes of the stories in this selection as much as we have enjoyed editing them.

LUCY EVANS, *Curator, Printed Heritage Collections*
TANYA KIRK, *Lead Curator, Printed Heritage Collections*

A NOTE FROM THE PUBLISHER

The original short stories reprinted in the British Library Tales of the Weird series were written and published in a period ranging across the nineteenth and twentieth centuries. There are many elements of these stories which continue to entertain modern readers; however, in some cases there are also uses of language, instances of stereotyping and some attitudes expressed by narrators or characters which may not be endorsed by the publishing standards of today. We acknowledge therefore that some elements in the stories selected for reprinting may continue to make uncomfortable reading for some of our audience. With this series British Library Publishing aims to offer a new readership a chance to read some of the rare material of the British Library's collections in an affordable paperback format, to enjoy their merits and to look back into the worlds of the past two centuries as portrayed by their writers. It is not possible to separate these stories from the history of their writing and as such the following stories are presented as they were originally published with minor edits only, made for consistency of style and sense. We welcome feedback from our readers, which can be sent to the following address:

British Library Publishing
The British Library
96 Euston Road
London, NW1 2DB
United Kingdom

THE GHOST AT THE CROSS-ROADS

—⌒ An Irish Christmas Night Story ⌒—

Frederick Manley

FIRST PUBLISHED IN THE
SOUTH LONDON PRESS, DECEMBER 1893

The Internet Speculative Fiction Database lists only one story by Frederick Manley, and this story is reproduced here. The *South London Press*, where this tale was printed, is still published today but little is known of Manley.

In 'The Ghost at the Cross-Roads' we have an Irish Christmas ghost story in the most traditional vein. The story begins: 'Night, and especially Christmas night, is the best time to listen to a ghost story' and as a reader you couldn't agree more. The vivid descriptions of the joyful Christmas scenes, the 'hills of potatoes, lakes of soups, mountains of roast beef' draw the reader in and only serves to heighten the chilling tale which unfolds when a stranger arrives in their midst.   —LE

Night, and especially Christmas night, is the best time to listen to a ghost story. Throw on the logs! Draw the curtains! Move your chairs nearer the fire and hearken!

Not one among the little group that sat in the snug parlour of Andy Sweeny's homestead, that wild Christmas of 1843, when Mrs Sweeny went to the window and drew the snow-white curtains very close, remarking at the same time, 'God shelter all poor travellers!' but whose thoughts were as plainly expressed in the general huddling-up which took place as though each one had told his neighbour his particular idea of comfort; and when, in answer to the good woman's prayer, they joined their voices in one deep, fervent 'Amen!' and huddled together in the brave glow of the turf fire, the general sentiment of the party was published by a red-haired, dapper little fellow named 'Reddy,' who said, in a rich voice:

"'Tis thanking God we should be for this comfort, not forgetting Mrs Sweeny!'

Although the Sweenys were known the county over for their hospitality, on this particular night they outdid all their previous efforts at entertaining. The oak table in the middle of the floor was covered from end to end with good things. We say good things, and we mean it so. There were no wafer-like sandwiches on that table, nor cold liquids in colder bottles, nor frail china-ware (no china-ware could stand food so substantial), not fancy salads, nor any of those dainties which as good as say to a hungry man, 'Come and eat me; I'm too nice to be lying here,' and which, when he has done them justice, spoil his evening's enjoyment and cause life to be a burden to him.

No; there were no such insidious edibles on Mrs Sweeny's table. To think of that supper is to be hungry. Hills of potatoes, all in their coats on account of the severe weather; lakes of soup, mountains of roast beef, with goose and turkey in the valleys between; pigeons, imprisoned in cells of crust, in which were little slits like loopholes, through which the inmates might peep—indeed, one brave bird that, we daresay, had become alarmed at the great number of diners, was attempting to escape, and actually succeeded in getting a leg through the bars, where he stuck and became discouraged; mounds of bread and butter; the whole Pie family, from plebeian Apple to rich Mrs Mince, were there in their crusty suits. The table mumbled and groaned. But who cared for the table's sorrows? In truth, who could think of anything but gladness in that home of light and joy on that frozen night?

Outside, the storm raged. The country around, a bleak stretch of moorland, was buried deep in snow. The winds had been busy, and many were the quaint mansions they had built, and strange and weird were the changes they had wrought. The sign-post at the four cross-roads—a most commonplace affair in clear weather—was now a terrible monster with four hideous arms, that were thrust out to seize the belated traveller. All traces of the road were lost, and it would have gone hard with a stranger had he been caught in the storm that December night. Derry Goland, in King's County, Ireland, is so drear and wild that the destroying elements have made it their meeting-place. Here the winds gather and plan their courses. Here they start from, and to this place return. Any winter's night you may hear them. At first they whisper among themselves as they map out their ways. Then may be heard deep murmurs, angry murmurs, shaking the boughs, as though the Storm King had given out orders which they did not like.

How the Storm King hated Andy Sweeny's snug home and the cheerful light shining from the windows, throwing a golden pathway into the night!

More turf for the fire! Every one has a glass of steaming punch in his hand; every one's face is lighted with love and radiant with joy; every one toasts every one, sings merry songs, dances with his sweetheart, or makes love to her in some shady corner, while the aged every-ones make matches for their boys and girls; and the blind fiddler plays away for dear life. The flames grow brighter as the storm without increases in violence. The punch glows a deeper red and sparkles as with delight. The old clock in the corner has a drowsier tick, and is at peace with the world, for the jolly round face on its dial smiles on the scene; and even the table, forgetful of its complaints, has ceased to groan. In short, there never was a happier home; there never were such music and such punch as Mrs Sweeny's, nor jollier souls to drink it.

The floor had just been cleared for dancing, and the fun was at its height, when out in the storm, seeming far away, there rose a cry— a terrible cry—a cry that spoke the anguish of a soul. Those within were silent, and listened with blanched faces to that cry without.

'God save us!' cried Andy. 'What was that?'

'The Lord bethune us and all harm! It was the banshee's cry!'

At this name, so fearful to an Irish ear, the children ran to their mothers and buried their little heads. Wives clung to their husbands, sweethearts to their sturdy lovers, and all waited anxiously for a repetition of the cry. Then something happened which caused all hearts to stand still and sent the cold blood rushing down the back. It was a human voice calling aloud for help! Soon after, the crunch of flying feet was heard. They came nearer and nearer.

'Open the door! Fling it wide!' cried Andy.

Willing hands soon had a broad pathway of firelight streaming from the doorway. The storm rushed in and scattered the turf and tore pictures from their places and made sad havoc with everything. But no one cared; no one noticed it. All eyes were watching a man who came flying towards the house; for though it was a blustering night, the moon peeped at intervals through the storm-rift clouds, casting a ghostly light. And now it shone down upon this figure that sped to the door and cried, in a voice made weak by fear and running, 'Save me!' then tottered across the threshold and fell prone upon the sanded floor.

Andy Sweeny turned quickly to the door, and, listening, peered long and searchingly into the darkness. At last he cried out:

'Who's there?'

The only answer was the soughing of the wind across the moor, and a gruesome answer it was.

'Who's there?' asked Andy again.

'Sure, no wan, avick,' returned his wife. 'Shut the door and be aisy.'

Andy cast a rueful, backward glance at the door, as Mrs Sweeny led him away from it.

'Look at the poor man foreninst ye!'

The poor man before the fire was unconscious. One motherly body was chafing his cold hands, another was bathing his forehead with punch she had seized in her hurry instead of water, and yet another forced the steaming liquor between his clenched teeth.

He was a young—a boy almost—whose age might have been guessed as twenty, and guessed correctly. That he was a stranger in Derry Goland was easily discovered, for the suit he wore was made of fine cloth and cut in the most approved style. Fashionable clothes were as common in Derry Goland as bears, and there wasn't a bear in the county. A silk-lined cloak, thrown back from his broad shoulders, disclosed a sparkling gem that winked and blinked at the firelight as though the sudden brilliancy was too much to stand. His features, although well formed and regular, had a suggestion of weakness in them, especially the chin and mouth, which lacked firmness, and wore a smiling expression of gentleness more fitted to a woman than a man. The people immediately divined that a gentleman, presumably an Englishman, judging from his dress, had fallen among them, and they went to work on him as though he were the dearest friend of each man who bent over him, or the husband, brother, or sweetheart of each good woman who carried pillows for the weary head and brought a glow of life into the pale face, so numerous were the little offices performed, so heartfelt and deep their solicitude. At length, to the great relief of all, the stranger slowly opened his eyes.

'Here ye are, sir, safe an' sound!' cried an old woman, cheeringly. 'Look up, sir; 'tis wid fri'nds y' are.'

The young man raised himself up, and asked Andy to assist him to a seat. He trembled violently as he moved with livid face to the chair which Andy had placed near the fire for his use. They stood at a respectful distance from the young man, regarding him with looks of half fear, half wonder. As the moments passed, he seemed to grow stronger; and presently he raised his head from his breast, in which position he had been gazing intently at the fire, and asked whether any one believed in ghosts.

17

'Ghosts, your honour?'

'Ghosts.'

'We do, your honour,' chimed in an old woman. ''Tis me well knows we do. Wasn't there Mary Doolan's mother—Lord rest her!—dead and gone ten years come next Ash Wednesday—as fine a woman as iver put foot to leather, as I've often said, and always will say, please God, if I die for it—an' I don't care who knows it—a fine lump of a girl when I first knew her. I knew her mother before her—a dacent body, too, who married Mike Carlin after he'd buried his first wife, and then married Pat Doolan when Mike kicked the bucket—God forgive him for a rascal! Didn't Mary Doolan—rest her soul!—didn't she meet a ghost at the cross-roads? Didn't she?'

As no one contradicted, the old woman was preparing to give the story in its entirety, when the stranger interrupted.

'At the cross-roads, did you say?'

'Tin years come Ash Wednesday. She—'

'There is a milestone near by'—he appeared to be murmuring to himself, as he kicked the blazing turf with the toe of his riding-boot—'a flat milestone, like a gravestone?'

'The same place, sir. And Mary Doolan—rest her soul!—a dacent, thrifty—'

'Which of you is the landlord of this place?'

'There's no landlord here,' said Andy Sweeny. 'This is my home. These are my friends and neighbours.'

'Will you give me a bed? I'll see that you are paid for it.'

'You are welcome to my place, sir, without money. I don't want that,' said Andy, rather sharply.

The young man noticed the touch of anger in Andy's voice.

'I beg your pardon. I did not mean to hurt you. I hardly know what I am saying.'

He buried his face in his hands, leaning his elbows on his knees.

Andy's guests, who but lately had stood in fear of the young stranger, now looked at him with great pity stamped on their kindly faces; and even the garrulous old woman whom he had interrupted so persistently ventured close to him, saying, in a friendly way:

'Is it on Christmas, sir, ye'd be givin' way so?'

'Christmas!'

'Av course. What else? Here, Mrs Sweeny, ma'am, if yez please, a glass o' punch for his honour!'

The young man had been stony hearted, indeed, could he have refused the steaming glass which comely Mrs Sweeny handed to him; hard as granite had he not melted before the expressions of homely sympathy that poured from all sides in a shy manner, as if they feared to offend, for only sufferers, brothers in sorrow, no matter what their station in life may be, know how to comfort sufferers.

The fiddler went to work once more, and played better than ever, too. The punch flowed again. The rough but sonorous voices joined in familiar airs that brought back many a half-forgotten holiday time. Hands were joined in reels and jigs, until it seemed that the storm had at last taken hold of Andy's cottage and was shaking it to pieces, so lively were the couples who 'lathered the flure wid their heels,' as Reddy remarked. The young people who had sought the terpsichorean honours of the evening, 'by holding out to tire each other down,' had at last tired themselves, and all sat round the fire, anxious for some other amusement than that which left them fatigued and short of breath. The old lady spoken of before, with the inherent instinct of a gossip—for gossips are born, not made—said to the stranger during a lull in the conversation:

'Did ye see a ghost tonight, sir?'

Andy Sweeny, imagining the old woman was annoying the gentleman, quickly interposed, and begged he would not mind her thoughtless questions.

'I am not offended,' said he. 'But I hardly know how to answer.'

'Who was it that chased you when you came running here, screaming for help?'

'Something in black.'

'How did it come to happen? You must pardon the question, sir, but as this is Christmas night, and knowing it is a time for great freedom, I thought you might be good enough to tell us all about it, sir—asking pardon once again, if I've offended you.'

Andy Sweeny, like most men of ordinary intelligence and education among the Irish peasantry, had the reputation of being a 'foine shpaker' and a 'shmart man;' and when he had finished his tentative address, his guests winked and nodded among themselves to express their great admiration, and Reddy even went so far as to say, 'There's for you.'

'It's all very strange, to be sure,' said the gentleman. Then he added, with a little forced laugh that would hardly come from a person whose nerves were in good condition, 'I will tell you all that happened.'

At these words, which promised the glorious entertainment always to be had from a ghost story, more especially when you sit in the midst of friends before a roaring, crackling fire, with a sparkling punch in your hand, listening to the storm that rattles the windows and doors, and hurls the snow down the broad chimney, hissing into the fire, as if it hated to see you so snug, and was determined to extinguish the cheerful blaze. It is then your mind wanders over dolorous, windswept moorland, trudges along the bleak path on the hillside, struggles with the storm on the highway, where every white-robed tree is a phantom and every rock a hiding-place of robbers and hideous somethings that await your approach and crouch in readiness to spring upon you.

Now every inoffensive oak is a terrible Briareus, stretching out its gaunt arms to seize you; now you feel certain a thing is dogging your footsteps while you fear to look behind, knowing that you would encounter its awful glance and be struck dead that instant, until the fancy becomes so strong that you break into a trot, from that to a run, and finally, with its footsteps but a few yards behind and gaining with every stride, coming so close you can feel its breath over your shoulder, your run quickens—faster—faster yet, till it ends in a wild flight, while you see nothing, think of nothing but it, and only stay the mad chase when the ruddy lights from some cottage window tell you that men, fellow-creatures, people of flesh and blood, are within hailing distance.

Now the fear, which up to this moment has paralysed your tongue, comes forth in one scream that startles the quiet villager, and brings him, candle in hand, to his door, where he finds you stretched insensible upon the snow, and whence he carries you to his blazing turf fire, beside which you slowly regain your senses, thanking Providence you are saved. No wonder the cottagers huddled round the fire! So Andy's guests being Irishmen, and having adamantine faith in the existence of all manner of 'uncanny' things, awaited the stranger's story with breathless interest.

'I may presume,' he began, 'that you all know Squire Goodfellow?'

'We do! Long life to his honour!'

'Well,' he continued, 'I was returning from his house to the inn at the village, where at present I am staying. What I had been doing there it is needless to say. The squire, who, as you all well know, is a downright good fel—gentleman, endeavoured to dissuade me from going home afoot in the storm, and invited me to sleep under his roof until morning. I, knowing he already had as many guests as his place could hold with comfort, thanked him for his kind offer, and started out for the inn—and bed, for I have been up— Well, I have been travelling for the past few days. I need not remind you of the weather. Suffice it to say that the snow was blown into my eyes until it blinded me and I wandered from the road. My fingers were stiff and frozen, so that I found it impossible to hold my cloak about me. I could not see an arm's length before me, the snow fell so thick and fast, the night was so dark. My eyes were growing heavy. I felt sleepy. But, knowing to lie down in the treacherous snow meant death, I made one last, mighty effort and struggled on. At length I got so weak I could only stumble forward, and three or four, maybe ten times I fell. Then I cried out for help—cried, screamed, yelled as I never did before. I called. How lonely, how awfully grave like the stillness was! My very voice seemed muffled. Then a feeling of rest, a sensation of great calm, came over me. I no longer felt the cold, nor heard the wind, nor knew fear, and I was about to sleep—it would have been my last—when some stories of travellers who had kept themselves awake by self-administered punishment came—most strange to tell—to my mind. The thought of death on that desolate moor, far from the hearts that loved me and awaited my homecoming, was so overpoweringly maddening, I tell you, that I tore my hair and shrieked out:

'"I will not die! I will not!"

'I pulled open my coat and found my pocket-knife. That saved me. See where my coat is punctured. It's a mercy I didn't run it up to the handle into myself in my efforts to stimulate myself. In spite of all my efforts, I was slowly but surely—oh, so surely—sinking, till I cried again in desperation:

"'Fool—fool! Why did you venture it? What wouldn't I give to be back at the squire's? All—everything! Anything to be saved—anything!"

"'I'll save you!"

'My good friends, the voice that uttered these words was so close to my ear that it seemed a whisper from another land, and I thought I was already dead. How was I to reason otherwise? In that moment of death, on that distant moor, the words were like a supernatural answer to my prayer. I trembled. The sound of the winds, the falling snow, brought me to myself. Then the words were repeated:

"'I'll save you!"

'I turned and looked at the speaker. His voice had sent a shiver—not like that produced by cold—through my frame, so that I was afraid to meet his gaze, which I know—I can't tell how—was fastened on me and pierced me through and through. Without venturing to meet his eye, I said:

"'Who are you?"

'And he answered:

"'One who will save you!"

"'Are you a farmer hereabouts?" I inquired, at a loss what to say.

"'Look and see," he answered.

'As he said this, I fancied he chuckled quietly. Then, though I had no desire to do so, despite my efforts to do otherwise, I felt myself turning to meet him—I felt myself do this, I say, while I endeavoured most strenuously to keep my back to him. Shall I ever forget his eyes? Shall I ever forget the devilish leer on his face? Never, though I live to be a thousand years old. He was a very tall, thin, middle-aged man, dressed all in black, from the beaver, on which, I remarked, not a snowflake fell, to what I could see of his lower parts. I noticed his appearance in a second; and while I glanced at him, he stood grinning at me with the greatest good humour. I dared not speak. I could not speak. It was he who broke the silence, asking me in a very deep, musical voice, whether he resembled a farmer. I admitted that there wasn't the faintest analogy—wishing deep down in my heart that there had been. You must not think I was frightened, for I wasn't. The place, the hour, the solitude, his sudden appearance, cast a sort of spell over me, and it was only by the putting forth of all my remaining strength that I had the heart to ask him to put me on the right path for home.

'"I will do so with pleasure," said he.

'I thanked him for his kindness, and off we started. He was so very affable, telling humorous stories to shorten our hard tramp; so extremely anxious regarding my comfort; so persistent in his efforts to please, and so polished and gentlemanly withal, that gradually I came to look upon him with less distaste, and before the cross-roads were reached, was actually exchanging addresses with him—verbally, of course. We had been speaking of the many ways which men have of amusing themselves, and I confessed that I was partial to card-playing as a pastime. He assured me it was his greatest pleasure. At length we came to the weird-looking post which stands at the cross-roads, pointing its long fingers in every direction in a most confusing manner. From that point my road was clear. "Now," said I to myself, "to bid him good night." And I proceeded to do so, holding out my hand and saying:

'"A thousand thanks for your timely assistance—a safe journey—and good-bye."

'He did not seem to notice my outstretched hand, but looked into my face with a steady, fascinating stare, for all the world like a snake trying to fix its prey.'

At this point the auditors gave vent to so many cries of surprise and fear that the narrator was forced to stop and wait until they became calm again.

"'We may never see each other again," I returned, though why I spoke those words is a mystery. They invited conversation, and knowing this, I could have torn out my tongue with rage at my thoughtlessness.

"'Oh," he said, "we shall surely meet once more—where there shall be neither snow nor frost, wind nor rain."

'I proffered my hand a second time, thinking he might not have seen it before—the night being so pitch-black— and I repeated my thanks and adieus.

"'Do you really wish to thank me for whatever small service I have been to you?" he asked.

"'If it be in my power to do so," I said.

"'The simplest thing in the world," he answered.

"'What is it?" I inquired.

"'Do you see this milestone?" said he, pointing towards a white mound.

"'I see something," was my reply.

"'It is a milestone;" and as he spoke he brushed away the snow, disclosing the long, flat slab beneath.

"'Well?" said I.

"'You can thank me by sitting down facing me on that stone and appeasing a craving—a hunger—which tortures me."

'By this time, as you may well suppose, I had grown very suspicious, and feeling certain that I had fallen in with a highwayman, whose dark purpose was to murder me for my money and jewellery, I determined to act with great circumspection—to humour his every whim, until a suitable opportunity of escape presented itself. Accordingly, I sat down on one end of the wet slab, and said to him in a voice which I endeavoured to make cheerful, "Here I am!" His grim words, "Appeasing a craving, a hunger," kept me from being at all cheerful, for I anticipated being eaten alive. I put the best face I could on the matter, assuring myself that it was better and more manly to die fighting than to sit down and calmly consent to be metamorphosed into a midnight supper for the pleasure of the gentleman in black. And reasoning thus, I felt for my knife—my only means of defence—opened the largest blade, and waited for him. You must remember, my good people, that I thought of all these things in a second, while he advanced to the milestone, on which he presently seated his black self. I clenched my teeth and clutched my knife in readiness for the fight I thought must surely come. But to my surprise, he took from his back pocket a pack of cards, placed them between us on the slab, and said:

"'I will play you a few games of forty-fives, at a sovereign a game, before we part."

"'Is this the craving you spoke of—this the hunger you must satisfy?" I asked him, almost too bewildered to articulate.

"'This," he answered, slowly, "is the first tool with which I worked my own ruin. Since I first had being, I have craved to win for myself all things which belong to others. The spirit of gaming was made part of me. It has grown with me, gained strength with years, until now it is all I live for. I began at an early age by wagering with another that the darker cloud of two which went sailing by in the heavens would disappear before the lighter one. He with whom I wagered won. Then, to regain what I had lost, I doubled the amount—I forget the subject of our bet. I lost again. I went on doubling and trebling, losing and winning alternately, until at last I found I was ruined. Then, indeed, I became desperate. Then was my whole mind given to the devising of schemes by which I was to recuperate my losses. I borrowed, I begged, I did everything to secure the necessary means wherewith to gamble. I have since gone on—sometimes living in luxury, sometimes in the most wretched penury; now sipping rich wine, again parching for a draught of clear water; today the guest of princes and lords, tomorrow the companion of filthy mendicants! But why waste time? Why tell you all this? Enough that last night I was lucky. I have money. On the way here you confessed a love of cards. Come; we will play!"

'These are his words as well as I can remember them. You may laugh at me when I tell you that, when he had finished speaking, I was seized with a desire to gamble and win the money he had mentioned. And there, on that wet milestone, in the dark night, with the storm raging round us, that and I began to play forty-fives for a sovereign a corner, with all the nonchalance and little amenities on his part which we observe when ladies and gentlemen play a rubber in the snug corner of a well-lighted parlour. I groped for the cards and cut them. He dealt. I picked up my five.

"'Look here, sir. I can't tell what I'm holding. It's too dark," I cried.

"'Wait," said he. With that his hand went down into the mysterious black pocket, and shortly afterwards, I heard a rattle as of iron.'

'God bless us!' ejaculated the listeners.

'Then,' continued the young man, 'I heard a scratching, a light spluttered and hissed; and before I could make out what he was about, a lighted lantern was casting a broad glow of light on the slab and extending a few yards round it until it melted in the blackness beyond. My wonderment was momentary only. My nature seemed to have undergone some startling change, for I thought of nothing, forgot everything—my late suffering, the desolate place, the hour, the cold that had but lately been turning my fingers to stone, my mysterious companion—all save that there was a small heap of gold near the stranger—two golden coins in the middle of the slab—and that I was to gamble and win. The first game I won; the second, too. In the third I was successful. Luck continued to be with me, and I was quickly transferring the heap of gold to my corner of the slab. Up to this neither of us had spoken, but when I had taken all but a few pieces from him he remarked:

"'You play a shrewd game.'

"'Thank you, sir,' said I.

'After that we went on playing in silence. My luck was changing. I lost repeatedly, and when we had played several hands, he succeeded in getting the gold back to his end, with five pounds of mine along with it. This angered me, and I proposed that we should raise the stakes and play for two pounds a side. He was quite agreeable. I lost another five. Then I said we had better play for six pounds each hand. Still I was unsuccessful; still he drew my money to his end, until the last piece of gold having been swept into his pile, we played for half-crowns, then for shillings, then for sixpences, and at last I had only a few coppers at stake. The cards were given out. Eagerly I grasped mine, with the hope of holding the better hand. Alas, it was worthless! He won! Every farthing of two hundred pounds was gone, and I was constrained to tell him I could play no longer.

"'Tut, man!' said he; "the game is young.'

"'Yes,' I answered, despondently; "but my last penny is lost. There's nothing left.'

"'Then I'll tell you what I'll do,' said he. "I'm anything but a bad man, so I'll give you a chance of getting your money back.'

"'You will?' cried I, delighted.

"'I will,' he replied. "What would you say if I were to wager all I have here"—he pushed the glittering pieces forward—"and all I have here"—taking a bag from his black pocket and emptying its golden contents on the slab—"that I will be victor in two games out of three?"

"'You would be very magnanimous,' I returned, burning to hear the conditions. "But I have absolutely nothing left."

"'You have your word.'

"'What do you mean?' I cried.

"'I mean that if you will pledge me your word to serve me hereafter at any time I may chance to call upon you, I will wager my gold against your word. If I lose, the gold is yours, all of it, every bright sovereign; and you may take back your vow, too.'

'As he spoke, he leaned forward, took the gold in his hand, letting it slip through his fingers in a sheeny, clinking stream. I did not hesitate to consider the import of his dreadful propositions. Gold I must have—not for its own sake, not because I am avaricious—simply because I hungered to gamble.

"'It's a bargain,' I said.

"'Then repeat these words after me,' he commanded.

"'I swear"—he dictated, and I repeated word after word to the end—"I swear to be the servant of this man from this hour unto the end of time, to renounce all other masters, and to serve him faithfully and well in all that he may command."

'I could hardly wait for him to finish, so eager was I to resume the play. Once more we seated ourselves on the milestone; again the cards were dealt out, and the strangest game that ever men played was begun. I won on the first hand. The cards came round a second time. He won. A game for each. Then I prepared myself for the last—the great struggle. Victory meant riches and freedom; defeat,

I know not what. My brain was on fire; my hands trembled so that in picking up the cards he had placed near me—the cards which were to decide for or against me—they fell out of my shaking fingers and dropped on the snow at my feet.' Here the speaker faltered and appeared reluctant to proceed. 'My good people, when just as my fingers were about to fasten on the cards, my eye saw something that caused my blood to turn as cold as this snow on the ground—something that took from me the power to move, to speak, that petrified me and left me gazing at it like a statue. Think of being alone with that man out on the snow, away from all help, in a place seemingly deserted by its Maker, and shudder to dream of what I saw—of it!'

He shuddered even then—even as he sat in the midst of Andy's guests—in Andy's cheerful parlour. But surely he is not to be termed a coward, when we know that the cottagers at this point of the recital turned their heads and cast many uneasy glances towards the door, drawing closer to the fire as they did so.

'I was telling you I was rooted to my seat. No wonder! Before me, with the sickly light from the lantern shining right down upon it, was—a cloven hoof!'

'A cloven hoof! The divil!' cried everybody.

'I closed my eyes, thinking I was dreaming. But no; for when I opened them, there was the cursed hoof before me!'

'Lord save us!'

'Then the awfulness of the compact I had made came to my mind with terrible force. I was bartering my soul for gold. Now I see that Providence watched over me, for it was the thought of what I was doing that caused me to leap to my feet with a cry for help, and run with feet of wind—feet winged with fear—away from that thing! Every moment I expected to feel his hand on my shoulder, to be dragged back to that hellish game of cards at which my soul would be lost to it—to the thing in black. You must have heard my screams, for as I ran I saw—and how I thanked God for it!—I saw a stream of glorious light burst in the blackness! It gave new courage to my heart and new strength to my limbs. After that I remember nothing. I suppose I became unconscious. The rest you already know; and, believe me when I say it, I cannot easily forget your prompt assistance and heartfelt sympathy. I have finished.'

With the stranger's adventure and all its hideous details fresh within the mind of every man, woman, and child present, the very idea of leaving that hospitable roof was thrilling in itself; so motherly Mrs Sweeny found resting-places for the women and children, while the men slept on improvised beds of chairs, tables, &c., the greater part of them lying on the floor before the fire. The stranger retired shortly after he had concluded his story, and it was not long until the Sweeny household was asleep and snoring.

To the reader:

If you doubt any part of this narrative, you may visit Mrs Sweeny and have it from her lips. Ask any one in Derry Goland, King's County, Ireland, the whereabouts of Andy Sweeny's house, and you will be sure to find it.

There were some cynics who said that the young man had been drinking freely at the squire's, had lost considerable money at playing cards, had wandered from the squire's in a maudlin state, had rested on the milestone and dreamed about the man in black, and that the only devil he saw was a creature of his drunken fancy, generally termed a 'blue devil.' But Mrs Sweeny and most of her guests maintain that the gentleman could not have related his adventure, and described it so graphically, too, had he been intoxicated. I give no opinion in the matter. The readers may take what view of it they please.

THE BLUE ROOM

Lettice Galbraith

FIRST PUBLISHED IN *MACMILLAN'S MAGAZINE*, OCTOBER 1897

Lettice Galbraith's life is as mysterious as the few stories thought to have been written by her. We don't know when she was born or died, or even whether Lettice Galbraith was her real name. Eight weird tales are credited to her, six of which appeared in her collection *New Ghost Stories* (1893). This story, 'The Blue Room', followed in 1897, and a further tale ('After Idem') appeared in the 1901 anthology *Strange Happenings*. After that, there's no further trace.

On the surface, this story uses a fairly common haunted room motif, but it's elevated by its spirited and courageous heroine.

—TK

I t happened twice in my time. It will never happen again, they say, since Miss Erristoun (Mrs Arthur, that is now,) and Mr Calder-Maxwell between them found out the secret of the haunted room, and laid the ghost; for ghost it was, though at the time Mr Maxwell gave it another name, Latin, I fancy, but all I can remember about it now is that it somehow reminded me of poultry-rearing. I am the housekeeper at Mertoun Towers, as my aunt was before me, and her aunt before her, and first of all my great-grandmother, who was a distant cousin of the Laird, and had married the chaplain, but being left penniless at her husband's death, was thankful to accept the post which has ever since been occupied by one of her descendants. It gives us a sort of standing with the servants, being, as it were, related to the family; and Sir Archibald and my Lady have always acknowledged the connection, and treated us with more freedom than would be accorded to ordinary dependants.

Mertoun has been my home from the time I was eighteen. Something occurred then of which, since it has nothing to do with this story, I need only say that it wiped out for ever any idea of marriage on my part, and I came to the Towers to be trained under my aunt's vigilant eye for the duties in which I was one day to succeed her.

Of course I knew there was a story about the blue tapestry room. Everyone knew that, though the old Laird had given strict orders that the subject should not be discussed among the servants, and always discouraged any allusion to it on the part of his family and guests. But there is a strange fascination about everything connected with the supernatural, and orders or no orders, people, whether gentle or simple, will try to gratify their curiosity; so a good deal of surreptitious talk went on both in the drawing-room and the servants' hall, and hardly a guest came to the house but would pay a visit to the Blue Room and ask all manner of questions about the ghost. The odd part of the business was that no one knew what the ghost was supposed to be, or even if there were any ghost at all. I tried hard to get my aunt to tell me some details of the legend, but she always reminded me of Sir Archibald's orders, and added that the tale most likely started with the superstitious fancy of people who lived long ago and were very ignorant, because a certain Lady Barbara Mertoun had died in that room.

I reminded her that people must have died, at some time or other, in pretty nearly every room in the house, and no one had thought of calling them haunted, or hinting that it was unsafe to sleep there.

She answered that Sir Archibald himself had used the Blue Room, and one or two other gentlemen, who had passed the night there for a wager, and they had neither seen nor heard anything unusual. For her part, she added, she did not hold with people wasting their time thinking of such folly, when they had much better be giving their minds to their proper business.

Somehow her professions of incredulity did not ring true, and I wasn't satisfied, though I gave up asking questions. But if I said nothing, I thought the more, and often when my duties took me to the Blue Room I would wonder why, if nothing had happened there, and there was no real mystery, the room was never used; it had not even a mattress on the fine carved bedstead, which was only covered by a sheet to keep it from the dust. And then I would steal into the portrait gallery to look at the great picture of the Lady Barbara, who had died in the full bloom of her youth, no one knew why, for she was just found one morning stiff and cold, stretched across that fine bed under the blue tapestried canopy.

She must have been a beautiful woman, with her great black eyes and splendid auburn hair, though I doubt her beauty was all on the outside, for she had belonged to the gayest set of the Court, which was none too respectable in those days, if half the tales one hears of it are true; and indeed a modest lady would hardly have been painted in such a dress, all slipping off her shoulders, and so thin that one can see right through the stuff. There must have been something queer about her too, for they do say her father-in-law, who was known as the wicked Lord Mertoun, would not have her buried with the rest of the family; but that might have been his spite, because he was angry that she had no child, and her husband, who was but a sickly sort of man, dying of consumption but a month later, there was no direct heir; so that with the old Lord the title became extinct, and the estates passed to the Protestant branch of the family, of which the present Sir Archibald Mertoun is the head. Be that as it may, Lady Barbara lies by herself in the churchyard, near the lych-gate, under a grand marble tomb indeed, but all alone, while her husband's coffin has its place beside those of his brothers who died before him, among their ancestors and descendants in the great vault under the chancel.

I often used to think about her, and wonder why she died, and how; and then It happened and the mystery grew deeper than ever.

There was a family-gathering that Christmas, I remember, the first Christmas for many years that had been kept at Mertoun, and we had been very busy arranging the rooms for the different guests, for on New Year's Eve there was a ball in the neighbourhood, to which Lady Mertoun was taking a large party, and for that night, at least, the house was as full as it would hold.

I was in the linen-room, helping to sort the sheets and pillow-covers for the different beds, when my Lady came in with an open letter in her hand.

She began to talk to my aunt in a low voice, explaining something which seemed to have put her out, for when I returned from carrying a pile of linen to the head-housemaid, I heard her say: 'It is too annoying to upset all one's arrangements at the last moment. Why couldn't she have left the girl at home and brought another maid, who could be squeezed in somewhere without any trouble?'

I gathered that one of the visitors, Lady Grayburn, had written that she was bringing her companion, and as she had left her maid, who was ill, at home, she wanted the young lady to have a bedroom adjoining hers, so that she might be at hand to give any help that was required. The request seemed a trifling matter enough in itself, but it just so happened that there really was no room at liberty. Every bedroom on the first corridor was occupied, with the exception of the Blue Room, which, as ill-luck would have it, chanced to be next to that arranged for Lady Grayburn.

My aunt made several suggestions, but none of them seemed quite practicable, and at last my Lady broke out: 'Well, it cannot be helped; you must put Miss Wood in the Blue Room. It is only for one night, and she won't know anything about that silly story.'

'Oh, my Lady!' my aunt cried, and I knew by her tone that she had not spoken the truth when she professed to think so lightly of the ghost.

'I can't help it,' her Ladyship answered: 'beside I don't believe there is anything really wrong with the room. Sir Archibald has slept there, and he found no cause for complaint.'

'But a woman, a young woman,' my aunt urged; 'indeed I wouldn't run such a risk, my Lady; let me put one of the gentlemen in there, and Miss Wood can have the first room in the west corridor.'

'And what use would she be to Lady Grayburn out there?' said her Ladyship. 'Don't be foolish, my good Marris. Unlock the door between the two rooms; Miss Wood can leave it open if she feels nervous; but I shall not say a word about that foolish superstition, and I shall be very much annoyed if any one else does so.'

She spoke as if that settled the question, but my aunt wasn't easy. 'The Laird,' she murmured; 'what will he say to a lady being put to sleep there?'

'Sir Archibald does not interfere in household arrangements. Have the Blue Room made ready for Miss Wood at once. *I* will take the responsibility,—if there is any.'

On that her Ladyship went away, and there was nothing for it but to carry out her orders. The Blue Room was prepared, a great fire lighted, and when I went round last thing to see all was in order for the visitor's arrival, I couldn't but think how handsome and comfortable it looked. There were candles burning brightly on the toilet-table and chimney-piece, and a fine blaze of logs on the wide hearth. I saw nothing had been overlooked, and was closing the door when my eyes fell on the bed. It was crumpled just as if someone had thrown themselves across it, and I was vexed that the housemaids should have been so careless, especially with the smart new quilt. I went round, and patted up the feathers, and smoothed the counterpane, just as the carriages drove under the window.

By and by Lady Grayburn and Miss Wood came upstairs, and knowing they had brought no maid, I went to assist in the unpacking. I was a long time in her Ladyship's room, and when I'd settled her I tapped at the next door and offered to help Miss Wood. Lady Grayburn followed me almost immediately to inquire the whereabouts of some keys. She spoke very sharply, I thought, to her companion, who seemed a timid, delicate slip of a girl, with nothing noticeable about her except her hair, which was lovely, pale golden, and heaped in thick coils all round her small head.

'You will certainly be late,' Lady Grayburn said. 'What an age you have been, and you have not half finished unpacking yet.' The young lady murmured something about there being so little time. 'You have had time to sprawl on the bed instead of getting ready,' was the retort, and as Miss Wood meekly denied the imputation, I looked over my shoulder at the bed, and saw there the same strange indentation I had noticed before. It made my heart beat faster, for without any reason at all I felt certain that crease must have something to do with Lady Barbara.

Miss Wood didn't go to the ball. She had supper in the schoolroom with the young ladies' governess, and as I heard from one of the maids that she was to sit up for Lady Grayburn, I took her some wine and sandwiches about twelve o'clock. She stayed in the schoolroom, with a book, till the first party came home soon after two. I'd been round the rooms with the housemaid to see the fires were kept up, and I wasn't surprised to find that queer crease back on the bed again; indeed, I sort of expected it. I said nothing to the maid, who didn't seem to have noticed anything out of the way, but I told my aunt, and though she answered sharply that I was talking nonsense, she turned quite pale, and I heard her mutter something under breath that sounded like 'God help her!'

I slept badly that night, for, do what I would, the thought of that poor young lady alone in the Blue Room kept me awake and restless. I was nervous, I suppose, and once, just as I was dropping off, I started up, fancying I'd heard a scream. I opened my door and listened, but there wasn't a sound, and after waiting a bit I crept back to bed, and lay there shivering till I fell asleep.

The household wasn't astir as early as usual. Every one was tired after the late night, and tea wasn't to be sent to the ladies till half-past nine. My aunt said nothing about the ghost, but I noticed she was fidgety, and asked almost first thing if anyone had been to Miss Wood's room. I was telling her that Martha, one of the housemaids, had just taken up the tray, when the girl came running in with a scared, white face. 'For pity's sake, Mrs Marris,' she cried, 'come to the Blue Room; something awful has happened!'

My aunt stopped to ask no questions. She ran straight upstairs, and as I followed I heard her muttering to herself, 'I knew it, I knew it. Oh Lord! what will my Lady feel like now?'

If I live to be a hundred I shall never forget that poor girl's face. It was just as if she'd been frozen with terror. Her eyes were wide open and fixed, and her little hands clenched in the coverlet on each side of her as she lay across the bed in the very place where that crease had been.

Of course the whole house was aroused. Sir Archibald sent one of the grooms post-haste for the doctor, but he could do nothing when he came; Miss Wood had been dead for at least five hours.

It was a sad business. All the visitors went away as soon as possible, except Lady Grayburn, who was obliged to stay for the inquest.

In his evidence, the doctor stated death was due to failure of heart's action, occasioned possibly by some sudden shock; and though the jury did not say so in their verdict, it was an open secret that they blamed her Ladyship for permitting Miss Wood to sleep in the haunted room. No one could have reproached her more bitterly than she did herself, poor lady; and if she had done wrong she certainly suffered for it, for she never recovered from the shock of that dreadful morning, and became more or less of an invalid till her death five years later.

All this happened in 184—. It was fifty years before another woman slept in the Blue Room, and fifty years had brought with them many changes. The old Laird was gathered to his fathers, and his son, the present Sir Archibald, reigned in his stead; his sons were grown men, and Mr Charles, the eldest, married, with a fine little boy of his own. My aunt had been dead many a year, and I was an old woman, though active and able as ever to keep the maids up to their work. They take more looking after now, I think, than in the old days before there was so much talk of education, and when young women who took service thought less of dress and more of dusting. Not but what education is a fine thing in its proper place, that is, for gentlefolk. If Miss Erristoun, now, hadn't been the clever, strong-minded young lady she is, she'd never have cleared the Blue Room of its terrible secret, and lived to make Mr Arthur the happiest man alive.

He'd taken a great deal of notice of her when she first came in the summer to visit Mrs Charles, and I wasn't surprised to find she was one of the guests for the opening of the shooting-season. It wasn't a regular house-party (for Sir Archibald and Lady Mertoun were away), but just half-a-dozen young ladies, friends of Mrs Charles, who was but a girl herself, and as many gentlemen that Mr Charles and Mr Arthur had invited. And very gay they were, what with lunches at the covert-side, and tennis-parties, and little dances got up at a few hours' notice, and sometimes of an evening they'd play hide-and-seek all over the house just as if they'd been so many children.

It surprised me at first to see Miss Erristoun, who was said to be so learned, and had held her own with all the gentlemen at Cambridge, playing with the rest like any ordinary young lady; but she seemed to enjoy the fun as much as any one, and was always first in any amusement that was planned. I didn't wonder at Mr Arthur's fancying her, for she was a handsome girl, tall and finely made, and carried herself like a princess. She had a wonderful head of hair, too, so long, her maid told me, it touched the ground as she sat on a chair to have it brushed. Everybody seemed to take to her, but I soon noticed it was Mr Arthur or Mr Calder-Maxwell she liked best to be with.

Mr Maxwell is a Professor now, and a great man at Oxford; but then he was just an undergraduate the same as Mr Arthur, though more studious, for he'd spend hours in the library poring over those old books full of queer black characters, that they say the wicked Lord Mertoun collected in the time of King Charles the Second. Now and then Miss Erristoun would stay indoors to help him, and it was something they found out in their studies that gave them the clue to the secret of the Blue Room.

For a long time after Miss Wood's death all mention of the ghost was strictly forbidden. Neither the Laird nor her Ladyship could bear the slightest allusion to the subject, and the Blue Room was kept locked, except when it had to be cleaned and aired. But as the years went by the edge of the tragedy wore off, and by degrees it grew to be just a story that people talked about in much the same way as they had done when I first came to the Towers; and if many believed in the mystery and speculated as to what the ghost could be, there were others who didn't hesitate to declare Miss Wood's dying in that room was a mere coincidence, and had nothing to do with supernatural agency. Miss Erristoun was one of those who held most strongly to this theory. She didn't believe a bit in ghosts, and said straight out that there wasn't any of the tales told of haunted houses which could not be traced to natural causes, if people had courage and science enough to investigate them thoroughly.

It had been very wet all that day, and the gentlemen had stayed indoors, and nothing would serve Mrs Charles but they should all have an old-fashioned tea in my room and 'talk ghosts,' as she called it. They made me tell them all I knew about the Blue Room, and it was then, when every one was discussing the story and speculating as to what the ghost could be, that Miss Erristoun spoke up. 'The poor girl had heart-complaint,' she finished by saying, 'and she would have died the same way in any other room.'

'But what about the other people who have slept there?' someone objected.

'They did not die. Old Sir Archibald came to no harm, neither did Mr Hawksworth, nor the other man. They were healthy, and had plenty of pluck, so they saw nothing.'

'They were not women,' put in Mrs Charles; 'you see the ghost only appears to the weaker sex.'

'That proves the story to be a mere legend,' Miss Erristoun said with decision. 'First it was reported that everyone who slept in the room died. Then one or two men did sleep there, and remained alive; so the tale had to be modified, and since one woman could be proved to have died suddenly there, the fatality was represented as attaching to women only. If a girl with a sound constitution and good nerve were once to spend the night in that room, your charming family-spectre would be discredited for ever.'

There was a perfect chorus of dissent. None of the ladies could agree, and most of the gentlemen doubted whether any woman's nerve would stand the ordeal. The more they argued the more Miss Erristoun persisted in her view, till at last Mrs Charles got vexed, and cried: 'Well, it is one thing to talk about it, and another to do it. Confess now, Edith, you daren't sleep in that room yourself.'

'I dare and I will,' she answered directly. 'I don't believe in ghosts, and I am ready to stand the test. I will sleep in the Blue Room tonight, if you like, and tomorrow morning you will have to confess that whatever there may be against the haunted chamber, it is not a ghost.'

I think Mrs Charles was sorry she'd spoken then, for they all took Miss Erristoun up, and the gentlemen were for laying wagers as to whether she'd see anything or not. When it was too late she tried to laugh aside her challenge as absurd, but Miss Erristoun wouldn't be put off. She said she meant to see the thing through, and if she wasn't allowed to have a bed made up, she'd carry in her blankets and pillows, and camp out on the floor.

The others were all laughing and disputing together, but I saw Mr Maxwell look at her very curiously. Then he drew Mr Arthur aside, and began to talk in an undertone. I couldn't hear what he said, but Mr Arthur answered quite short:

'It's the maddest thing I ever heard of, and I won't allow it for a moment.'

'She will not ask your permission perhaps,' Mr Maxwell retorted. Then he turned to Mrs Charles, and inquired how long it was since the Blue Room had been used, and if it was kept aired. I could speak to that, and when he'd heard that there was no bedding there, but that fires were kept up regularly, he said he meant to have the first refusal of the ghost, and if he saw nothing it would be time enough for Miss Erristoun to take her turn.

Mr Maxwell had a kind of knack of settling things, and somehow with his quiet manner always seemed to get his own way. Just before dinner he came to me with Mrs Charles, and said it was all right, I was to get the room made ready quietly, not for all the servants to know, and he was going to sleep there.

I heard next morning that he came down to breakfast as usual. He'd had an excellent night, he said, and never slept better.

It was wet again that morning, raining 'cats and dogs,' but Mr Arthur went out in it all. He'd almost quarrelled with Miss Erristoun, and was furious with Mr Maxwell for encouraging her in her idea of testing the ghost-theory, as they called it. Those two were together in the library most of the day, and Mrs Charles was chaffing Miss Erristoun as they went upstairs to dress, and asking her if she found the demons interesting. Yes, she said, but there was a page missing in the most exciting part of the book. They could not make head or tail of the context for some time, and then Mr Maxwell discovered that a leaf had been cut out. They talked of nothing else all through dinner, the butler told me, and Miss Erristoun seemed so taken up with her studies, I hoped she'd forgotten about the haunted room. But she wasn't one of the sort to forget. Later in the evening I came across her standing with Mr Arthur in the corridor. He was talking very earnestly, and I saw her shrug her shoulders and just look up at him and smile, in a sort of way that meant she wasn't going to give in. I was slipping quietly by, for I didn't want to disturb them, when Mr Maxwell came out of the billiard-room. 'It's our game,' he said; 'won't you come and play the tie?'

'I'm quite ready,' Miss Erristoun answered, and was turning away, when Mr Arthur laid his hand on her arm. 'Promise me first,' he urged, 'promise me that much, at least.'

'How tiresome you are!' she said quite pettishly. 'Very well then, I promise; and now please, don't worry me any more.'

Mr Arthur watched her go back to the billiard-room with his friend, and he gave a sort of groan. Then he caught sight of me and came along the passage. 'She won't give it up,' he said, and his face was quite white. 'I've done all I can; I'd have telegraphed to my father, but I don't know where they'll stay in Paris, and anyway there'd be no time to get an answer. Mrs Marris, she's going to sleep in that d— room, and if anything happens to her—I—' he broke off short, and threw himself on to the window-seat, hiding his face on his folded arms.

I could have cried for sympathy with his trouble. Mr Arthur has always been a favourite of mine, and I felt downright angry with Miss Erristoun for making him so miserable just out of a bit of bravado.

'I think they are all mad,' he went on presently. 'Charley ought to have stopped the whole thing at once, but Kate and the others have talked him round. He professes to believe there's no danger, and Maxwell has got his head full of some rubbish he has found in those beastly books on Demonology, and he's backing her up. She won't listen to a word I say. She told me point-blank she'd never speak to me again if I interfered. She doesn't care a hang for me; I know that now, but I can't help it; I—I'd give my life for her.'

I did my best to comfort him, saying Miss Erristoun wouldn't come to any harm; but it wasn't a bit of use, for I didn't believe in my own assurances. I felt nothing but ill could come of such tempting of Providence, and I seemed to see that other poor girl's terrible face as it had looked when we found her dead in that wicked room. However, it is a true saying that 'a wilful woman will have her way,' and we could do nothing to prevent Miss Erristoun's risking her life; but I made up my mind to one thing, whatever other people might do, *I* wasn't going to bed that night.

I'd been getting the winter-hangings into order, and the upholstress had used the little boudoir at the end of the long corridor for her work. I made up the fire, brought in a fresh lamp, and when the house was quiet, I crept down and settled myself there to watch. It wasn't ten yards from the door of the Blue Room, and over the thick carpet I could pass without making a sound, and listen at the keyhole. Miss Erristoun had promised Mr Arthur she would not lock her door; it was the one concession he'd been able to obtain from her. The ladies went to their rooms about eleven, but Miss Erristoun stayed talking to Mrs Charles for nearly an hour while her maid was brushing her hair. I saw her go to the Blue Room, and by and by Louise left her, and all was quiet. It must have been half-past one before I thought I heard something moving outside. I opened the door and looked out, and there was Mr Arthur standing in the passage. He gave a start when he saw me. 'You are sitting up,' he said, coming into the room; 'then you do believe there is evil work on hand tonight? The others have gone to bed, but I can't rest; it's no use my trying to sleep. I meant to stay in the smoking-room, but it is so far away; I couldn't hear there even if she called for help. I've listened at the door; there isn't a sound. Can't you go in and see if it's all right? Oh, Marris, if she should—'

I knew what he meant, but I wasn't going to admit *that* possible,—yet. 'I can't go into a lady's room without any reason,' I said; 'but I've been to the door every few minutes for the last hour and more. It wasn't till half-past twelve that Miss Erristoun stopped moving about, and I don't believe, Mr Arthur, that God will let harm come to her, without giving those that care for her some warning. I mean to keep on listening, and if there's the least hint of anything wrong, why I'll go to her at once, and you are at hand here to help.'

I talked to him a bit more till he seemed more reasonable, and then we sat there waiting, hardly speaking a word except when, from time to time, I went outside to listen. The house was deathly quiet; there was something terrible, I thought, in the stillness; not a sign of life anywhere save just in the little boudoir, where Mr Arthur paced up and down, or sat with a strained look on his face, watching the door.

As three o'clock struck, I went out again. There is a window in the corridor, angle for angle with the boudoir-door. As I passed, some one stepped from behind the curtains and a voice whispered: 'Don't be frightened Mrs Marris; it is only me, Calder-Maxwell. Mr Arthur is there, isn't he?' He pushed open the boudoir door. 'May I come in?' he said softly. 'I guessed you'd be about, Mertoun. I'm not at all afraid myself, but if there *is* anything in that little legend, it is as well for some of us to be on hand. It was a good idea of yours to get Mrs Marris to keep watch with you.'

Mr Arthur looked at him as black as thunder. 'If you didn't *know* there was something in it,' he said, 'you wouldn't be here now; and knowing that, you're nothing less than a blackguard for egging that girl on to risk her life, for the sake of trying to prove your insane theories. You are no friend of mine after this, and I'll never willingly see you or speak to you again.'

I was fairly frightened at his words, and for how Mr Maxwell might take them; but he just smiled, and lighted a cigarette, quite cool and quiet.

'I'm not going to quarrel with you, old chap,' he said. 'You're a bit on the strain tonight, and when a man has nerves he mustn't be held responsible for all his words.' Then he turned to me. 'You're a sensible woman, Mrs Marris, and a brave one too, I fancy. If I stay here with Mr Arthur, will you keep close outside Miss Erristoun's door? She may talk in her sleep quietly; that's of no consequence; but if she should cry out, go in at once, *at once*, you understand; we shall hear you, and follow immediately.'

At that Mr Arthur was on his feet. 'You know more than you pretend,' he cried. 'You slept in that room last night. By Heaven, if you've played any trick on her I'll—'

Mr Maxwell held the door open. 'Will you go, please, Mrs Marris?' he said in his quiet way. 'Mertoun, don't be a d— fool.'

I went as he told me, and I give you my word I was all ears, for I felt certain Mr Maxwell knew more than we did, and that he expected something to happen.

It seemed like hours, though I know now it could not have been more than a quarter of that time, before I could be positive someone was moving behind that closed door.

At first I thought it was only my own heart, which was beating against my ribs like a hammer; but soon I could distinguish footsteps, and a sort of murmur like someone speaking continuously, but very low. Then a voice (it was Miss Erristoun's this time) said, 'No, it is impossible; I am dreaming, I must be dreaming.' There was a kind of rustling as though she were moving quickly across the floor. I had my fingers on the handle, but I seemed as if I'd lost power to stir; I could only wait for what might come next.

Suddenly she began to say something out loud. I could not make out the words, which didn't sound like English, but almost directly she stopped short. 'I can't remember any more,' she cried in a troubled tone. 'What shall I do? I can't—' There was a pause. Then—'No, *no!*' she shrieked. 'Oh, Arthur, Arthur!'

At that my strength came back to me, and I flung open the door.

There was a night-lamp burning on the table, and the room was quite light. Miss Erristoun was standing by the bed; she seemed to have backed up against it; her hands were down at her sides, her fingers clutching at the quilt. Her face was white as a sheet, and her eyes staring wide with terror, as well they might,—I know I never had such a shock in my life, for if it was my last word, I swear there was a man standing close in front of her. He turned and looked at me as I opened the door, and I saw his face as plain as I did hers. He was young and very handsome, and his eyes shone like an animal's when you see them in the dark.

'Arthur!' Miss Erristoun gasped again, and I saw she was fainting. I sprang forward, and caught her by the shoulders just as she was falling back on to the bed.

It was all over in a second. Mr Arthur had her in his arms, and when I looked up there were only us four in the room, for Mr Maxwell had followed on Mr Arthur's heels, and was kneeling beside me with his fingers on Miss Erristoun's pulse. 'It's only a faint,' he said, 'she'll come round directly. Better take her out of this at once; here's a dressing gown.' He threw the wrapper round her, and would have helped to raise her, but Mr Arthur needed no assistance. He lifted Miss Erristoun as if she'd been a baby, and carried her straight to the boudoir. He laid her on the couch and knelt beside her, chafing her hands. 'Get the brandy out of the smoking-room, Maxwell,' he said. 'Mrs Marris, have you any salts handy?'

I always carry a bottle in my pocket, so I gave it to him, before I ran after Mr Maxwell, who had lighted a candle, and was going for the brandy. 'Shall I wake Mr Charles and the servants?' I cried. 'He'll be hiding somewhere, but he hasn't had time to get out of the house yet.'

He looked as if he thought I was crazed. 'He—who?' he asked.

'The man,' I said; 'there was a man in Miss Erristoun's room. I'll call up Soames and Robert.'

'You'll do nothing of the sort,' he said sharply. 'There was no man in that room.'

'There was,' I retorted, 'for I saw him; and a great powerful man too. Someone ought to go for the police before he has time to get off.'

Mr Maxwell was always an odd sort of gentleman, but I didn't know what to make of the way he behaved then. He just leaned against the wall, and laughed till the tears came into his eyes.

'It is no laughing matter that I can see,' I told him quite short, for I was angry at his treating the matter so lightly; 'and I consider it no more than my duty to let Mr Charles know that there's a burglar on the premises.'

He grew grave at once then. 'I beg your pardon, Mrs Marris,' he said seriously; 'but I couldn't help smiling at the idea of the police. The vicar would be more to the point, all things considered. You really must not think of rousing the household; it might do Miss Erristoun a great injury, and could in no case be of the slightest use. Don't you understand? It was not a man at all you saw, it was an—well, it was what haunts the Blue Room.'

Then he ran downstairs leaving me fairly dazed, for I'd made so sure what I'd seen was a real man, that I'd clean forgotten all about the ghost.

Miss Erristoun wasn't long regaining consciousness. She swallowed the brandy we gave her like a lamb, and sat up bravely, though she started at every sound, and kept her hand in Mr Arthur's like a frightened child. It was strange, seeing how independent and stand-off she'd been with him before, but she seemed all the sweeter for the change. It was as if they'd come to an understanding without any words; and, indeed, he must have known she had cared for him all along, when she called out his name in her terror.

As soon as she'd recovered herself a little, Mr Maxwell began asking questions. Mr Arthur would have stopped him, but he insisted that it was of the greatest importance to hear everything while the impression was fresh; and when she had got over the first effort, Miss Erristoun seemed to find relief in telling her experience. She sat there with one hand in Mr Arthur's while she spoke, and Mr Maxwell wrote down what she said in his pocket-book.

She told us she went to bed quite easy, for she wasn't the least nervous, and being tired she soon dropped off to sleep. Then she had a sort of dream, I suppose, for she thought she was in the same room, only differently furnished, all but the bed. She described exactly how everything was arranged. She had the strangest feeling too, that she was not herself but someone else, and that she was going to do something,—something that must be done, though she was frightened to death all the time, and kept stopping to listen at the inner door, expecting someone would hear her moving about and call out for her to go to them. That in itself was queer, for there was nobody sleeping in the adjoining room. In her dream, she went on to say, she saw a curious little silver brazier, one that stands in a cabinet in the picture-gallery (a fine example of *cinque cento* work, I think I've heard my Lady call it), and this she remembered holding in her hands a long time, before she set it on a little table beside the bed. Now the bed in the Blue Room is very handsome, richly carved on the cornice and frame, and especially on the posts, which are a foot square at the base and covered with relief-work in a design of fruit and flowers. Miss Erristoun said she went to the left-hand post at the foot, and after passing her hand over the carving, she seemed to touch a spring in one of the centre flowers, and the panel fell outwards like a lid, disclosing a secret cupboard out of which she took some papers and a box. She seemed to know what to do with the papers, though she couldn't tell us what was written on them; and she had a distinct recollection of taking a pastille from the box, and lighting it in the silver brazier. The smoke curled up and seemed to fill the whole room with a heavy perfume, and the next thing she remembered was that she awoke to find herself standing in the middle of the floor, and,—what I had seen when I opened the door was there.

She turned quite white when she came to that part of the story, and shuddered. 'I couldn't believe it,' she said; 'I tried to think I was still dreaming, but I wasn't, I wasn't. It was real, and it was there, and,— oh, it was horrible!'

She hid her face against Mr Arthur's shoulder. Mr Maxwell sat, pencil in hand, staring at her. 'I was right then,' he said. 'I felt sure I was; but it seemed incredible.'

'It is incredible,' said Miss Erristoun; 'but it is true, frightfully true. When I realized that I was awake, that it was actually real, I tried to remember the charge, you know, out of the office of exorcism, but I couldn't get through it. The words went out of my head; I felt my will-power failing; I was paralysed, as though I could make no effort to help myself and then,—then I—,' she looked at Mr Arthur and blushed all over her face and neck. 'I thought of you, and I called,—I had a feeling that you would save me.'

Mr Arthur made no more ado about us than if we'd been a couple of dummies. He just put his arms round her and kissed her, while Mr Maxwell and I looked the other way.

After a bit, Mr Maxwell said: 'One more question, please; what was it like?'

She answered after thinking for a minute. 'It was like a man, tall and very handsome. I have an impression that its eyes were blue and very bright.' Mr Maxwell looked at me inquiringly, and I nodded. 'And dressed?' he asked. She began to laugh almost hysterically. 'It sounds too insane for words, but I think,—I am almost positive it wore ordinary evening dress.'

'It is impossible,' Mr Arthur cried. 'You were dreaming the whole time, that proves it.'

'It doesn't,' Mr Maxwell contradicted. 'They usually appeared in the costume of the day. You'll find that stated particularly both by Scott and Glanvil; Sprenger gives an instance too. Besides, Mrs Marris thought it was a burglar, which argues that the,—the manifestation was objective, and presented no striking peculiarity in the way of clothing.'

'What?' Miss Erristoun exclaimed. 'You saw it too?' I told her exactly what I had seen. My description tallied with hers in everything, but the white shirt and tie, which from my position at the door I naturally should not be able to see.

Mr Maxwell snapped the elastic round his note-book. For a long time he sat silently staring at the fire. 'It is almost past belief,' he said at last, speaking half to himself, 'that such a thing could happen at the end of the nineteenth century, in these scientific rationalistic times that we think such a lot about, we, who look down from our superior intellectual height on the benighted superstitions of the Middle Ages.' He gave an odd little laugh. 'I'd like to get to the bottom of this business. I have a theory, and in the interest of psychical research and common humanity, I'd like to work it out. Miss Erristoun, you ought, I know, to have rest and quiet, and it is almost morning; but will you grant me one request? Before you are overwhelmed with questions, before you are made to relate your experience till the impression of tonight's adventure loses edge and clearness, will you go with Mertoun and myself to the Blue Room, and try to find the secret panel?'

'She shall never set foot inside that door again,' Mr Arthur began hotly, but Miss Erristoun laid a restraining hand on his arm.

'Wait a moment, dear,' she said gently; 'let us hear Mr Maxwell's reasons. Do you think,' she went on, 'that my dream had a foundation in fact; that something connected with that dreadful thing is really concealed about the room?'

'I think,' he answered, 'that you hold the clue to the mystery, and I believe, could you repeat the action of your dream, and open the secret panel, you might remove for ever the legacy of one woman's reckless folly. Only if it is to be done at all, it must be soon, before the impression has had time to fade.'

'It shall be done now,' she answered; 'I am quite myself again. Feel my pulse; my nerves are perfectly steady.'

Mr Arthur broke out into angry protestations. She had gone through more than enough for one night, he said, and he wouldn't have her health sacrificed to Maxwell's whims.

I have always thought Miss Erristoun handsome, but never, not even on her wedding-day, did she look so beautiful as then when she stood up in her heavy white wrapper, with all her splendid hair loose on her shoulders.

'Listen,' she said; 'if God gives us a plain work to do, we must do it at any cost. Last night I didn't believe in anything I could not understand. I was so full of pride in my own courage and common-sense, that I wasn't afraid to sleep in that room and prove the ghost was all superstitious nonsense. I have learned there are forces of which I know nothing, and against which my strength was utter weakness. God took care of me, and sent help in time; and if He has opened a way by which I may save other women from the danger I escaped, I should be worse than ungrateful were I to shirk the task. Bring the lamp, Mr Maxwell, and let us do what we can.' Then she put both hands on Mr Arthur's shoulders. 'Why are you troubled?' she said sweetly. 'You will be with me, and how can I be afraid?'

It never strikes me as strange now that burglaries and things can go on in a big house at night, and not a soul one whit the wiser. There were five people sleeping in the rooms on that corridor while we tramped up and down without disturbing one of them. Not but what we went as quietly as we could, for Mr Maxwell made it clear that the less was known about the actual facts, the better. He went first, carrying the lamp, and we followed. Miss Erristoun shivered as her eyes fell on the bed, across which that dreadful crease showed plain, and I knew she was thinking of what might have been, had help not been at hand.

Just for a minute she faltered, then she went bravely on, and began feeling over the carved woodwork for the spring of the secret panel. Mr Maxwell held the lamp close, but there was nothing to show any difference between that bit of carving and the other three posts. For full ten minutes she tried, and so did the gentlemen, and it seemed as though the dream would turn out a delusion after all, when all at once Miss Erristoun cried, 'I have found it,' and with a little jerk, the square of wood fell forward, and there was the cupboard just as she had described it to us.

It was Mr Maxwell who took out the things, for Mr Arthur wouldn't let Miss Erristoun touch them. There were a roll of papers and a little silver box. At the sight of the box she gave a sort of cry; 'That is it,' she said, and covered her face with her hands.

Mr Maxwell lifted the lid, and emptied out two or three pastilles. Then he unfolded the papers, and before he had fairly glanced at the sheet of parchment covered with queer black characters, he cried, 'I knew it, I knew it! It is the missing leaf.' He seemed quite wild with excitement. 'Come along,' he said. 'Bring the light, Mertoun; I always said it was no ghost, and now the whole thing is as clear as daylight. You see,' he went on, as we gathered round the table in the boudoir, 'so much depended on there being an heir. That was the chief cause of the endless quarrels between old Lord Mertoun and Barbara. He had never approved of the marriage, and was for ever reproaching the poor woman with having failed in the first duty of an only son's wife. His will shows that he did not leave her a farthing in event of her husband dying without issue. Then the feud with the Protestant branch of the family was very bitter, and the Sir Archibald of that day had three boys, he having married (about the same time as his cousin) Lady Mary Sarum, who had been Barbara's rival at Court and whom Barbara very naturally hated. So when the doctors pronounced Dennis Mertoun to be dying of consumption, his wife got desperate, and had recourse to black magic. It is well known that the old man's collection of works on Demonology was the most complete in Europe. Lady Barbara must have had access to the books, and it was she who cut out this leaf. Probably Lord Mertoun discovered the theft and drew his own conclusions. That would account for his refusal to admit her body to the family vault. The Mertouns were staunch Romanists, and it is one of the deadly sins, you know, meddling with sorcery. Well, Barbara contrived to procure the pastilles, and she worked out the spell according to the directions given here, and then,— Good God! Mertoun, what have you done?'

For before any one could interfere to check him, Mr Arthur had swept papers, box, pastilles, and all off the table and flung them into the fire. The thick parchment curled and shrivelled on the hot coals, and a queer, faint smell like incense spread heavily through the room. Mr Arthur stepped to the window and threw the casement wide open. Day was breaking, and a sweet fresh wind swept in from the east which was all rosy with the glow of the rising sun.

'It is a nasty story,' he said; 'and if there be any truth in it, for the credit of the family and the name of a dead woman, let it rest for ever. We will keep our own counsel about tonight's work. It is enough for others to know that the spell of the Blue Room is broken, since a brave, pure-minded girl has dared to face its unknown mystery and has laid the ghost.'

Mr Calder-Maxwell considered a moment. 'I believe you are right,' he said, presently, with an air of resignation. 'I agree to your proposition, and I surrender my chance of world-wide celebrity among the votaries of Psychical Research; but I *do* wish, Mertoun, you would call things by their proper names. It was *not* a ghost. It was an—'

But as I said, all I can remember now of the word he used is, that it somehow put me in mind of poultry-rearing.

NOTE.—The reader will observe that the worthy Mrs Marris, though no student of Sprenger, unconsciously discerned the root-affinity of the *incubator* of the hen-yard and the *incubus* of the MALLEUS MALEFICARUM.

ON THE NORTHERN ICE

Elia Wilkinson Peattie

FIRST PUBLISHED IN *THE SHAPE OF FEAR
AND OTHER GHOSTLY TALES*, 1898

Elia Wilkinson (1862–1935) was born in Kalamazoo, Michigan and relocated to Chicago with her family while still young. She began her career by writing short stories and later became a reporter for the *Chicago Tribune*. Like many of the writers included in this volume her output was prolific. Among other works she produced a children's guide to the history of the USA and a guidebook to Alaska. In the eight years she worked at the *Omaha World-Herald* she published eight hundred editorials, stories, and columns as well as many works of fiction, including two serialized novels. She was considered an accomplished and respected journalist who promoted independence for women.

In 'On the Northern Ice', Peattie's ghostly tale brings a chill with no warmth of a Christmas fireside to lighten the story. This lonely atmospheric tale about a benevolent ghost still brings a feeling of unease to the reader.   —LE

The winter nights up at Sault Ste. Marie are as white and luminous as the Milky Way. The silence which rests upon the solitude appears to be white also. Even sound has been included in Nature's arrestment, for, indeed, save the still white frost, all things seem to be obliterated. The stars have a poignant brightness, but they belong to heaven and not to earth, and between their immeasurable height and the still ice rolls the ebon ether in vast, liquid billows.

In such a place it is difficult to believe that the world is actually peopled. It seems as if it might be the dark of the day after Cain killed Abel, and as if all of humanity's remainder was huddled in affright away from the awful spaciousness of Creation.

The night Ralph Hagadorn started out for Echo Bay—bent on a pleasant duty—he laughed to himself, and said that he did not at all object to being the only man in the world, so long as the world remained as unspeakably beautiful as it was when he buckled on his skates and shot away into the solitude.

He was bent on reaching his best friend in time to act as grooms-man, and business had delayed him till time was at its briefest. So he journeyed by night and journeyed alone, and when the tang of the frost got at his blood, he felt as a spirited horse feels when it gets free of bit and bridle. The ice was as glass, his skates were keen, his frame fit, and his venture to his taste! So he laughed, and cut through the air as a sharp stone cleaves the water. He could hear the whistling of the air as he cleft it.

As he went on and on in the black stillness, he began to have fancies. He imagined himself enormously tall—a great Viking of the Northland, hastening over icy fiords to his love. And that reminded him that he had a love—though, indeed, that thought was always present with him as a background for other thoughts. To be sure, he had not told her that she was his love, for he had seen her only a few times, and the auspicious occasion had not yet presented itself. She lived at Echo Bay also, and was to be the maid of honour to his friend's bride—which was one more reason why he skated almost as swiftly as the wind, and why, now and then, he let out a shout of exultation.

The one cloud that crossed Hagadorn's sun of expectancy was the knowledge that Marie Beaujeu's father had money, and that Marie lived in a house with two stories to it, and wore otter skin about her throat and little satin-lined mink boots on her feet when she went sledding. Moreover, in the locket in which she treasured a bit of her dead mother's hair, there was a black pearl as big as a pea. These things made it difficult—perhaps impossible—for Ralph Hagadorn to say more than, 'I love you.' But that much he meant to say though he were scourged with chagrin for his temerity.

This determination grew upon him as he swept along the ice under the starlight. Venus made a glowing path toward the west and seemed eager to reassure him. He was sorry he could not skim down that avenue of light which flowed from the love-star, but he was forced to turn his back upon it and face the black northeast.

It came to him with a shock that he was not alone. His eyelashes were frosted and his eyeballs blurred with the cold, so at first he thought it might be an illusion. But when he had rubbed his eyes hard, he made sure that not very far in front of him was a long white skater in fluttering garments who sped over the ice as fast as ever werewolf went.

He called aloud, but there was no answer. He shaped his hands and trumpeted through them, but the silence was as before it was complete. So then he gave chase, setting his teeth hard and putting a tension on his firm young muscles. But go however he would, the white skater went faster. After a time, as he glanced at the cold gleam of the north star, he perceived that he was being led from his direct path. For a moment he hesitated, wondering if he would not better keep to his road, but his weird companion seemed to draw him on irresistibly, and finding it sweet to follow, he followed.

Of course it came to him more than once in that strange pursuit, that the white skater was no earthly guide. Up in those latitudes men see curious things when the hoar frost is on the earth. Hagadorn's own father—to hark no further than that for an instance!—who lived up there with the Lake Superior Indians, and worked in the copper mines, had welcomed a woman at his hut one bitter night, who was gone by morning, leaving wolf tracks on the snow! Yes, it was so, and John Fontanelle, the half-breed, could tell you about it any day—if he were alive. (Alack, the snow where the wolf tracks were, is melted now!)

Well, Hagadorn followed the white skater all the night, and when the ice flushed pink at dawn, and arrows of lovely light shot up into the cold heavens, she was gone, and Hagadorn was at his destination. The sun climbed arrogantly up to his place above all other things, and as Hagadorn took off his skates and glanced carelessly lakeward, he beheld a great wind-rift in the ice, and the waves showing blue and hungry between white fields. Had he rushed along his intended path, watching the stars to guide him, his glance turned upward, all his body at magnificent momentum, he must certainly have gone into that cold grave.

How wonderful that it had been sweet to follow the white skater, and that he followed!

His heart beat hard as he hurried to his friend's house. But he encountered no wedding furore. His friend met him as men *meet* in houses of mourning.

'Is this your wedding face?' cried Hagadorn. 'Why, man, starved as I am, I look more like a bridegroom than you!'

'There's no wedding today!'

'No wedding! Why, you're not—'

'Marie Beaujeu died last night—'

'Marie—'

'Died last night. She had been skating in the afternoon, and she came home chilled and wandering in her mind, as if the frost had got in it somehow. She grew worse and worse, and all the time she talked of you.'

'Of me?'

'We wondered what it meant. No one knew you were lovers.'

'I didn't know it myself; more's the pity. At least, I didn't know—'

'She said you were on the ice, and that you didn't know about the big breaking-up, and she cried to us that the wind was off shore and the rift widening. She cried over and over again that you could come in by the old French creek if you only knew—'

'I came in that way.'

'But how did you come to do that? It's out of the path. We thought perhaps—'

But Hagadorn broke in with his story and told him all as it had come to pass.

That day they watched beside the maiden, who lay with tapers at her head and at her feet, and in the little church the bride who might have been at her wedding said prayers for her friend. They buried Marie Beaujeu in her bridesmaid white, and Hagadorn was before the altar with her, as he had intended from the first! Then at midnight the lovers who were to wed whispered their vows in the gloom of the cold church, and walked together through the snow to lay their bridal wreaths upon a grave.

Three nights later, Hagadorn skated back again to his home. They wanted him to go by sunlight, but he had his way, and went when Venus made her bright path on the ice.

The truth was, he had hoped for the companionship of the white skater. But he did not have it. His only companion was the wind. The only voice he heard was the baying of a wolf on the north shore. The world was as empty and as white as if God had just created it, and the sun had not yet coloured nor man defiled it.

THE BLACK CAT

W. J. Wintle

FIRST PUBLISHED IN *GHOST GLEAMS:
TALES OF THE UNCANNY* (1921)

William James Wintle (1861–1934) was born in Gloucestershire but moved to London as a child and lived there for most of his life. His first profession was as a teacher, and his obituary (in the *Journal of Molluscan Studies*) notes that 'he was so young when he acquired his first headmastership that he had to grow a beard to hide his youthful appearance'. Later he worked as a journalist and his final role was as a publishing director and literary advisor. At the same time as this busy and varied career he somehow also found time to volunteer for his local Roman Catholic church in Chiswick, west London; to have a keen interest in naturalism (including a Fellowship at the Royal Zoological Society and the secretariat of the Malacological Society of London); and to write an impressive number of ghost stories.

'The Black Cat', featuring a man whose cat phobia takes on an altogether more sinister aspect, was published in Wintle's only anthology, *Ghost Gleams: Tales of the Uncanny*. He wrote the contents during a stint as a lay brother at the Abbey on Caldey Island in Wales, intending the stories to entertain the eight boys who attended the Abbey's school. In his foreword to the collection, Wintle paints a vivid picture of the book's origin, explaining that the tales 'were told on Sunday nights to the little group crouching round a wood fire on a windswept island off the Western shore... Truth to tell, the gruesome ones met with the best reception.'

—TK

If there was one animal that Sydney disliked more than another it was a cat. Not that he was not fond of animals in a general way—for he had a distinct affection for an aged retriever that had formerly been his—but somehow a cat seemed to arouse all that was worst in him. It always appeared to him that if he had passed through some previous stage of existence, he must have been a mouse or a bird and thus have inherited—so to speak—an instinctive dread and hatred for the enemy of his earlier days.

The presence of a cat affected him in a very curious fashion. There was first of all a kind of repulsion. The idea of the eyes of the animal being fixed on him; the thought of listening for a sound-less tread; and the imagined touch of the smooth fur; all this made him shudder and shrink back. But this feeling quickly gave place to a still stranger fascination. He felt drawn to the creature that he feared—much as a bird is supposed, but quite erroneously, to be charmed by a snake. He wanted to stroke the animal and to feel its head rubbing against his hand: and yet at the same time the idea of the animal doing so filled him with a dread passing description. It was something like that morbid state in which a person finds actual physical pleasure in inflicting pain on himself. And then there was sheer undisguised fear. Pretend as he might, Sydney was in deadly fear when a cat was in the room. He had tried and tried, time and again, to overcome it; but without success. He had argued from the well-known friendliness of the domestic cat; from its notorious timidity; and from its actual inability to do any very serious harm to a strong and active man. But it was all of no use. He was afraid of cats; and it was useless to deny it.

At the same time, Sydney was no enemy to cats. He was the last man in the world to hurt one. No matter how much his slumber might be disturbed by the vocal efforts of a love-sick marauder on the roof in the small hours of the morning, he would never think of hurling a missile at the offender. The sight of a half-starved cat left behind when its owner was away in the holiday season filled him with a pity near akin to pain. He was a generous subscriber to the Home for Lost Cats. In fact, his whole attitude was inconsistent and contradictory. But there was no escape from the truth—he disliked and feared cats.

Probably this obsession was to some extent fostered by the fact that Sydney was a man of leisure. With more urgent matters to occupy his thoughts, he might have outgrown these fancies with the advance of middle age. But the possession of ample means, an inherited dislike for any kind of work calling for energy, and two or three interesting hobbies which filled up his time in an easy and soothing fashion, left him free to indulge his fancies. And fancies, when indulged, are apt to become one's masters in the end; and so it proved with Sydney.

He was engaged in writing a book on some phase of Egyptian life in the olden days, which involved considerable study of the collections in the British Museum and elsewhere, as well as much search for rare books among the antiquarian bookshops. When not out on these pursuits, he occupied an old house which like most old and rambling places of its kind was the subject of various queer stories among the gossips of the neighbourhood. Some tragedy was supposed to have happened there at some date not defined, and in consequence something was supposed to haunt the place and to do something from time to time. Among local gossips there was much value in that nebulous term 'something', for it covered a multitude of inaccurate recollections and of foggy traditions. Probably Sydney had never heard the reputation of his house, for he led a retired life and had little to do with his neighbours. But if the tales had reached his ears, he gave no sign; nor was he likely to do so. Apart from the cat obsession, he was a man of eminently balanced mind. He was about the last person to imagine things or to be influenced by any but proved facts.

The mystery which surrounded his untimely end came therefore as a great surprise to his friends: and the horror that hung over his later days was only brought to partial light by the discovery of a diary and other papers which have provided the material for this history. Much still remains obscure, and cannot now be cleared up; for the only man who could perhaps throw further light on it is no longer with us. So we have to be content with such fragmentary records as are available.

It appears that some months before the end, Sydney was at home reading in the garden, when his eyes happened to rest upon a small heap of earth that the gardener had left beside the path. There was nothing remarkable about this; but somehow the heap seemed to fascinate him. He resumed his reading; but the heap of earth was insistent in demanding his attention. He could not keep his thoughts off it, and it was hard to keep his eyes off it as well. Sydney was not the man to give way to mental dissipation of this kind, and he resolutely kept his eyes fixed on his book. But it was a struggle; and in the end he gave in. He looked again at the heap; and this time with some curiosity as to the cause of so absurd an attraction.

Apparently there was no cause; and he smiled at the absurdity of the thing. Then he started up suddenly, for he saw the reason of it. The heap of earth was exactly like a black cat! And the cat was crouching as if to spring at him. The resemblance was really absurd, for there were a couple of yellow pebbles just where the eyes should have been. For the moment, Sydney felt all the repulsion and fear that the presence of an actual cat would have caused him. Then he rose from his chair, and kicked the heap out of any resemblance to his feline aversion. He sat down again and laughed at the absurdity of the affair—and yet it somehow left a sense of disquiet and of vague fear behind. He did not altogether like it.

It must have been about a fortnight later when he was inspecting some Egyptian antiquities that had recently reached the hands of a London dealer. Most of them were of the usual types and did not interest him. But a few were better worth attention; and he sat down to examine them carefully. He was specially attracted by some ivory tablets, on which he thought he could faintly trace the remains of handwriting. If so, this was a distinct find, for private memoranda of this sort are very rare and should throw light on some of the more intimate details of private life of the period, which are not usually recorded on the monuments. Absorbed in this study, a sense of undefined horror slowly grew upon him and he found himself in a kind of day dream presenting many of the uncanny qualities of nightmare. He thought himself stroking an immense black cat which grew and grew until it assumed gigantic proportions. Its soft fur thickened around his hands and entwined itself around his fingers like a mass of silky, living snakes; and his skin tingled with multitudinous tiny bites from fangs which were venomous; while the purring of the creature grew until it became a very roar like that of a cataract and overwhelmed his senses. He was mentally drowning in a sea of impending catastrophe, when, by an expiring effort, he wrenched himself free from the obsession and sprang up. Then he discovered that his hand had been mechanically stroking a small unopened animal mummy, which proved on closer examination to be that of a cat.

The next incident that he seems to have thought worth recording happened a few nights later. He had retired to rest in his usual health and slept soundly. But towards morning his slumbers were disturbed by a dream that recalled the kind of nocturnal fear that is common in childhood. Two distant stars began to grow in size and brilliancy until he saw that they were advancing through space towards him with incredible speed. In a few moments they must overwhelm him in a sea of fire and flame. Onwards they came, bulging and unfolding like great flaming flowers, growing more dazzling and blinding at every moment; and then, just as they were upon him, they suddenly turned into two enormous cat's eyes, flaming green and yellow. He sprang up in bed with a cry, and found himself at once wide awake. And there on the window-sill lay a great black cat, glowering at him with lambent yellow eyes. A moment later the cat disappeared.

But the mysterious thing of it was that the window-sill was not accessible to anything that had not wings. There was no means by which a cat could have climbed to it. Nor was there any sign of a cat in the garden below.

The date of the next thing that happened is not clear, for it does not appear to have been recorded at the time. But it would seem to have been within a few days of the curious dream. Sydney had occasion to go to a cupboard which was kept locked. It contained manuscripts and other papers of value; and the key never left his possession. To his knowledge the cupboard had not been

75

opened for at least a month past. He now had occasion to refer to a collection of notes in connection with his favourite study. On opening the cupboard, he was at once struck by a curious odour. It was not exactly musky, but could only be described as an animal odour, slightly suggestive of that of a cat. But what at once arrested Sydney's notice and caused him extreme annoyance was the fact that the papers had been disturbed. The loose papers contained in some pigeon-holes at the back had been drawn forwards into a loose heap on the shelf. They looked for all the world like a nest, for they had been loosely arranged in a round heap with a depression in the middle. It looked as if some animal had coiled itself up to sleep there; and the size of the depression was just such as would be made by a cat.

Sydney was too much annoyed by the disturbance of his papers to be greatly impressed at the moment by their curious arrangement; but it came home to him as a shock when he began to gather the papers together and set them in order. Some of them seemed to be slightly soiled, and on closer examination he found that they were besprinkled with short black hairs like those of a cat.

About a week afterwards he returned later in the evening than usual, after attending a meeting of a scientific society to which he belonged. He was taking his latch key from his pocket to open the door when he thought that something rubbed against his leg. Looking down, he saw nothing; but immediately afterwards he felt it again, and this time he thought he saw a black shadow beside his right foot. On looking more closely, nothing was to be seen; but as he went into the house he distinctly felt something soft brush against his leg. As he paused in the hall to remove his overcoat, he saw a faint shadow which seemed to go up the stairs. It was certainly only a shadow and nothing solid, for the light was good and he saw it clearly. But there was nothing in motion to account for the passing shadow. And the way the shadow moved was curiously suggestive of a cat.

The next notes in the book that Sydney seems to have devoted to this curious subject appear to be a series of mere coincidences: and the fact that he thought them worth recording shows only too clearly to what an extent his mind was now obsessed. He had taken the numerical value of the letters C, A, T, in the alphabet, 3, 1, and 20 respectively, and by adding them together had arrived at the total 24. He then proceeded to note the many ways in which this number had played its part in the events of his life. He was born on the 24th of the month, at a house whose number was 24; and his mother was 24 years old at the time. He was 24 years old when his father died and left him the master of a considerable fortune. That was just 24 years ago. The last time he had balanced his affairs, he found that he was worth in invested funds—apart from land and houses—just about 24 thousand pounds. At three different periods, and in different towns, he had chanced to live at houses numbered 24; and that was also the number of his present abode. Moreover the number of his ticket for the British Museum Reading Room ended with 24, and both his doctor and his solicitor were housed under that same persistent number. Several more of these coincidences had been noted by him; but they were rather far-fetched and are not worth recording here. But the memoranda concluded with the ominous question, 'Will it all end on the 24th?'

Soon after these notes were written, a much more serious affair had to be placed on record. Sydney was coming downstairs one evening, when he noticed in a badly lighted corner of the staircase something that he took to be a cat. He shrank back with his natural dislike for the animal; but on looking more closely he saw that it was nothing more than a shadow cast by some carving on the stair-head. He turned away with a laugh; but, as he turned, it certainly seemed that the shadow moved! As he went down the stairs he twice stumbled in trying to save himself from what he thought was a cat in danger of being trodden upon; and a moment later he seemed to tread on something soft that gave way and threw him down. He fell heavily and shook himself badly.

On picking himself up with the aid of his servant he limped into his library, and there found that his trousers were torn from a little above the ankle. But the curious thing was that there were three parallel vertical tears—just such as might be caused by the claws of a cat. A sharp smarting led to further investigation; and he then found that there were three deep scratches on the side of his leg, exactly corresponding with the tears in the trousers.

In the margin of the page on which he recorded this accident, he has added the words, 'This cat means mischief.' And the whole tone of the remaining entries and of the few letters that date from this time shows only too clearly that his mental outlook was more or less tinged and obscured by gloomy forebodings.

It would seem to have been on the following day that another disturbing trifle occurred. Sydney's leg still pained him, and he spent the day on a couch with one or two favourite books. Soon after two o'clock in the afternoon, he heard a soft thud, such as might be caused by a cat leaping down from a moderate height. He looked up, and there on the window-sill crouched a black cat with gleaming eyes; and a moment later it sprang into the room. But it never reached the floor—or, if it did, it must have passed through it! He saw it spring; he saw it for the moment in mid-air; he saw it about to alight on the floor; and then—it was not there!

He would have liked to believe that it was a mere optical delusion; but against that theory stood the awkward fact that the cat in springing down from the window knocked over a flower-pot; and there lay the broken pieces in evidence of the fact.

He was now seriously scared. It was bad enough to find himself seeing things that had no objective reality; but it was far worse to be faced by happenings that were certainly real, but not to be accounted for by the ordinary laws of nature. In this case the broken flower-pot showed that if the black cat was merely what we call a ghost for lack of any more convenient term, it was a ghost that was capable of producing physical effects. If it could knock a flower-pot over, it could presumably scratch and bite—and the prospect of being attacked by a cat from some other plane of existence will hardly bear being thought of.

Certainly it seemed that Sydney had now real ground for alarm. The spectre cat—or whatever one likes to call it—was in some way gaining power and was now able to manifest its presence and hostility in more open and practical fashion. That same night saw a proof of this. Sydney dreamed that he was visiting the Zoological Gardens when a black leopard of ferocious aspect escaped from its cage and sprang upon him. He was thrown backwards to the ground and pinned down by the heavy animal. He was half crushed by its weight; its claws were at his throat; its fierce yellow eyes were staring into his face; when the horror of the thing brought the dream to a sudden end and he awoke. As consciousness returned he was aware of an actual weight on his chest; and on opening his eyes he looked straight into the depths of two lambent yellow flames set in a face of velvet black. The cat sprang off the bed and leaped through the window. But the window was closed and there was no sound of breaking glass.

79

Sydney did not sleep much more that night. But a further shock awaited him on rising. He found some small bloodstains on his pillow; and an inspection before the looking glass showed the presence of two groups of tiny wounds on his neck. They were little more than pin-pricks; but they were arranged in two semi-circular groups, one on either side of the neck and just such as might be caused by a cat trying to grasp the neck between its two forepaws.

This was the last incident recorded in Sydney's diary; and the serious view that he took of the situation is shown by certain letters that he wrote during the day, giving final instructions to his executors and settling various details of business—evidently in view of his approaching end.

What happened in the course of the final scene of the tragedy we can only guess from the traces left behind: but there is sufficient evidence to show that the horror was an appalling one.

The housekeeper seems to have been awakened once during the night by a strange noise which she could only describe as being like an angry cat snarling; while the parlour maid, whose room was immediately above that occupied by Sydney, says that she dreamt that she heard her master scream horribly once or twice.

In the morning, Sydney did not answer when called at his usual hour; and, as the door was found to be locked, the housekeeper presently procured assistance and had it broken open. He was found crouching on the floor and leaning against the wall opposite the window. The carpet was saturated with blood; and the cause was quickly evident. The unfortunate man's throat had been torn open on either side, both jugular veins being severed. So far as could be made out, he had retired to bed and had been attacked during sleep, for the sheets were bespattered with blood. He had apparently got out of bed in his struggles to overcome the Thing that had him fast in its fearful grip. The look of horror on his distorted face was said by the witnesses to be past description.

Both window and door were fastened, and there was nothing to show how the assailant entered. But there was something to show how it left. The bloodstains on the floor recorded the footprints of a gigantic cat. They led across the floor from the corpse to the opposite wall—and there they ceased. The cat never came back; but whether it passed through the solid wall or melted into thin air, no one knows. In some mysterious way it came and went; and in passing it did this deed of horror.

It was a curious coincidence that the tragedy took place on Christmas Eve—the 24th day of the month!

GANTHONY'S WIFE

E. Temple Thurston

FIRST PUBLISHED IN *THE ROSETTI
AND OTHER TALES*, 1926

Ernest Temple Thurston (1879–1933) was known as a poet and playwright in his early career before becoming a prolific author of fiction. His best known novel was *The City of Beautiful Nonsense* (1909) which was adapted for two different film versions. His private life was not without its complications—he was married three times—but this doesn't seem to have interrupted the production of a dauntingly large bibliography.

'Ganthony's Wife' is a tale told in that old tradition, gathered around the fire with family, and Thurston puts his narrator at the heart of the story. However, the action takes us to the plantations of Sri Lanka and then back to London at Christmas to snow which is falling like 'a muslin curtain'. The evocative descriptions of the capital in the 1920s are the backdrop for an unexpected and chilling appearance.   —LE

The custom of telling stories round the fire on Christmas Eve is dying out, like letter-writing and all the amateur domestic arts of the last century. Our stories are told us by professionals and broadcast to thousands by the printing machine. We give our letters to a dictaphone or a stenographer. The personal touch is going out of life, if it has not already gone. In an age where every conceivable machine is invented to save time and labour, we have no time to spare for these things. We are too exhausted from working our machines to give them our attention.

We were saying all this last year as we sat round a blazing wood fire at that little house party the Stennings give every Christmas in that Tudor house of theirs on the borders of Kent and Sussex.

The children had gone to bed. There were five of us grown-ups left round the broad open fireplace where huge oak logs were burning on the glowing heart of a pile of silver ashes that had been red-hot for a week or more.

Miss Valerie Brett, the actress, was sitting inside the chimney corner warming first one toe, then the other. She comes there every Christmas. The children love her. She can make funny noises with her mouth. Also by facial contortion, she can look like Queen Victoria on the heads of all the pennies that ever were minted. In a semi-circle outside we sat, the rest of us, Stenning and his wife, Northanger and myself, smoking our various smokes and sipping that punch, the secret of which Stenning learnt from an old wine merchant in Winthrop Street, Cork. I think he relies on it to secure the few select guests he always has at his Christmas parties.

'Come down for Christmas. Punch.'

This is a common form of his invitation.

We had been playing games with the children, hide-and-seek being the most popular. We were all a bit exhausted. It was Mrs Stenning who opened the discussion by complaining that there was no one qualified to tell children ghost stories nowadays.

'We had a man here last Christmas,' she said, 'and he began one, but the children guessed the end of it before it was halfway through.'

'Bless 'em,' said Miss Brett.

'It was a rotten story, anyhow,' said Stenning. 'You can't make a mystery now by just rattling a chain and slamming a door and blowing out the candle. When the candle went out, young John said, "Why didn't he shut the window?" Our amiable story teller assured John that he did, but he wasn't convincing about it, because Emily said, "'Spect it was like that window up in my bedroom. The wind comes through there when it's shut and blows the curtains about."'

Mrs Stenning sighed.

'I suppose they know too much,' she said—'and all I've done, you don't know, to try and keep them simple.'

'They don't know too much,' said Northanger. 'It's more likely we who know too little. We don't believe in the rattling chain and the extinguished candle ourselves. We've been laughing at them for the last twenty years, and they've caught up with us.'

'Do you mean this civilization's at the end of its evolution?' I asked.

'Either that,' said he, 'or we're in one of those hanging pauses, like a switchback when it gets to the top of a crest and just crawls over the top till it gathers a fresh impetus to rise to a higher crest. It's only pessimists who say we're finished. Shedding an old skin is a proper process of nature. There are signs of the old skin going.'

Northanger is a queer chap. He talks very little. This was voluble for him. As usually happens with a man like that, we listened.

'What signs?' asked Miss Brett.

'All sorts,' said he. 'There's even a new ghost. I saw one last Christmas.'

'You saw one?'

Two or three of us spoke at once.

'I saw one,' he repeated.

If a man like Northanger admits to seeing a ghost, we felt there must be something in it. It would not be a mere turnip head with a candle inside.

'Why didn't you tell us when the children were here?' asked Mrs Stenning immediately.

'It's not a story for children,' he replied. 'Though I don't know why it shouldn't be. They wouldn't understand it, and that's the first quality required of a ghost story.'

'Tell us.'

This was practically simultaneous from everybody. Miss Brett pulled her feet up on to the chimney-corner seat. Stenning slipped over to the table and brought round the punch bowl to fill our glasses. I say 'slipped over' because he moved like a man who does not want to disturb an atmosphere. Somehow that chap Northanger had put a grip on us. We felt he knew that what he was going to tell us was unknowable. He had indeed created an atmosphere, the atmosphere that Stenning was careful not to disturb. There was the proper sort of hush in the air while he was filling our glasses. No one had lit the lights since we had been playing at hide-and-seek. We were all grouped around the light of the fire. Then Northanger began.

'Do any of you know Ganthony—Ganthony's a tea planter in Ceylon?'

None of us did.

'Well—that makes it better,' said he. Then he looked across at Miss Brett. 'You and I haven't met before, Miss Brett,' he said, 'till our good friends brought us together this Christmas. I've seen you on the stage, but not being one of those admirers who have the courage to offer their congratulations without introduction, you haven't seen me till now.'

In that prelude, I suddenly had a glimpse of Northanger's way with women, an odd sardonic sort of way, too subtle for most of them, but conveying with it an impression that he was not unsusceptible.

She smiled as he continued:

'In case our good friends haven't told you then,' he went on, 'it's necessary to say I'm a bachelor. I have rooms in Stretton Street, Piccadilly. I've been there seventeen years. When they pull down Devonshire House, they pull me off my perch. That'll be the end of Stretton Street. I don't mean my going. But without the restraining influence of the Baroness Burdett-Coutts and the Duke of Devonshire, Stretton Street will become anybody's street. A cinema theatre in those new buildings they are going to put up on the site of Devonshire House will send Stretton Street to the dogs. It's like that with people. Ninety per cent of us live by example. However, my story's about Ganthony.

'It was last Christmas. I mean 1923. I was staying in town. I often do. I like London on Christmas Day.'

Miss Brett shuddered.

'Yes—I know,' said Northanger. 'London seems dead to lots of people when the shops are shut, and the theatres are closed. It doesn't get me like that. It seems alive to me.'

'What with?' It was Mrs Stenning who asked this.

'With the spirits of people. We were talking about ghosts. Well, how could you expect a ghost to clank a chain when the rattle of motor buses would drown the noise of it out of existence? What's the good of blowing out candles when the streets are daylight with night signs? There's one thing I always do when I'm in London on Christmas Day. I go to my club. It used to be one of the old gaming houses before the Regency. Modern interior decoration has hidden all that, but on Christmas Day, when some of the rooms are absolutely empty, they come back, the old gamesters. You can feel them about you. Imagination, I know—but who has properly defined what imagination is? Memory's impulse of association isn't good enough. Where does the impulse come from?

'I always go to my club. I went there that afternoon and to my amazement found Ganthony in the smoking-room writing letters. Ganthony is one of those men who belong to a London club and appear in it, somewhat like a comet, at rare intervals. Suddenly he walks in, gets his letters from the hall porter, fills a waste-paper basket with the accumulated rubbish, and writes a pile of answers. For the next week or so you can find him practically at any moment on the premises. Then one day, you say to the hall porter, "Mr Ganthony in the club?" "Mr Ganthony, sir? He's gone."

'Perhaps as much as three years go by before you see him again. That Christmas Day I hadn't seen him for four years at least. He was surrounded with letters and was writing for all he was worth. I think he was as glad to see me as I was to see him. He'd just come home from Ceylon—didn't know how long he was going to stay. He never does. I picked out a comfortable chair and we talked. Presently I inquired about his wife, whether he'd brought her with him—how she was. His eyes went like pebbles when the water's dried off them.

'"My wife died nearly a year ago," said he.

'I must tell you about Ganthony's wife. He had met and married her during the War. But the War had nothing to do with it. We've got into the habit of putting those hurried marriages down to the War. Whenever they'd met, Ganthony would have married her. It was the case of a man meeting the fate that was in store for him and rushing to it like a bit of steel to a magnet. What he had meant to her I've never been able to quite satisfy my mind about. The relationships that circumstance contrives between individuals must have some sort of scheme about them. But I'm blowed if it's possible to begin to think what it is or how it's regulated.

'Ganthony met her in a restaurant. He'd just come out of hospital. Been knocked out by a shell burst on Vimy Ridge. His face had been cut about and was still all wrapped in bandages. One side of his face was fairly clear—on the other, his eye just peeped out of a mass of lint. He didn't care what he looked like. In fact I think it rather amused him to go and dine in public. He went alone.

'She was dining at a table a few yards away with a man. Like everyone else she was attracted by the sight of this bandaged face of Ganthony's. She drew her companion's attention. I had all this from Ganthony himself just before he was married. It was as though she said, "They've been knocking him about— haven't they?"

'The man looked at him for a moment or two. Wounded men were pretty common those days. He was a soldier himself. He was in khaki. He took no more notice. But the woman went on looking. Every other second Ganthony caught her eye. More than that, he could see she didn't want her companion to notice it. Something about it intrigued Ganthony. The scheme, whatever it is, was beginning to work. The fate was beginning to draw him. He smiled—so far as that was possible with half his face in bandages. She smiled in return—one of those smiles a woman can hide from everyone but the person for whom it is intended. In a few minutes they were talking to each other with their eyes, that sort of conversation that isn't hampered with the expression and meaning of mere words.

'Ganthony cut a course out and finished his meal before they did. He ordered his bill when she was looking at him. He paid it, looked at the door, then at her, then he got up and went out. He hadn't to wait more than two seconds before she was outside on the pavement beside him. She'd made some excuse to her companion. She had for decency's sake to go back and finish her dinner. They arranged to meet later.

'They were married in a week. No need to tell you more than that. You can put it down to the War if you like. But Ganthony wasn't the sort of man to marry that sort of woman just because there was a war on. He did it with his eyes open even if his face was bandaged. He knew the kind she was. He knew he wasn't the first, but I suppose he may have thought that when he took her out to Ceylon after he was quit of the War, he would be the last. I never thought so. But it was no good telling him that. When a man runs into his fate as he did, platitudes and speculations about morals don't stop him. He has to find things out for himself. God disposes sometimes, it seems to me before and after a man's proposal.

'Anyhow that's as much as it has to do with this story. Ganthony had married and now his wife was dead. I confess to a feeling of satisfaction when I heard it. She was a beautiful woman no doubt—intensely attractive. I had never seen her, but he had sent me a snapshot of himself and her from Ceylon after they got out there. However, attraction isn't everything. It invites, but it doesn't always entertain.'

'It doesn't sound very much like a ghost story,' said Mrs Stenning. Northanger apologized.

'I warned you it wasn't a ghost story for children,' said he. 'I told you they wouldn't understand it. I doubt if I understand it myself.'

'Shove a log on, Valerie,' said Stenning, 'and don't interrupt him, Grace. The man's earning his punch with me anyhow. Go on, Northanger. You tell it your own way. Women always want to see the last page. Ganthony's wife was dead.'

'Yes—dead,' Northanger went on. 'Ganthony saw her dead. They had lived in Colombo for the first six or eight months and apparently in that short time, he came to know how attractive she was. And yet, it was not only her physical attraction for men, he told me, as a sort of fatality about her that drew them as it had drawn him.

'Apparently he knew nothing in fact. She was not so much secretive about it, as almost mysterious. As far as I can make out, it was as though she had a vocation for that sort of life, like the sacred women in the temple of Osiris at Thebes. I can imagine her having been extraordinarily mysterious with that other man in the restaurant when she first met Ganthony. She must have just slipped away from him when that dinner was over. At one moment he may have thought she was his for the evening. The next she was gone.

'It was the beginning of that feeling in Ganthony that at any moment he might lose her, made him leave Colombo and take her up country to a spot close to his plantations. She made no complaint. It was not as though she were a gay woman and were being torn away from her gaiety. She went without a word. He was terribly fond of her. Any fool could have seen that. Notwithstanding the way he had met her, it had not continued to be promiscuous with him. She was a sacred women to him right enough. He told me about her death, in that slow, measured sort of way as a man walks at the end of a journey. Whatever she'd been, her death had left a wound in his life that wouldn't heal in a hurry.'

'Are we to hear how she did die?' I asked.

'Yes—I want to hear how she died,' said Miss Brett.

'I'm coming to that,' said Northanger. 'Away there up country, Ganthony felt she was safe. Except down at the plantations, there were no Englishmen about. After a few months up there, when she seemed to be quite contented, Ganthony had to go down to Colombo on business. He was gone three days. When he came back, she was gone. The native servants were in a panic. He scoured the country for two days. They'd heard nothing of her down at the plantations. She'd vanished—slipped away. On the third day, coming back after a fruitless search, he found a Buddhist priest waiting for him at his bungalow. All the man would say was, "I've come to bring you to see the memsahib." Ganthony followed him. Again and again he asked the fellow what was the matter, threatened him, tried to frighten him, but he'd say nothing except—"You shall see the memsahib."

'On the side of a hill about three miles from Ganthony's bungalow, there was a Buddhist monastery. He was taken there, and there on a rough sort of bed in one of the rooms—it was a rest place—he found his wife lying—dead. There was no question of getting a doctor. There was not a doctor within miles.

'I asked him if he was sure she was dead, and he turned those stone eyes of his on me.

'"You have to be your own doctor out there," said he, "and there are one or two things you can't fail to recognize. Death's one of 'em. She'd been dead some time. She was quite cold. There's no mistaking when the spirit's gone out of the body. Hers was gone. I could feel it had. She lay there, just a dead body, and I felt I couldn't touch her then—it seemed repulsive without her spirit."

'I asked him how she got there, what he thought she'd died of, how long he imagined she'd been dead. None of his answers were very elaborate. He made it out to be fever. She had walked by herself into the monastery. She must have been dead two days. He arrived at that decision apart from what the monks told him.

'Then he said an extraordinary thing which made me realize the repulsion he had felt for that body bereft of its spirit.

'"I left her there," he said—"they buried her."

'Well, that was Ganthony's story as he told it me that Christmas afternoon in the club. We had tea together while we talked. After that he went back to finish his letters. I went into the reading-room till about a quarter to seven. It was snowing then, coming down like a white fog over the black darkness outside. There was hardly a taxi moving in the streets. I'd ordered my dinner for eight o'clock at my rooms. I went out of the reading-room to make a move towards Stretton Street and then I thought of Ganthony, probably dining there in the club by himself. I looked into the smoking-room and asked him to come along. He pushed his hand through his bundle of letters.

'"Only half finished," said he.

'"Finish 'em tomorrow."

"'No,' he said, "I'll get 'em done now while I'm at it. If I get finished before ten, I'll look in and have a drink with you. But no more raising from the dead. That's buried."

'I nodded my head. It was plain he wasn't coming. When a man wants to do a thing, he does it without ifs and buts. Those are feminine prerogatives. I left him to his letters. I walked out of the club, pushed my way through that white storm across the black gape of Trafalgar Square, up the Haymarket, and turned off into Jermyn Street.

'I always think Jermyn Street is a queer street. I've known odd men living there, in little rooms over little shops. It keeps an atmosphere about it which the rest of London is losing as fast as a woman loses self-respect directly she takes to drink. It has dark, sunken doorways. The houses are so close together that you hardly ever look up at the windows as you pass along its narrow thoroughfare. I never used to think of the existence of those windows till an odd chap I knew invited me to his rooms there. There was something so queer about them that after that, I spent a morning walking along the north side of Jermyn Street looking up at the houses on the opposite side. They're nearly all of them funny. They're hiding places. And the street itself has got that feeling. So much has it got it, that it is one of the favourite walking places of that band of sisters who count the world well lost for—why shouldn't they call it love?

'I never expected to see one of them that night. There wasn't a soul anywhere. The snow was coming down like a muslin curtain of a big design. A policeman passed me. His footsteps and mine were silent in the snow. I wished him a happy Christmas as I went by. His answer was like the voice of a man with a respirator on. The snow had dressed him in white. He just appeared and disappeared.

'I was getting near the St James's end, just about where old Cox's Hotel used to stand when through that muslin curtain of snow, just as through the curtains you can dimly see someone moving about inside a room, I saw a figure coming towards me. I felt a moment's surprise. It was a woman.

'There were not many steps for us to approach each other before we met. With that snow the whole of London was cramped up into the dimensions of a narrow, little room. As we passed, it was just as though she had pulled the curtains for an instant and looked through the window at me. Then, like the policeman, she was gone.'

It might have been the instinct of a raconteur to heighten the suspense, but here Northanger stopped and looked at Valerie Brett.

'Go on,' we said.

'Well,' said he, 'I'm considering this young lady's feeling. To give you the proper impression of what happened, I have to be what the novelists call—psychological here. Will she mind?'

'Don't be an ass,' said Stenning. 'You know jolly well you're only trying to tantalize us. Go on with your psychology. She's on the stage. They're full of psychology there.'

'I only felt it necessary,' said Northanger, 'to describe a man's attitude towards encounters like this. Perhaps it would be more accurate to say my own towards this particular one. Because though, as far as the story is, she'd gone by, there had been that half-instant's pause—the moment as I said when she seemed to have pulled the muslin curtains and looked at me out of the window. That pause was indescribable. It was an encounter. Most often a woman like that says something—a fatuous word of endearment—a challenge—a salute as if you were old friends. This woman didn't say anything. She just looked through that pause at me, and though I could not have described her for the life of me, I felt clearly conscious of her personality.

'I don't know what a woman feels like about her own sex of that class. I expect most men would have felt what I did then, a sort of demand for consideration, quite unsupported by the conscience or moral standards of a county councillor. Christmas Day and that snowstorm when most people were sitting beside a warm fire awaiting the announcement of a comfortable meal! I felt pretty sorry for her. I suppose it was this and that consciousness of her personality made me turn. If she had said anything I should have walked straight on. She had gone by in silence, and I turned.

'She had not only turned as well. She had stopped. With all that snow on the ground I hadn't heard her. We stood there looking at each other and then she came back.

'"Going to your club?" she said.

'"Coming from it," said I.

'"Going home, I suppose?"

'I nodded my head.

'"And all the family expecting you back to dinner?"

'I told her there was no family—merely dinner.

'"Alone?" she asked.

'"Quite alone," said I.

'That didn't deter her. She started walking in my direction. I should have looked a fool if I had refused to accompany her. Besides that, there's a considerable excitement of interest in talking to an absolute stranger of the other sex. Men and women too would indulge more frequently in that kind of adventure if they weren't so afraid of appearances. Probably the snowstorm gave me courage. We walked into St James's Street together and up into Piccadilly.

'"I live just in Stretton Street," said I. "If you come much farther, a mere common politeness will compel me to ask you in to dinner."

'"If you did," said she, "a mere common appetite for a comfortable meal would compel me to accept."

'The human voice is an extraordinary thing. It is an unfailing indication of character and personality. You can't really fake it. The best actor or actress in the world'—he made a sweep of his hand excluding Valerie Brett—'can only make up their face. They can't make up their voice. They can imitate. But that's not the same thing. There was something in this woman's voice that guaranteed me against feeling ashamed of myself before my man, Charles. Charles is essentially a diplomat, but he has taste. How she was dressed didn't matter so much. How she was dressed I couldn't see, covered as she was with the snow that was falling. I don't know anything about women's dress, but I was conscious of the impression that she was what a man calls—all right.

'"Allow me to invite you then," said I, and when she accepted I felt I had done a thing which you do, not so much because you want to, as because of some arrangement of things which needs a certain act from you at a certain given moment. I felt that Ganthony's refusal to come and dine with me was an essential part of that whole arrangement. I felt that my will was not concerned in the matter. I walked up the steps and opened the door with my latchkey, and it seemed as though it were a mere act of obedience on my part. When she passed me into the hall it was as though she had the control of the situation, not I.

'I am trying to convey my impressions to you in the light of what happened, yet I don't want to exaggerate those impressions because, up to the last moment, there was no reason why it should not have appeared absolutely natural. A little unconventional perhaps—but that's all.

'I have only four rooms at Stretton Street—a dining-room, a sitting-room and two bedrooms. Charles showed her along to the spare bedroom to take her coat off and tidy up. It was ten minutes off dinner. And here is another impression I'm sure I don't exaggerate. Charles's manner from the moment he saw her was by no means that of the incomparable diplomat. It was not that he objected to her coming to a meal in the flat so much as that he would have avoided the situation if he could. When I taxed him with it afterwards, he said:

"'I make my apologies, sir, if I showed anything."

"'You disapproved, Charles?" I asked him.

"'No, sir—why should I disapprove?"

"'Then what was it?"

"'I just felt awkward, sir—I felt as though the lady knew more about things than what I did, which is an uncomfortable feeling, sir, when it's a woman."

'Well—that's that. Charles has no reason to exaggerate his impressions, because I've never told him anything. Anyhow, we don't matter. She's the centre of the tale. She came into the sitting-room in about five minutes with her coat and hat off. I suppose she was well-dressed. I can only tell you there was nothing of Jermyn Street about her appearance. At the same time, there she was, unmistakably the courtesan. I don't mean that she was rouged or dyed. I don't mean that she made advances to me. I don't mean that her conversation was anything but what any woman's might have been who found herself dining with a man completely strange to her. She was perfectly natural, and yet there was this extraordinary suggestion about her that she was not just one of a type, but the type itself embodied in one person.

'Added to this was the impression I received directly she entered the room, that I had seen her before. Again and again through dinner, stealing glances, because I had a strong reluctance to show how interested I was, I tried to place her somewhere in my life. I failed so completely that for a time I gave it up. We just talked—oh, about all sorts of things. It came to jewellery. She was wearing a big cabochon ruby in a ring. It was the only bit of jewellery she had. I admired it and asked her where it came from.

'"I got that in Ceylon," said she.

'Suddenly my memory quickened. I held my tongue till we got into the sitting-room. Then, while we were drinking coffee, I looked straight at her and said: "Did you know a man named Ganthony in Ceylon?"

'If I had expected any flutter of surprise I was disappointed. Very serenely she looked at me and she said:

'"Are you trying to place me?"

'I admit for the moment I was disconcerted. I didn't know whether to apologize—or frankly agree that I was.

'"My inquisitiveness is not as rude as it appears," I said. "I have a reason for asking."

'She inquired quite placidly what it was.

'For answer I went straight across to my desk. Somewhere in one of the drawers was that snapshot Ganthony had sent me from Ceylon. I fished it out, satisfied myself first, and then brought it across to her. So far as a snapshot can be said to be a likeness in its minute dimensions and unposed effect, that picture of Ganthony's wife was the picture of the woman who was sitting there in my room. I'll swear to that.

'She took it from my hand. For quite a long while she sat there looking at it, a slow smile spreading over her face as I watched her. At the sound of the door-bell of my flat, she looked up, straight at me.

'"Docs this man named Ganthony come here?" she asked.

'Then it suddenly occurred to me. This was Ganthony. It couldn't be anyone else—and somehow she knew it. I hurried out of the room before Charles could open the door. It was Ganthony. Despite his ifs and buts he'd come. And all this seemed part of the arrangement—part of some scheme of things which none of us could have prevented. I caught his arm as he passed through the door.

'"Are you prepared for a shock?" I said as quietly as I could.

'I don't know why he should have looked distressed so quickly, but he did.

'"What is it?" he asked.

'I pointed to my sitting-room door.

'"Your wife's in there," said I.

'"My wife's dead," he said, and there was a sharp note of anger in his voice. "I told you she was dead. I saw her dead"—and thrusting my arm away before I could stop him, he strode to the door, opened it and went in. For a moment I wondered whether I should follow. There's a sound principle about not interfering between a husband and wife. I was just about to go into the dining-room when the sense of an odd silence got me. There were no voices. I followed him. Ganthony was standing in the middle of the room staring at the little photograph of her. There was no one else there.

'Without a word to him I went to the little bedroom that opened off the sitting-room. Her hat and coat were gone. I came back and walked across to the window. My flat is on the ground floor. I opened the window. There were no signs of her having gone that way, though certainly the snow was falling so fast that if there had been, her footsteps outside would have been covered by them.

'I turned back and looked at Ganthony.

'"I'll swear," I began.

'He just smiled at me, a thin sort of a smile, the smile of a man who has plumbed the depths of suffering and knows that nothing more can hurt him.

'"Don't bother," said he. "I've seen her myself. Nearly a year ago it was, at Monte Carlo. Last September I was in London. Just for three days. I saw her then. She's dead," he added, "I saw her dead—as dead as that sort of women ever dies."'

Northanger passed his glass to Stenning to be replenished. All our minds were battling through the subsequent silence to ply him with our questions.

'It's no good asking me any more about it,' said he—'that's all I know and I don't pretend to understand.'

MR HUFFAM

Hugh Walpole

FIRST PUBLISHED IN *STRAND MAGAZINE*, DECEMBER 1933

Sir Hugh Seymour Walpole (1884–1941) was born in Auckland, New Zealand to English parents, and spent his childhood in New York and at various English boarding schools. He was related to two important Gothic writers—Horace Walpole, who wrote the first Gothic novel *The Castle of Otranto* in 1764, and Richard Harris Barham, author of *The Ingoldsby Legends*. He became a prolific novelist himself, publishing his most famous book *Rogue Herries*, an historical novel set near his home in Cumbria, in 1930. He was shocked that same year when his friend Somerset Maugham included a satirical portrait of him in the novel *Cakes and Ale*, saying 'I could think of no one among my contemporaries who had achieved so considerable a position on so little talent.' This shook his confidence and he wrote sadly in his diary in 1935, 'shall I have any lasting reputation? Like every author in history who has seriously tried to be an artist, I sometimes consider the question. Fifty years from now I think the Lake stories will still be read locally, otherwise I shall be mentioned in a small footnote to my period in literary history.' However, he was admired by writers including Arnold Bennett, Clemence Dane, J. B. Priestley and Joseph Conrad, and he was a close friend of Virginia Woolf. He was in a long-term relationship until his death with a former policeman called Harold Cheevers who was known officially as his chauffeur.

'Mr Huffam' is a classic Christmas ghost story which draws on the Victorian tradition, and is light-hearted and warming rather than terrifying.   —TK

Once upon a time (it doesn't matter when it was except that it was long after the Great War) young Tubby Winsloe was in the act of crossing Piccadilly just below Hatchard's bookshop. It was three days before Christmas and there had been a frost, a thaw, and then a frost again. The roads were treacherous, traffic nervous and irresponsible, while against the cliff-like indifference of brick and mortar a thin, faint snow was falling from a primrose-coloured sky. Soon it would be dusk and the lights would come out. Then things would be more cheerful.

It would, however, take more than lights to restore Tubby's cheerfulness. Rubicund of face and alarmingly stout of body for a youth of twenty-three, he had just then the spirit of a damp face-towel, for only a week ago Diana Lane-Fox had refused to consider for a moment the possibility of marrying him.

'I like you, Tubby,' she had said. 'I think you have a kind heart. But marry you! You are useless, ignorant and greedy. You're disgracefully fat, and your mother worships you.'

He had not known, until Diana refused him, how bitterly alone he would find himself. He had money, friends, a fine roof above his head; he had seemed to himself popular wherever he went.

'Why, there's old Tubby!' everyone had cried.

It was true that he was fat, it was true that his mother adored him. He had not, until now, known that these were drawbacks. He had seemed to himself until a week ago the friend of all the world. Now he appeared a pariah.

Diana's refusal of him had been a dreadful shock. He had been quite sure that she would accept him. She had gone with him gladly to dances and the pictures. She had, it seemed approved highly of his mother, Lady Winsloe, and his father, Sir Roderick Winsloe, Bart. She had partaken, again and again, of the Winsloe hospitality.

All, it seemed to him, that was needed was for him to say the word. He could choose his time. Well, he *had* chosen his time— at the Herries dance last Wednesday evening. This was the result.

He had expected to recover. His was naturally a buoyant nature. He told himself, again and again, that there were many other fish in the matrimonial sea. But it appeared that there were not. He wanted Diana and only Diana.

He halted at the resting-place halfway across the street, and sighed so deeply that a lady with a little girl and a fierce-looking Chow dog looked at him severely, as though she would say:

'Now this is Christmas time—a gloomy period for all concerned. It is an unwarranted impertinence for anyone to make it yet more gloomy.'

There was someone else clinging to this small fragment of security. A strange-looking man. His appearance was so .unusual that Tubby forgot his own troubles in his instant curiosity. The first unusual thing about this man was that he had a beard. Beards were then very seldom worn. Then his clothes, although they were clean and neat, were most certainly old-fashioned. He was wearing a high sharp-pointed collar, a black stock with a jewelled tie-pin, and a most remarkable waistcoat, purple in colour, and covered with little red flowers. He was carrying a large, heavy-looking brown bag. His face was bronzed and he made Tubby think of a retired sea captain.

But the most remarkable thing of all about him was the impression that he gave of restless, driving energy. It was all that he could do to keep quiet. His strong, wiry figure seemed to burn with some secret fire. The traffic rushed madly past, but, at every moment when there appeared a brief interval between the cars and the omnibuses, this bearded gentleman with the bag made a little dance and once he struck the Chow with his bag and once nearly thrust the small child into the road.

The moment came when, most unwisely, he darted forth. He was almost caught by an imperious, disdainful Rolls-Royce. The lady gave a little scream and Tubby caught his arm, held him, drew him back.

'That nearly had you, sir!' Tubby murmured, his hand still on his arm. The stranger smiled—a most charming smile that shone from his eyes, his beard, his very hands.

'I must thank you,' he said, bowing with old-fashioned courtesy. 'But damn it, as the little boy said to the grocer, "there's no end to the dog," as he saw the sausages coming from the sausage machine.'

At this he laughed very heartily and Tubby had to laugh, too, although the remark did not seem to him very amusing.

'The traffic's very thick at Christmas-time,' Tubby said. 'Everyone doing their shopping, you know.'

The stranger nodded.

'Splendid time, Christmas!' he said. 'Best of the year!'

'Oh, do you think so?' said Tubby. 'I doubt if you'll find people to agree with you. It isn't the thing to admire Christmas these days.'

'Not the thing!' said the stranger, amazed. 'Why, what's the matter?'

This was a poser because so many things were the matter, from Unemployment to Diana. Tubby was saved for the moment from answering.

'Now there's a break,' he said. 'We can cross now.' Cross they did, the stranger swinging his body as though at any instant he might spring right off the ground.

'Which way are you going?' Tubby asked. It astonished him afterwards when he looked back and remembered this question. It was not his way to make friends of strangers, his theory being that everyone was out to 'do' everyone, and in these days especially.

'To tell you the truth I don't quite know,' the stranger said. 'I've only just arrived.'

'Where have you come from?' asked Tubby.

The stranger laughed.

'I've been moving about for a long time. I'm always on the move. I'm considered a very restless man by my friends.'

They were walking along very swiftly, for it was cold and the snow was falling fast now.

'Tell me,' said the stranger, '—about its being a bad time. What's the matter?'

What was the matter? What a question!

Tubby murmured:

'Why, everything's the matter—unemployment—no trade— *you* know.'

'No, I don't. I've been away. I think everyone looks very jolly.'

'I say, don't you feel cold without an overcoat?' Tubby asked.

'Oh, that's nothing,' the stranger answered. 'I'll tell you when I *did* feel cold though. When I was a small boy I worked in a factory putting labels on to blacking-bottles. It was cold *then*. Never known such cold. Icicles would hang on the end of your nose!'

'No!' said Tubby.

'They did, I assure you, and the blacking-bottles would be coated with ice!'

By this time they had reached Berkeley Street. The Winsloe mansion was in Hill Street.

'I turn up here,' said Tubby.

'Oh, do you?'

The stranger looked disappointed. He smiled and held out his hand.

Then Tubby did another extraordinary thing. He said:

'Come in and have a cup of tea. Our place is only five yards up the street.'

'Certainly,' the stranger said. 'Delighted.'

As they walked up Berkeley Street, he went on confidentially:

'I haven't been in London for a long time. All these vehicles are very confusing. But I like it—I like it immensely. It's so lively, and then the town's so quiet compared with what it was when I lived here.'

'Quiet!' said Tubby.

'Certainly. There were cobbles, and the carts and drays screamed and rattled like the damned.'

'But that's years ago!'

'Yes. I'm older than I look.'

Then, pointing, he added:

'But that's where Dorchester House was. So they've pulled it down. What a pity!'

'Oh, everything's pulled down now,' said Tubby.

'I acted there once—a grand night we had. Fond of acting?'

'Oh, I'd be no good,' said Tubby modestly, 'too self-conscious.'

'Ah, you mustn't be self-conscious,' said the stranger. 'Thinking of yourself only breeds trouble, as the man said to the hangman just before they dropped him.'

'Isn't that bag a terrible weight?' Tubby asked.

'I've carried worse things than this,' said the stranger. 'I carried a four-poster once, all the way from one end of the Marshalsea to the other.'

They were outside the house now and Tubby realized for the first time his embarrassment. It was not his way to bring anyone into the house unannounced, and his mother could be very haughty with strangers. However, here they were and it was snowing hard and the poor man was without a coat. So in they went. The Winsloe mansion was magnificent, belonging in all its features to an age that was gone. There was a marble staircase and up this the stranger almost ran, carrying his bag like a feather. Tubby toiled behind him but was, unhappily, not in time to prevent the stranger from entering through the open doors of the drawing-room.

Here, seated in magnificent state, was Lady Winsloe, a roaring fire encased with marble on one side of her, a beautiful tea-table in front of her, and walls hung with magnificent imitations of the great Masters.

Lady Winsloe was a massive woman with snow-white hair, a bosom like a small skating rink, and a little face that wore a look of perpetual astonishment. Her dress of black-and-white silk fitted her so tightly that one anticipated with pleasure the moment when she would be compelled to rise. She moved as little as possible, she said as little as possible, she thought as little as possible. She had a very kind heart and was sure that the world was going straight to the devil.

The stranger put his bag on the floor and went over to her with his hand outstretched.

'How are you?' he said. 'I'm delighted to meet you!'

By good fortune, Tubby arrived in the room at this moment.

'Mother,' he began, 'this is a gentleman—'

'Oh, of course,' said the stranger, 'you don't know my name. My name's Huffam,' and he caught the small white podgy hand and shook it. At this moment, two Pekinese dogs, one brown and one white, advanced from somewhere violently barking. Lady Winsloe found the whole situation so astonishing that she could only whisper:

'Now, Bobo—now, Coco!'

'You see, Mother,' Tubby went on, 'Mr Huffam was nearly killed by a motor-car and I rescued him and it began to snow heavily.'

'Yes, dear,' Lady Winsloe said, in her queer husky little voice that was always a surprise coming from so vast a bosom. Then she pulled herself together. For some reason Tubby had done this amazing thing, and whatever Tubby did was right.

'I do hope you'll have some tea, Mr—?' She hesitated.

'Huffam, ma'am. Yes, thank you. I *will* have some tea!'

'Milk *and* sugar?'

'All of it!' Mr Huffam laughed and slapped his knee. 'Yes, milk *and* sugar. Very kind of you indeed. A perfect stranger as I am. You have a beautiful place here, ma'am. You are to be envied.'

'Oh, do you think so?' said Lady Winsloe, in her husky whisper. 'Not in these days—not in these terrible days. Why, the taxes alone! You've no idea, Mr—?'

'Huffam.'

'Yes. How stupid of me! Now, Bobo! Now, Coco!'

Then a little silence followed and Lady Winsloe gazed at her strange visitor. Her manners were beautiful. She never looked *directly* at her guests. But there was something about Mr Huffam that *forced* you to look at him. It was his energy. It was his obvious happiness (for happy people were so very rare). It was his extraordinary waistcoat.

Mr Huffam did not mind in the least being looked at. He smiled back at Lady Winsloe, as though he had known her all his life.

'I'm so very fortunate,' he said, 'to find myself in London at Christmas-time. And snow, too! The very thing. Snowballs, Punch and Judy, mistletoe, holly, the pantomime—nothing so good in life as the pantomime!'

'Oh, do you think so?' said Lady Winsloe faintly. 'I can't, I'm afraid, altogether agree with you. It lasts such a *very* long time and is often so exceedingly vulgar!'

'Ah, it's the sausages!' said Mr Huffam, laughing. 'You don't like the sausages! For my part I dote on 'em. I know it's silly at my age, but there it is—Joey and the sausages. I wouldn't miss them for anything.'

At that moment a tall and exceedingly thin gentleman entered. This was Sir Roderick Winsloe. Sir Roderick had been once an Under Secretary, once a Chairman of a Company, once famous for his smart and rather vicious repartees. All these were now glories of the past. He was now nothing but the husband of Lady Winsloe, the father of Tubby, and the victim of an uncertain and often truculent digestion. It was natural that he should be melancholy, although perhaps not so melancholy as he found it necessary to be. Life for him was altogether without savour. He now regarded Mr Huffam, his bag and his waistcoat, with unconcealed astonishment.

'This is my father,' said Tubby.

Mr Huffam rose at once and grasped his hand.

'Delighted to meet you, sir,' he said.

Sir Roderick said nothing but 'Ah'—then he sat down. Tubby was suffering now from a very serious embarrassment. The odd visitor had drunk his tea and it was time that he should go. Yet it seemed that he had no intention of going. With his legs spread apart, his head thrown back, his friendly eyes taking everyone in as though they were all his dearest friends, he was asking for his second cup.

Tubby waited for his mother. She was a mistress of the art of making a guest disappear. No one knew quite how she did it. There was nothing so vulgarly direct as a glance at the clock or a suggestion as to the imminence of dressing for dinner. A cough, a turn of the wrist, a word about the dogs, and the thing was done. But *this* guest, Tubby knew, was a little more difficult than the ordinary. There was something old-fashioned about him. He took people naively at their word. Having been asked to tea, he considered that he *was* asked to tea. None of your five minutes' gossip and then hastening on to a cocktail-party. However, Tubby reflected, the combination of father, mother *and* the drawing-room, with its marble fireplace and row of copied Old Masters, was, as a rule, enough to ensure brief visitors. On this occasion also it would have its effect.

And then—an amazing thing occurred! Tubby perceived that his mother *liked* Mr Huffam, that she was smiling and even giggling, that her little eyes shone, her tiny mouth was parted in expectation as she listened to her visitor.

Mr Huffam was telling a story—an anecdote of his youth. About a boy whom he had known in his own childhood, a gay, enterprising, and adventurous boy who had gone as page-boy to a rich family. Mr Huffam described his adventures in a marvellous manner, his *rencontre* with the second footman, who was a snob and Evangelical, of how he had handed biscuits through the pantry window to his little sister, of the friendship that he had made with the cook. And, as Mr Huffam told these things, all these people lived before your eyes, the pompous mistress with her ear-trumpet, the cook's husband who had a wooden leg, the second footman who was in love with a pastrycook's daughter. The house of this young page-boy took on life, and all the furniture in it, the tables and chairs, the beds and looking-glasses, everything down to the very red woollen muffler that the footman wore in bed, because he was subject to colds in the neck. Then Lady Winsloe began to laugh and Sir Roderick Winsloe even laughed, and the butler, a big, red-faced man, coming in to remove the tea, could not believe his parboiled eyes, but stood there, looking first of all at his mistress, then at his master, then at Mr Huffam's bag, then at Mr Huffam himself, until he remembered his manners and, with a sudden apologetic cough, set sternly (for himself this disgraceful behaviour of his employers was no laughing matter) about his proper duties.

But best of all perhaps was the pathos at the end of Mr Huffam's story. Pathos is a dangerous thing in these days. We so easily call it sentimentality. Mr Huffam was a master of it. Quite easily and with no exaggeration he described how the sister of the little page-boy lost some money entrusted to her by her only too bibulous father, of her terror, her temptation to steal from her aged aunt's purse, her final triumphant discovery of the money in a band-box!

How they all held their breaths! How vividly they saw the scene! How real was the sister of the little page-boy! At last the story was ended. Mr Huffam rose.

'Well, ma'am, I must thank you for a very happy hour,' he said.

Then the most remarkable thing of all occurred, for Lady Winsloe said:

'If you have not made any other arrangements, why not stay here for a night or two—while you are looking about you, you know? I'm sure we should be delighted—would we not, Roderick?'

And Sir Roderick said:

'Ah—ah—certainly.'

II

On looking back, as he so often did afterwards, into the details of this extraordinary adventure, Tubby was never able to arrange the various incidents in their proper order. The whole affair had the inconsequence, the coloured fantasy, of a dream—one of those rare and delightful dreams that are so much more true and reasonable than anything in one's waking life.

After that astounding invitation of Lady Winsloe's, in what order did the events follow—the cynical luncheon-party, the affair of Mallow's young woman (Mallow was the butler), the extraordinary metamorphosis of Miss Allington? All of these were certainly in the first twenty-four hours after Mr Huffam's arrival. The grand sequence of the Christmas Tree, the Mad Party, the London Vision, were all parts of the tremendous climax.

At once, Tubby realized, the house itself changed. It had never been a satisfactory house; always one of those places rebelliously determined not to live. Even the rooms most often inhabited—the drawing-room, the long, dusky dining-room, Sir Roderick's study, Tubby's own bedroom—sulkily refused to play the game. The house was too large, the furniture too heavy, the ceilings too high. Nevertheless, on the first evening of Mr Huffam's visit, the furniture began to move about. After dinner on that evening there was only the family present. (Miss Agatha Allington, an old maid, a relation with money to be left, an unhappy old woman, suffering from constant neuralgia, had not yet arrived.) There they were in the drawing-room and, almost at once, Mr Huffam had moved some of the chairs away from the wall, had turned the sofa with the gilt, spiky back more cosily towards the fire. He was not impertinent nor officious. Indeed, on this first evening, he was very quiet, asking them some questions about present-day London, making some rather odd social enquiries about prisons and asylums and the protection of children. He was interested, too, in the literature of the moment and wrote down in a little note-book an odd collection of names, for Lady Winsloe told him that Ethel M. Dell, Warwick Deeping, and a lady called Wilhelmina Stitch who wrote poetry, were her favourite writers, while Tubby suggested that he should look into the work of Virginia Woolf, D. H. Lawrence and Aldous Huxley. They had, in fact, a quiet evening which ended with Mr Huffam having his first lesson in Bridge. (He had been, he told them, when he had last 'tried' cards, an enthusiastic whist player.) It was a quiet evening, but, as Tubby went up the long, dark staircase to his room, he felt that, in some undefined way, there was excitement in the air. Before undressing he opened his window and looked out on to the roofs and chimney-pots of London. Snow glittered and sparkled under a sky that quivered with stars. Dimly he heard the recurrent waves of traffic, as though the sea gently beat at the feet of the black, snow-covered houses.

'*What* an extraordinary man!' was his last thought before he slept. Before he had known that he would have Mr Huffam as his guest, Tubby had invited a few of his clever young friends to luncheon—Diana, Gordon Wolley, Ferris Band, Mary Polkinghorne. Gathered round the Winsloe luncheon-table, Tubby regarded them with new eyes. Was it because of the presence of Mr Huffam? He, gaily flaunting his tremendous waistcoat, was in high spirits. He had, all morning, been revisiting some of his old haunts. He was amazed. He could not conceal, he did not attempt to conceal, his amazement. He gave them, as they sat there, languidly picking at their food, a slight notion of what East London had once been—the filth, the degradation, the flocks of wild, haggard-eyed, homeless children—Mary Polkinghorne, who had a figure like an umbrella-handle, an Eton crop and an eye-glass, gazed at him with bemused amazement.

'But they say our slums are awful. I haven't been down there myself, but Bunny Carlisle runs a Boys' Club and *he* says...!'

Mr Huffam admitted that he had seen some slums that morning, but they were nothing, nothing at all, to the things he had seen in his youth.

'Who is this man?' Ferris Band whispered to Diana.

'I don't know,' she answered. 'Someone Tubby picked up. But I like him.'

And then this Christmas!

'Oh dear,' young Wolley sighed, 'here's Christmas again! Isn't it awful! I'm going to bed. I shall sleep, and I hope dream, until this dreadful time is over.'

Mr Huffam looked at him with wonder.

'Hang up your stocking and see what happens,' he said.

Everyone screamed with laughter at the idea of young Wolley hanging up his stocking. Afterwards, in the drawing-room, they discussed literature.

'I've just seen,' Ferris Band explained, 'the proofs of Hunter's new novel. It's called *Pigs in Fever*. It's quite marvellous. The idea is, a man has scarlet fever and it's an account of his ravings. Sheer poetry.'

There was a book on a little table. He picked it up. It was a first edition of *Martin Chuzzlewit* bound in purple leather.

'Poor old Dickens,' he said. 'Hunter has a marvellous idea. He's going to rewrite one or two of the Dickens books.'

Mr Huffam was interested.

'Rewrite them?' he asked.

'Yes. Cut them down to about half. There's some quite good stuff in them hidden away, he says. He'll cut out all the sentimental bits, bring the humour up to date, and put in some stuff of his own. He says it's only fair to Dickens to show people that there's something there.'

Mr Huffam was delighted.

'I'd like to see it,' he said. 'It will make quite a new thing of it.'

'That's what Hunter says,' Band remarked. 'People will be surprised.'

'I should think they will be,' Mr Huffam remarked.

The guests stayed a long time. Mr Huffam was something quite new in their experience. Before she went, Diana said to Tubby:

'What a delightful man! Where *did* you find him?'

Tubby was modest. She was nicer to him than she had ever been before.

'What's happened to you, Tubby?' she asked. 'You've woken up suddenly.'

During the afternoon, Miss Agatha Allington arrived with a number of bags and one of her worst colds.

'How are you, Tubby? It's kind of you to ask me. What horrible weather! What a vile thing Christmas is! You won't expect me to give you a present, I hope?'

Before the evening, Mr Huffam made friends with Mallow the butler. No one knew quite how he did it. No one had ever made friends with Mallow before. But Mr Huffam went down to the lower domestic regions and invaded the world of Mallow, Mrs Spence, the housekeeper, Thomas the footman, Jane and Rose the housemaids, Maggie the scullery-maid. Mrs Spence, who was a little round woman like a football, was a Fascist in politics, said that she was descended from Mary Queen of Scots, and permitted no one, except Lady Winsloe, in her sitting-room. But she showed Mr Huffam the photographs of the late Mr Spence and her son, Damley, who was a steward on the Cunard Line. She laughed immeasurably at the story of the organ-grinder and the lame monkey. But Mallow was Mr Huffam's great conquest. It seemed (no one had had the least idea of it) that Mallow was hopelessly in love with a young lady who assisted in a flower shop in Dover Street. This young lady, apparently, admired Mallow very much and he had once taken her to the pictures. But Mallow was shy. (No one had conceived it!) He wanted to write her a letter, but simply hadn't the courage. Mr Huffam dictated a letter for him. It was a marvellous letter, full of humour, poetry and tenderness.

'But I can't live up to this, sir,' said Mallow. 'Sho'll find me out in no time.'

'That's all right,' said Mr Huffam. 'Take her out to tea tomorrow, be a little tender. She won't worry about letters after that!'

He went out after tea and returned powdered with snow, in a taxi-cab filled with holly and mistletoe.

'Oh dear,' whispered Lady Winsloe, 'we haven't decorated the house for years. I don't know what Roderick will say. He thinks holly so messy.'

'I'll talk to him,' said Mr Huffam. He did, with the result that Sir Roderick came himself and assisted. Through all this, Mr Huffam was in no way dictatorial. Tubby observed that he had even a kind of shyness—not in his opinions, for here he was very clear-minded indeed, seeing exactly what he wanted, but he seemed to be aware, by a sort of ghostly guidance, of the idiosyncrasies of his neighbours. How did he know, for instance, that Sir Roderick was afraid of a ladder? When he, Mallow, Tubby and Sir Roderick were festooning the hall with holly, he saw Sir

Roderick begin timidly, with trembling shanks, to climb some steps. He went to him, put his hand on his arm, and led him safely to ground again.

'I know you don't like ladders,' he said. 'Some people can't stand 'em. I knew an old gentleman once terrified of ladders, and his eldest son, a bright, promising lad, *must* become a steeple-jack. Only profession he had a liking for.'

'Good heavens!' cried Sir Roderick, paling. 'What a horrible pursuit! Whatever did his father do?'

'Persuaded him to be a diver instead,' said Mr Huffam. 'The lad took to it like a duck to water. Up or down, it was all the same to him, he said.'

In fact, Mr Huffam looked after Sir Roderick as a father his child, and, before the day was out, the noble Baronet was asking Mr Huffam's opinion on everything—the right way to grow carnations, the Gold Standard, how to breed dachshunds, and the wisdom of Lord Beaverbrook. The Gold Standard and Lord Beaverbrook were new to Mr Huffam, but he had his opinions all the same. Tubby, as he listened, could not help wondering where Mr Huffam had been all these years. In some very remote South Sea island surely! So many things were new to him. But his kindness and energy carried him forward through everything. There was much of the child about him, much of the wise man of the world also, and behind these a heart of melancholy, of loneliness.

'He has, it seems,' thought Tubby, 'no home, no people, nowhere especially to go.' And he had visions of attaching him to the family as a sort of secretarial family friend. Tubby was no sentimentalist about his own sex, but he had to confess that he was growing very fond of Mr Huffam. It was almost as though he had known him before. There were, in fact, certain phrases, certain tones in the voice that were curiously familiar and reminded Tubby in some dim way of his innocent departed childhood.

And then, after dinner, there was the conquest of Agatha Allington. Agatha had taken an instant dislike to Mr Huffam. She prided herself on her plain speech.

'My dear,' she said to Lady Winsloe, 'what a ruffian! He'll steal the spoons.'

'I don't think so,' said Lady Winsloe with dignity. 'We like him very much.'

He seemed to perceive that Agatha disliked him. He sat beside her at dinner—he wore a tail-coat of strange, old-fashioned cut, and carried a large gold fob. He was, as Tubby perceived, quite different from Agatha. He was almost, you might say, an old maid himself—or, rather, a confirmed old bachelor. He discovered that she had a passion for Italy—she visited Rome and Florence every year—and he described to her some of his own Italian journeys, taken many years ago: confessed to her that he didn't care for frescoes, which he described as 'dim virgins with mildewed glories'. But Venice! Ah! Venice! with its prisoners and dungeons and lovely iridescent waters! All the same, he was always homesick when he was out of London, and he described the old London to her, the fogs and the muffin-bells and the 'growlers,' and enchanted her with a story about a shy little bachelor, and how he went out one evening to dine with a vulgar cousin and be kind to a horrible godchild. Indeed they all listened spellbound: even Mallow stood, with a plate in his hand and his mouth open, forgetting his duties. Then, after dinner, he insisted that they should dance. They made a space in the drawing-room, brought up a gramophone, and set about it. Then how Mr Huffam laughed when Tubby showed him a one-step.

'Call that dancing!' he cried. Then, humming a polka, he caught Agatha by the waist and away they polkaed! Then Lady Winsloe, who had adored the polka once, joined in. Then the Barn Dance. Then, few though they were, Sir Roger.

'I know!' Mr Huffam cried. 'We must have a party!'

'A party!' almost screamed Lady Winsloe. 'What kind of a party?'

'Why, a children's party, of course. On Christmas night.'

'But we don't know any children! And children are bored with parties. And they'll all be engaged anyway.'

'Not the children *I'll* ask!' cried Mr Huffam. 'Not the party *I'll* have! It shall be the best party London has seen for years!'

III

It is well known that good-humoured, cheerful, and perpetually well-intentioned people are among the most tiresome of their race. They are avoided by all wise and comfort-loving persons. Tubby often wondered afterwards why Mr Huffam was *not* tiresome. It was perhaps because of his childlikeness; it was also, most certainly, because of his intelligence. Most of all it was because of the special circumstances of the case. In ordinary daily life, Mr Huffam *might* be a bore—most people are at one time or another. But on this occasion no one was a bore, not even Agatha.

It was as though the front wall of the Hill Street House had been taken away and all the detail and incidents of these two days, Christmas Eve and Christmas Day, became part of it. It seemed that Berkeley Square was festooned with crystal trees, that candles—red and green and blue—blazed from every window, that small boys, instead of chanting 'Good King Wenceslas' in the usual excruciating fashion, carolled with divine voices, that processions of Father Christmases, with snowy beards and red gowns, marched from Selfridges and Harrods and Fortnum's, carrying in their hands small Christmas trees, and even attended by reindeer, as though brown-paper parcels tied with silver bands and decorated with robins fell in torrents through the chimney, and gigantic Christmas puddings rolled on their own stout bellies down Piccadilly, attended by showers of almonds and raisins. And upon all this, first a red-faced sun, then a moon, cherry-coloured and as large as an orange, smiled down, upon a world of crusted, glittering snow, while the bells pealed and once again the Kings of the East came to the stable with gifts in their hands...

Of course, it was not like that—but most certainly the Winsloe house was transformed. For one thing, there was not the usual present-giving. At breakfast on Christmas Day, everyone gave everyone else presents that must not by order cost more than sixpence apiece. Mr Huffam had discovered some marvellous things—toy dogs that barked, Father Christmases glistening with snow, a small chime of silver bells, shining pieces of sealing-wax.

Then they all went to church at St James's, Piccadilly At the midday meal Sir Roderick had turkey and Christmas pudding, which he hadn't touched for many a day.

In the evening came the Party. Tubby had been allowed to invite Diana—for the rest the guests were to be altogether Mr Huffam's. No one knew what was in his mind. At 7.15 exactly came the first ring of the door-bell. When Mallow opened the portals, there on the steps were three very small children, two girls and a boy.

'Please, sir, this was the number the gentleman said,' whispered the little girl, who was very frightened. Then up Hill Street the children came, big children, little children, children who could scarcely walk, boys as bold as brass, girls mothering their small relations, some of them shabby, some of them smart, some with shawls, some with mufflers, some with collars, some brave, some frightened, some chattering like monkeys, some silent and anxious—all coming up Hill Street, crowding up the stairs, passing into the great hall.

It was not until they had all been ushered up the stairs by Mallow, were all in their places, that Sir Roderick Winsloe, Bart., Lady Winsloe, his wife, Tubby Winsloe, their son, were permitted to see their own drawing-room. When they did they gasped with wonder. Under the soft and shining light the great floor had been cleared, and at one end of the room all the children were gathered. At the other end was the largest, the strongest, the proudest Christmas Tree ever beheld, and this Tree shone and gleamed with candles, with silver tissue, with blue and gold and crimson balls, and so heavily weighted was it with dolls and horses and trains and parcels that it was a miracle that, Tree as it was, it could support its burden. So there it was, the great room shining with golden light, the children massed together, the gleaming floor like a sea, and only the crackle of the fire, the tick of the marble clock, the wondering whispers of the children for sound.

A pause, and from somewhere or other (but no one knew whence) Father Christmas appeared. He stood there, looking across the floor at his guests.

'Good evening, children,' he said, and the voice was the voice of Mr Huffam.

'Good evening, Father Christmas,' the children cried in chorus.

'It's all his own money,' Lady Winsloe whispered to Agatha. 'He wouldn't let me spend a penny.'

He summoned them then to help with the presents. The children (who behaved with the manners of the highest of the aristocracy—even *better* than that, to be truthful) advanced across the shining floor. They were told to take turn according to size, the smallest first. There was no pushing, no cries of 'I want *that!*' as so often happens at parties, no greed and satiety. At last the biggest girl (who was almost a giantess), and the biggest boy (who might have been a heavyweight boxing champion) received their gifts. The Tree gave a little quiver of relief at its freedom from its burden, and the candles, the silver tissue, the red and blue and golden balls shook with a shimmer of pleasure because the present-giving had been so successful.

Games followed. Tubby could never afterwards remember what the games had been. They were no doubt Hunt the Slipper, Kiss in the Ring, Cross-your-Toes, Last Man Out, Blind Man's Buff, Chase the Cherry, Here Comes the Elephant, Count Your Blessings, and all the other games. But Tubby never knew. The room was alive with movement, with cries of joy and shouts of triumph, with songs and kisses and forfeits. Tubby never knew. He only knew that he saw his mother with a paper cap on her head, his father with a false nose, Agatha beating a child's drum—and on every side of him children and children and children, children dancing and singing and running and sitting and laughing.

There came a moment when Diana, her hair dishevelled, her eyes shining, caught his arm and whispered:

'Tubby, you are a dear. Perhaps—one day—if you keep this up—who knows?'

And there was a sudden quiet. Mr Huffam, no longer Father Christmas, arranged all the children round him. He told them a story, a story about a circus and a small child who, with her old grandfather, wandered into the company of those strange people— of the fat lady and the Living Skeleton, the jugglers and the beautiful creatures who jumped through the hoops, and the clown with the broken heart and how his heart was mended.

'And so they all lived happily ever after,' he ended. Everyone said good-night. Everyone went away.

'Oh dear, I *am* tired!' said Mr Huffam. 'But it has been a jolly evening!'

Next morning when Rose the housemaid woke Lady Winsloe with her morning cup of tea she had startling news.

'Oh dear, my lady, the gentleman's gone!'

'What gentleman?'

'Mr Huffam, my lady. His bed's not been slept in and his bag's gone. There isn't a sign of him anywhere.'

Alas, it was only too true. Not a sign of him anywhere. At least one sign only.

The drawing-room was as it had always been, every chair in its proper place, the copied Old Masters looking down solemnly from the dignified walls.

One thing alone was different. The first edition of *Martin Chuzzlewit* in its handsome purpose binding was propped up against the marble clock.

'How very strange!' said Lady Winsloe. But, opening it, she found that on the fly-leaf these words were freshly written:

> For Lady Winsloe
> with gratitude
> from her Friend
> the Author—

And, under this, the signature, above a scrawl of thick black lines, 'Charles Dickens'.

THE MAN WHO CAME BACK

Margery Lawrence

FIRST PUBLISHED IN *THE SPHERE*, NOVEMBER 1935

Margery Lawrence (1889–1969) was an English writer from Wolverhampton whose first published work was a volume of poetry published by her father in 1913. Later she turned her hand to fantasy, detective and adventure stories. She is now remembered primarily for her ghost stories. Her best known series were styled as the case histories of an occult detective. They were said to be inspired by the works of Algernon Blackwood and Dion Fortune. Alongside her fictional work, Lawrence was a committed spiritualist and contributed many 'true' stories and observations about the occult. Lawrence was a member of The Ghost Club, an organization which is still in operation today and is dedicated to paranormal investigation. Lawrence sometimes used the experiences of fellow members to inspire her fiction.

'The Man Who Came Back' could be one such story. First published in *The Sphere*, which ran from 1900–1964, the story later appeared in Lawrence's short story collection *The Floating Café*. The tale begins with a jolly Christmas party which takes a turn when, waiting in the wings in the manner of the fortune teller in Jane Eyre, a celebrated medium is produced. Initial enthusiasm turns to horror as some decidedly non-festive revelations occur.   —LE

I t was a very merry house-party. The givers of it, Colonel and
Lady Garrison, were two pleasant, gregarious souls. Not peculiarly interesting in themselves, but possessing that priceless
gift, that, in my opinion should be subsidized, when found, by the
government of the country to which the owner of it belongs—that
gift that the Americans crisply describe as 'mixing!'

Tho Garrisons, childless, well-to-do and middle-aged, gave, it
was well known, by far the most amusing parties in their particular
coterie, and fierce was the competition for invitations, especially
to the annual Christmas house-party, held in their country house,
a rambling, old-fashioned, but supremely comfortable old manor
in a well-known hunting county. The Colonel was a keen man to
hounds, and despite his increasing years and weight, still easily
held his own with the younger men, and several of his rivals in
the hunting field were members of the present party who, sitting
round a blazing fire in the drawing-room after dinner, were eating
chestnuts and cracking jokes, well pleased with themselves, their
dinner and their hosts.

Ted Boulter, the M.F.H., and his pretty little wife, whose
Dresden-china beauty belied her pluck across country. The two
Symons, brother and sister. Londoners, dark, given to odd clothes
and odder Bohemian jargon; altogether too 'arty and crafty' in the
Colonel's private opinion. But indubitably young people to know,

since they were rapidly becoming the only people who counted in the matter of smart house decoration. The Todhunters, travellers and explorers, Cecily Fleet, a county beauty, just embarking on a film career, and her two admirers, Len Ponsonby and Terry Walters; a couple of young nephews, all bounce and brawn, and two new acquaintances that Lady Garrison had picked up at the bridge club she frequented in town. Doctor and Mrs Playfair—charming people, thought the Colonel, as, with his glasses perched precariously on his forehead and his dinner-jacket rumpled as usual between his shoulders, he twiddled with the knobs on his beloved radio in a vain endeavour to get Rome or Milan. Charming people! Playfair himself was a brilliant young feller; one of the coming men in Harley Street, everybody said. And his wife was a dam' pretty woman! Small and slim and exquisitely dressed, with hair the colour of a new chestnut and golden hazel eyes.

The two were complete love-birds. At least, Playfair was obviously madly in love with his wife, never let her out of his sight unless he could help it; while she seemed sincerely fond of him—but between love and mere fondness lies a world of difference! Still, it seemed to be working all right, thought the Colonel to himself, as he struggled with the wireless. But neither Rome nor Milan responded, and, defeated, he turned to his guests.

'Something wrong with the blasted thing! Not that it matters. Anybody care for a game of billiards?' he demanded.

A chorus of assent came from the younger men, but Lady Garrison's motherly voice rose above them.

'Not a bit of it! I'm not going to let one of you out of here yet. I've got a surprise!'

'Not another ghost?' demanded Cecily Fleet, who had been at last year's gathering, and still retained vivid memories of the amazingly well-staged 'ghost' scare that Lady Garrison had got up for the amusement of her Christmas guests. Lady Garrison, plump and matronly in plum-coloured satin, shook her well-marcelled grey head.

'Nothing so ordinary!' She looked round the expectant circle with a smile of satisfaction. 'I've got another "stunt"—as you young people call it. I've got—what do you think? I've persuaded Madame Esperanza, the famous medium, to come and give us a sitting!'

There was a general chorus of acclaim.

'How splendid! How perfectly *marvellous!*'

The Boulters, who had a passion for bridge and considered any evening not spent at cards an evening wasted, smiled with tempered enthusiasm and said nothing. Cecily Floot pressed her fingers, long and slender and tipped with shining scarlet nails, to her correspondingly scarlet lips and rolled scared blue eyes over them at the company in general.

'I shall be simply *terrified!*' she proclaimed, but from his post at one side of the fire Ned Playfair responded, smiling indulgently.

'No need to be in the least alarmed, Miss Fleet!' His rich, pleasant voice was comfortingly reassuring. 'It's only an amusing game, of course. I assure you there's nothing whatever in these so-called mediums. Nothing supernatural, that is.'

'What do you mean by "nothing whatever"?'

Lady Garrison's tone was faintly nettled. With a bend of his handsome head in her direction the young doctor deprecatingly replied.

'Please forgive me, Lady Garrison. But really, you see, as a doctor we know what this kind of thing is worth. And surely you, of all people, only regard a thing like this—this sitting, seance, whatever one likes to call it—as an amusing sort of game? You don't think there's really anything in it?'

There was a pause. Lady Garrison's plump face was faintly flushed, and her lips were pressed together. She was sharply irritated, in truth. Not that she herself was an ardent believer in spiritualism, in which, to be honest, she was merely a dabbler, half believing and half sceptical. But Playfair's undisguised contempt stung her at least momentary championship.

'I don't know.' She spoke defiantly. 'I'm not clever enough to argue the point, Doctor Playfair, and I freely admit that I, personally, haven't done enough of it to be able to speak with any authority. But if people like Marshall Hall and Oliver Lodge and—er, Conan Doyle, and so on—find something worth considering in it, it surely can't be dismissed so easily as that?'

There was an awkward pause. Cecily Fleet broke it, with a little gush of girlish earnestness.

'I'm sure the doctor didn't mean… er… that?' she said, skilfully skimming over what precisely she meant by 'that'. 'But I'm sure that the rest of us want to see Madame What's-her-name most frightfully! *I* do, for one.'

'We do!' chorused the Symons eagerly, and a general murmur of enthusiasm arose. It was obvious that the doctor's attitude of antagonism was not popular, and he was clever enough to see the wisdom of retreating at least a little way. He had no desire to quarrel with the Garrisons and their very well-to-do circle. He smiled disarmingly.

'I'm sure I apologize, Lady Garrison, if inadvertently I said anything you might have construed into a sneer or a slight on your "surprise".'

He smiled again at the old lady where she sat stiffly braced, upright in her favourite red satin Victorian chair, and against her will she thawed, smiling reluctantly back. Certainly Playfair knew how to handle women, reflected the Colonel, amused. Repute had it he had had plenty of experience with 'em! Even that his large practice was due to his extraordinary influence over—and charm for—women. But that was gossip in all probability. Mere jealousy directed against a rising man, and the Colonel, who was strictly fair-minded, scouted the idea almost as soon as it raised its head. Yet it would not be entirely banished... like a sardonic imp it sat there, in the remotest corner of his mind, listening and watching as the young doctor smoothed down the ruffled feelings of his hostess and re-established himself in her good graces.

'You know I didn't mean to be at all rude, Lady Garrison—far from it! I spoke on impulse, that's all—and I had no idea you took the thing so seriously. But since you do—why, then, I withdraw! Of course, I shall be only too pleased to join in anything you like to arrange.'

Lady Garrison arose, appeased.

'That's all right,' she said. 'I'll go and fetch Madame Esperanza. She's here already—resting and preparing in my room.'

Mrs Boulter gave a little squeak of delighted fear.

'Oh, is she here? Have you kept her hidden until this moment! Oh, Ted, how *thrilling*!'

'I only hope,' said Lady Garrison, 'that the sitting *will* be thrilling. But mind—I don't promise anything. She said herself that unless the conditions were favourable she couldn't guarantee anything at all.'

'The usual guff!' muttered Ned Playfair to his wife, as the Colonel, ever courteous, shuffled after his plump wife to open the door for her. Ida Playfair glanced up at him curiously, her hazel eyes starry under the shadow of her fringe of chestnut hair.

'Don't you like it, Ned? If you'd rather not sit, I'm sure we can get out of it. I'm a little bit scared, to be honest!'

He shook his head and glanced round the rest of the group, their eyes fixed expectantly on the door.

'I'm afraid not. I've rather foolishly put the old girl's back up by joking about it, and since I want to get 'em as patients, or at least, some of their friends—they've a hell of a lot of influence—I suppose we shall have to sit through it. But you've no reason to feel scared, Ida. It's all rot. Clever posing, with a spot of telepathy or hypnotism or guesswork thrown in as make-weight!'

He smiled down at her reassuringly, but her eyes were on the fire. Her expression was faintly dissatisfied.

'I don't know,' she began. 'If, as Lady Garrison says, all these brilliant men have come to the conclusion that there *is* something in it, surely it can't be *all* rubbish? And Tillie van Heyden told me...'

Impatiently he interrupted, his black brows drawn together in a dangerous-looking scowl.

'I don't care what Tillie van Heyden said. She's a silly twittering fool, anyway—just the type that likes to mess about with what it describes as "the occult". I tell you, it's fraud, and when it's not deliberate fraud it's a mixture of hysteria and self-delusion and hypnotism, and I don't know what all! If it didn't mean that I can't afford to offend the old folks—we've only just got to know 'em—I'd go upstairs to bed right away, and not waste time on their damn silly seance. But, however...'

He paused, for the door opened and Lady Garrison entered, followed by a strange woman. An insignificant little woman wearing a shabby black velvet dress ornamented with a conglomeration of cheap beads about the neck; she had greying hair, untidily bundled into a 'bun' at the back of her head, pince-nez, and a small, faded, indefinite face behind large horn-rimmed glasses. An almost audible hush of disappointment ran round the room, for nobody less like a professional sybil could possibly be imagined—but Lady Garrison, experienced hostess, instantly filled in the awkward moment with a flood of introductions.

'Madame Esperanza—Mrs Boulter, Miss Fleet, Mr and Mrs Todhunter...'

The little woman, warming her meagre hands at the fire, nodded and smiled vaguely at each fresh name until Lady Garrison ended her litany with:

'Dr and Mrs Playfair. And that's the lot!'

The medium, raising her eyes from the fire, surveyed the owners of the last two names—he still standing with one arm on the mantel-piece, watching the proceedings with a quizzical eye, she crouched on a black velvet pouffe at his feet, her white tulle frock billowing about her like a summer cloud. For a moment Madame Esperanza eyed the pretty woman at her feet, then spoke suddenly.

'Are you going to be at the sitting?' she asked.

Her voice was reedy, and she spoke with a faintly uneducated twang. Ida Playfair regarded her with a slight sense of distaste min-gled with wonder and a rising sense of incredulity. Surely nothing that this common, shabby little woman could say could be really worth while! Probably as Ned declared, she was just a clever *poseuse*, some back-street pythoness who had somehow managed to impress dear old Thedosia Garrison—but quite obviously nobody to feel afraid of. She laughed breezily.

'Certainly I am! I'm not going to miss shaking hands with a spook!'

The medium looked down at her in silence. Behind, the room was in a cheerful uproar as chairs were hastily arranged in a circle, tables, cushions and whatnots pushed into corners, the door locked and a length of scarlet silk draped over the chandelier to dim its brightness to the requisite subdued glow; Lady Garrison, in her element, was bustling about directing operations, and for the moment the three beside the fire were alone, unnoticed, the shabby little woman with the intent eyes and the handsome young doctor and his wife. As if hypnotized by that strange, steady stare, for a moment Ida stared back without speaking—then Madame Esperanza spoke, suddenly and decidedly.

'I wouldn't, if I were you,' she said.

Ida's eyes flew wide with amazement, and her husband laughed drily.

'Why not?' he said curtly.

The medium looked at him, opened her mouth to speak, and changing her mind, looked back at the fire and went on warming her hands in silence.

But Ida Playfair's curiosity was aroused. Moreover, she felt faintly irritated that the woman's warning should coincide with a deep-seated sense of reluctance in her own heart. She did not want to take part in the sitting, in truth—but it was odd that Madame What's-her-name should have voiced, echoed, that feeling!

'Why don't you think I should go to the sitting?' she persisted.

The medium lifted her thin shoulders in an oddly foreign shrug. Perhaps, reflected the doctor sardonically, she actually deserved the name under which she worked. 'Esperanza!' It was a convincing name with which to tickle the groundlings, and she was quite a good actress, anyway. All this, of course, was according to type. She wouldn't be able to say *why* she had said that to Ida; would only hedge and hint. Yet...

'I can't tell you why I said that,' the medium said, almost brusquely, 'but sometimes before a sitting I get the feeling that for a certain person it would be better if they didn't join in. I don't know why—but it's always right.' She raised eyes, suddenly piercing behind their horn-rimmed glasses, to Playfair, standing leaning against the mantelpiece with his hands in his pockets, a barely-concealed smile of derision on his dark face. 'It applies to you, too, you know,' she said bluntly. 'I'd keep away from this sitting if I were you!'

Playfair's mouth fell open—then he laughed aloud and scornfully.

'My *dear* lady! What on earth have I to fear?'

Again that dark glance, and again the shrug.

'You know best. I don't know a thing about your life, of course. But if you've a secret in your life—if you've something to hide, or if you've done something—well, that you don't like to look back on—then if so, I'd find some excuse not to join in this circle.'

Ida Playfair's hand flew to clasp her husband's.

'Something to hide?' Her voice was sharp with affectionate resentment. 'What a perfectly idiotic idea! Darling...'

But for once an appeal by his adored wife passed Ned Playfair by. He did not hear, for he was staring at the woman with sudden attention. Staring fixedly—and for a moment it seemed as though his handsome brown face was a trifle white and strained. Then with a brusque laugh he seemed to dismiss the whole thing and turned away.

'Absurd! But I congratulate you,' he spoke coldly over his shoulder. 'I congratulate you on playing the part excellently, from the very first minute you came on the stage. Brilliant, really. You ought to go on the stage proper.'

The taunt was blatantly rude, but the medium did not seem to hear. She was staring down into the fire, apparently lost in thought—flushed with excitement, Lady Garrison bustled up, talking as usual at the top of her voice.

'Come on now—come along! It's all ready. That's right, isn't it, Madame?'

The medium turned, and surveying the room, nodded briefly.

'That's right—you have the door locked, so that servants can't come in and interrupt? Good. Then we'll start.'

Entering the circle she seated herself in the central chair, the hug leather 'grandfather' generally sacred to the Colonel, and glanced round the ring of eager faces that surrounded her. Taking off her glasses, she put them neatly away, like any maiden aunt, in a leather spectacle-case, and tucked them into the beaded bag that swung from her waist—and for a moment Ida Playfair blinked, surprised. For the eyes that the horn-rimmed glasses had hidden were dark and amazing, set in deep hollows that emphasized their darkness—piercing, oddly dominant eyes. Eyes that—suddenly—seemed to promise all sorts of possibilities... a faint sense of fear touched her once more like a passing wing, and she reached for her husband's hand and gave it a quick squeeze to give herself courage as she settled into her place. He glanced at her, surprised and touched—for as the Colonel had shrewdly surmised, their relations were definitely, as the old French song says, '*l'un qui baise, et l'autre qui tend la joue.*' Despite his desperate love of her, it was still, with her, only a gentle turning of the cheek.

'There is one thing I must ask of you all, please.'

It was the medium speaking, and her voice already sounded oddly drowsy and slow. 'That is, that when I am once *in* trance you keep your places until I come *out* of trance.'

She blinked and paused, as though collecting thoughts already growing hazy.

'I—it may be very dangerous to me for anyone to leave their seat without permission from my control. If he gives it—all right, but not otherwise. I can't explain the—conditions but I am sure you will accept my assurance that this rule is necessary.'

A subdued murmur of assent arose from the circle, and settling back into the chair with her head against the padded back, Madame Esperanza closed her eyes, and drawing a long breath, appeared to go to sleep. Playfair smiled faintly to himself as he watched her. Of course! The usual thing. Talk a lot of vague stuff about 'conditions' in order to *impose* conditions that made it utterly impossible for anybody to investigate the thing! The usual thing... except that it was odd that she had said... that; but here Dr Playfair, like the Colonel, hustled a certain thought deliberately and firmly into the background and settled down to watch events.

Everything was quiet. At first an excited giggle or two from one of the women broke out, a rustle of movement as somebody changed their position, a subdued whisper—but now, as though hypnotized, everyone sat very still, and dead silence lay like a deep unfathomable pool over the dimly-lit room. In the great chair the medium lay sunk in sleep, and the red light, falling almost directly upon her, etched curious lights and shadows on her shrunken little face. Watching, Ida Playfair shivered suddenly, thinking the face had changed, gained a curious dignity and power; the lines down each side of the mouth, the deep hollows about the eyes, looked as though carved in stone—the whole face looked, indeed, like the face of some old Crusader reclining 'mansize in marble' upon his tomb. Or the death-mask, stern, immovable, of some ancient king, long forgotten of mankind... even as Ida Playfair stared and shivered, clutching her husband's hand, the medium shuddered violently, gave a smothered ejaculation in some unknown tongue, and then with an indescribable majesty sat upright in her chair. With eyes still shut she turned her head slowly from side to side, following the ring of faces as though she saw, indeed, through those fast-closed lids; and her face was sternly unfamiliar.

Mrs Boulter clutched her husband's arm.

'It's—it's not the same woman!' she whispered agitatedly. 'It's a man's face! Oh, Tony, I wish we hadn't started, I'm frightened...'

A deep voice broke the silence, uttering a few unintelligible words. 'The usual bastard Hebrew or Egyptian,' muttered the doctor under his breath, but he dared not speak aloud. Although he was still utterly convinced that the whole thing was nothing but a clever fraud, against his will he was impressed. Impressed at least into silence... and that change in the face, that voice, heavy, masculine, rich, was certainly amazingly well done. Who'd have thought that shabby little Aunt Jane had it in her?

The voice was speaking again, but now in English.

'Peace be to this house!' The head bowed gravely in the direction of Lady Garrison, sitting upright, clutching the hands of her neighbours, her wholesome pink face flushed with excitement and nervousness. 'Peace!' The blind eyes went round the circle again as though seeking something, then paused. 'Peace and greetings to all, from the world of Spirit. I know what you would have—you would hold talk with those whom you call dead. With those who are on *this* side. And that is well—when you take care to whom you talk.'

There was a pause while the sitters, bewildered, looked at each other. Lady Garrison broke it at last.

'Er—how do you do?' The lame modern phrase sounded incredibly foolish. 'I—we are very glad to see you, and of course you are quite right about what we want to do. But we don't quite understand...'

'I will explain!'

The deep voice paused, then continued.

'I am what you call the "control" of this instrument here on earth—and the name I use is Sekhet. On this side we do not like to allow these instruments—what you call mediums—to be used by anyone who chooses. We try to keep back those whom we do not think should speak to you; yet our powers are limited, and if the force is very strong—we must stand aside and permit it to speak. But—in this case I do not think it would be wise.'

'What *do* you mean?'

It was Ned Playfair's voice, brusque, unbelieving, that broke the puzzled silence that had followed on the control's speech. The figure bowed its head.

'I mean, that there is here, amongst other souls who wish to speak, one soul that I would try to keep from speaking. And for that reason I think it would be wise,' he bowed once more, with ineffable grace and courtesy, towards Lady Garrison, 'to what you call "break up" the meeting? Release your hands, thus shutting the current off, and I will bring the medium out of trance at once.'

A chorus of astonished and indignant voices answered him.

'Give it up—just when it's getting interesting? *What* an idea! But why?'

The chorus rolled round the circle while Ned Playfair sat back and smiled. Just as he had expected! The woman, seeing from the outset that he was not to be fooled like the others, had tried to frighten him—first through Ida, then directly away from the sitting;

and now, finding he was not to be so frightened, she had recourse to this childish expedient! She was prepared to break up the circle, to lose her fee, and disappoint a group of eminently worth-while people sooner than risk discovery—now nothing in the world would persuade him to allow the circle to be broken, and he added his sharply-cut drawl to the chorus.

'Surely, Mr—er—Sekhet—you don't think you can frighten us in that way? I can assure you that we are prepared for any and everything that may happen! But we are not prepared to abandon the sitting.'

There was a momentary pause. The others looked gratefully at their champion, but Ida Playfair, suddenly white, half rose from her seat.

'I—I want to go!' she whispered. Her face was curiously strained, her great eyes ringed like a doe's. 'I don't know why—but I want to go.'

The deep voice answered from the centre of the circle.

'That is wise, little lady! You may go. But for you others—close the circle in as she leaves, friends, so that the current is broken as little as possible.' Without a word the white-clad figure rose and fled, and as the door closed behind her the voice resumed.

'With regard to what you say, my son,' the blind eyes seemed to pierce right through the dark young doctor where he sat, 'if you insist—all have free will, and if it is the will of all to go on with this sitting, so be it! But—I still advise you against it.'

There was a faint pause. Lady Garrison, more impressed than she cared to admit, glanced uncertainly round the circle. The Boulters looked doubtful, the Todhunters puzzled, the Symons cynically amused, Cecily Fleet and her attendant swains definitely disappointed—a very little would have persuaded the good lady to take the mysterious Sekhet's advice and dissolve the circle altogether, but Ned Playfair's voice rose again, brusque, antagonistic.

'I suggest we are rather wasting time, Lady Garrison? I, for one, refuse to be alarmed by vague hints and warnings. We formed this circle for the definite purpose of seeing signs and wonders. And if Madame Esperanza feels that for some reasons' (the sneer was patent) 'she cannot tonight produce these signs and wonders, then let her say so plainly and candidly. But if she is *not* prepared to say so—why, then let her carry on!'

'And we'll take the consequences,' suggested Cecily Fleet with a giggle. 'If there are any?'

'And,' agreed Playfair suavely, 'we'll take the consequences. At least, if there are any consequences we shall all agree not to blame you, Mr Sekhet!'

The sternly upright figure in the centre of the circle bowed its head resignedly.

'So be it. You have, as I said, free will. And if you will insist, against my advice, upon opening this door tonight, then I will do my best to control the soul that already beats upon it, desiring to re-establish contact with the earth he has left. Be still, all! I go to prepare the way.'

There was a slight convulsion of the body, and the medium, drooped together, fell back into the chair. In the red light her face was again the face of a weary little middle-aged woman, lined and tired—Cecily Fleet, who was sitting on the other side of Ned Playfair, nudged him eagerly as she whispered.

'Look, isn't that odd! Her face looked just like a man when *That* was talking—and now it's herself again! Isn't that queer?'

But there was no time to answer, for the medium, muttering rapidly and unintelligibly to herself, was rising upright in her chair again. Her face was twisted and distressed, and the voice that came through her lips was hoarse, with a rattle now and then—like the voice of somebody striving, through the stress of furious excitement, to speak clearly and connectedly. A voice entirely and utterly different from the measured, level tones of Sekhet! Suddenly the hoarseness left it and it came clear, ringing, a strong masculine voice—and at the sound of it Ned Playfair bounded in his chair, his face suddenly chalk-white, his eyes blazing.

Yet the voice was not addressing him—it seemed to be arguing with someone unseen, so that it sounded for all the world like a human voice arguing with a telephone operator.

'Let me get through, will you—oh yes, I'll remember! I'll keep steady—at least, I'll do my best, but don't lecture me now, d'you hear? I've *got* to get through—I tell you I must, I know she's there!' Then, in a ringing shout that rang through the room like a clarion call: '*I want my wife, I say! I want my wife!*'

The call was so electric, so painful in its intensity, that a loud and startled gasp ran round the circle, Cecily Fleet, her flippancy vanished, gave a pitiful little cry that echoed Mrs Boulter's, and the hot tears pricked behind Lady Garrison's eyes, as in a strangled voice she stammered.

'Your wife? I'm afraid... who is it speaking?'

'Neil Ramsay!' came the answer instantly, sharp and clear, and Cecily Fleet, hearing a quick-drawn breath at her shoulder, turned and peered at the man beside her. Odd that Ned Playfair, who, of all people, had been at the start the hardest, the most defiantly sceptical, should be so shaken now! Even in the dusky red glow from the scarlet-draped lamp one could see how white he was.

'Did you know Neil Ramsay?' she whispered. But Playfair shook his head.

'No! No!' he muttered feverishly—and the entire circle started with amazement and alarm as the voice came again, this time in a furious shout.

'*Liar!* You to say you don't know me, Ned Playfair?'

With a huge effort the medium staggered from the chair and, standing planted firmly on her feet, faced the white-faced doctor. Half risen from his chair, Playfair stood shaking, endeavouring to steady himself with one hand upon his chair-back, but with the sweat of sheer terror running down his face, while within him two things fought fiercely for mastery. Cynicism—the bitter atheism that refused, even at this moment, to believe that he beheld anything other than a horribly brilliant *tour de force* of acting—and fear. That dreadful aching fear that turns a man's bones to water and his soul to a stone that sinks therein... madly he snatched at his vanishing self-control, and tried to laugh. But all that came was a cracked whisper, a ghastly echo of a laugh.

'Ha, ha! Of course I remember you now, old fellow. Neil Ramsay! But why...'

'You know why I come. You don't need to ask.'

The little figure in black was menacing now. Frail as a shadow, yet charged with a dreadful shattering power.

'*You* know why I come, Playfair. To find my wife. My wife—of whom you robbed me!'

A terrified shuddering ran round the circle, and Mrs Boulter slipped quietly to the ground in a faint—but held in the steel grip of sheer fascinated horror nobody could either move or speak. Playfair stood as though turned to stone, his eyes fixed on the grim little figure before him as the voice thundered on.

'Of whom you robbed me, Ned Playfair. *The wife for whom you murdered me!*'

With a spring like that of a coiled snake, on the last word she was on him, her lean fingers knotted in his throat. Shrieking, hysterical with fear, the women sprang up and scattered as the two fought, swaying and staggering wildly about in the centre of the circle, while the men, flinging chairs aside, seized the combatants and tried to force them apart—then suddenly in their arms the woman went limp and a great voice spoke, it seemed, from over their heads.

'Put her down—there, in the chair—and leave her to come round. I have removed the poor love-crazed soul who just possessed her—I warned you, I, Sekhet, but you would not be warned. Yet retribution is just... see to *him* now. Farewell!'

It ceased, and in silence the shaken group gathered about the prone form of the young doctor, lying just where he had fallen, among a welter of fallen chairs, scattered bags and scarves and fans, stark in the brilliance of the white light from which the shrouding red drapery had been removed. His face was set in a terrible expression of fear and rage, and there were red marks round his throat where the thin, vicious fingers had clutched—he lay deadly still, and with a sudden fear catching at his heart Colonel Garrison beckoned Todhunter over to his side. As becomes an explorer, the brown-faced man had a good working knowledge of medicine. Kneeling, in a dead and awful silence he opened the prostrate man's shirt, tested his heart and held a mirror to his lips, then looked up with a grave face. Cecily Fleet, reading the news in his eyes, burst into tears, and a general murmur of horror ran round the room as, soberly, Todhunter rose to his feet.

'Dead—of heart failure, as far as I can judge,' he said gravely. 'Those marks on the throat are nothing—only superficial. Although the spirit that moved her to attack him was a man—or so it seems— she was only a frail little woman, and it wasn't her attack that killed

146

or even injured him. He died of shock. And if tonight's experience is as genuine as I believe it to be—no wonder!'

'But what is it all about—and who was Ramsay?' breathed the Colonel his healthy red face palpably pale with horror.

Todhunter hesitated for a moment.

'I don't like to say much,' he said. 'Especially as the man's dead now—and has paid for his sins. But—whoever spoke through the woman's mouth spoke what is thought, by many people, to be the sober truth. Ida Playfair was Ida Ramsay—the wife of Neil Ramsay—until a year or two ago, and they adored each other. Playfair met them and fell desperately in love with her. But she wouldn't look at him, so Playfair played a waiting game. Cultivated Ramsay, who was rather a simple soul; became his doctor as well as his bosom friend, and, one summer, about two years ago, they went on a fishing expedition together, and upon that expedition Ramsay was taken ill and died. Through—so Playfair said—eating tinned food that wasn't quite good. Playfair gave the certificate of death—natural causes—so that was O.K. for Playfair. And when he came back to London he made himself so indispensable to poor little Ida, who was completely lost and bewildered without Ramsay, that at last she married him. Though there were not lacking folks who said that Ramsay's convenient death, that left a charming and wealthy wife ready, as it were, to Playfair's hand, was rather too convenient to be convincing! That's the story. And—in view of what has happened tonight—it looks very much as though it were true.'

THE THIRD SHADOW

H. Russell Wakefield

FIRST PUBLISHED IN *WEIRD TALES*, NOVEMBER 1950

Herbert Russell Wakefield (1888–1964) was the son of a clergy-man from Kent. Wakefield was a sporting man who served in the First World War as a Captain. In the 1920s Wakefield turned to publishing, working as the chief editor for William Collins, Sons and Co. His work as a publisher inspired several of his short stories but he was reportedly inspired to write ghost stories after a stay in a haunted house. As well as his ghost stories, Wakefield also produced several non-fiction works on criminology and three detective novels.

Wakefield's stories often featured vengeful ghosts, and 'The Third Shadow' is no exception. Featuring a summer rather than a winter snow, the story is narrated by an unreconstructed pro-tagonist. The slow ascent of the mountain intensifies the feelings of loneliness and isolation for both the characters and the reader, and the final vengeance is terrifying to behold.　　　—LE

'A nd the other man on the rope, Andrew,' I asked, 'did you ever encounter him?'

He gave me a quick glance and tapped the ash from his cigarette.

'Well, *is* there such a one?' he asked, smiling.

'I've many times read of him,' I replied. 'Didn't Smythe actually see him on the Brenva Face and again on that last dread lap of Everest?'

Sir Andrew paused before replying.

No one glancing casually at that eminent and superbly discreet civil servant, Sir Andrew Poursuivant, would have guessed that in his day and prime he had been the second-best amateur mountaineer, of all time, with a dozen first ascents to his immortal fame; and many more than a dozen of the closest looks at death vouchsafed to any man. One who had leaped almost from the womb on to his first hill, a gravity defier by right of birth, soon to revolutionize the technique of rock-climbing and later to write two of the very finest books on his exquisite art. Yet there was something about that uncompromising buttress, his chin, the superbly modelled arête, his nose, those unflinching blue tarns, his eyes, and the high wide cliff of his brow to persuade the reader of faces that here was a born man of action, endowed with that strange and strangely named faculty, presence of mind, which ever finds in great emergency and peril the stimulus to a will and a cunning to meet and conquer them.

We were seated in my stateroom in the *Queen Elizabeth* bound for New York, he for some recurrent brawl, I on the interminable quest for dollars. The big tub was pitching hard into a nor-west blizzard and creaking her vast length.

I am but an honorary member of the corps of mountaineers, having no head for the game. But I love it dearly by proxy, and as the sage tells us, 'He who *thinks on* Himalcha shall have pardon for all sins,' and the same is true, I hope, of lesser ranges.

I dined with Sir Andrew perhaps half a dozen times a year and usually persuaded him on these felicitous occasions to tell me some great tale of the past. Hence on this felicitous occasion my 'fishing' enquiry.

'Yes, so I remember,' he presently said, 'but are there not nice, plausible explanations for that? The illusions consequent on great height, great strain? You may remember Smythe, who is highly psychic, saw something else from Everest, very strange wings beating the icy air.'

'He isn't the only one,' I said, 'it's a well-documented tradition.'

'It is, I agree. Guides, too, have known his presence, and always at moments of great stress and danger, and he has left them when these moments passed. And if they do not pass, the fanciful might suggest he meets them on the other side. But who he is no one knows. I grant you, also, I myself have sometimes felt that over, say, twelve thousand feet, one moves into a realm, where nothing is quite the same, or, perhaps, and more likely, it is just one's mind that changes and becomes more susceptible and exposed to—well, certain *oddities*.'

'But you have never encountered this particular oddity?' I insisted.

'What an importunate bag-man you are.'

'I believe you have, Andrew, and you must tell me of it!'

'That is not quite so,' he replied, 'but—it will be thirty-five long years ago next June, I did once have a very terrible experience that had associated with it certain subsidiary experiences somewhat recalcitrant to explanation.'

'That is a very cautious pronouncement, Andrew.'

'Phrased in the jargon of my trade, Bill.'

'And you are going to relate it to me.'

'I suppose so. I've never actually told it to another, and it will give me no pleasure to rouse it from my memory. But perhaps I owe it to you.'

'Fill your glass, mind that lurch, and proceed.'

'I haven't told it before,' said Sir Andrew, 'partly, because it's distasteful to recall, and partly, for the reason that the prudent sea-captain turns his blind eye on a sea serpent and keeps a buttoned lip over the glimpse he caught; no one much appreciates the grin of incredulous derision.'

'I promise to keep a straight face,' I assured him.

'Yes, I rather think you will. Well, all those years ago, in that remote and golden time, I knew and climbed with a man I will call Brown. He was about my age. He had inherited considerable position and fortune and he was heir, also, to that irresistible and consuming passion for high places, their conquest and company, which, given the least opportunity, will never be denied, and only decrepitude or death can frustrate. Technically, he was a master in all departments, a finished cragsman and just as expert on snow and ice. But there was just occasionally an un-mastered streak of recklessness in him which flawed him as a leader, and everyone, including myself, preferred to have him lower down the rope.

'It was, perhaps, due to one of these reckless seizures that, after our fourth season together, he proposed to a wench, who replied promptly in the affirmative. He was a smallish fellow, though immensely lithe, active, strong and tough. She was not far short of six feet and tipped the beam at one hundred and sixty-eight pounds, mostly muscle. With what suicidal folly, my dear Bill, do these infatuate pigmies, like certain miserable male insects, doom themselves with such Boadiceas, and how pitilessly and jocundly do those monsters bounce upon their prey! This particular specimen was terribly, viciously, "County," immensely handsome, and intolerably authoritarian. Speaking evil of the dead is often the only revenge permitted us and I have no intention of refraining from saying that I have seldom, almost certainly *never*, disliked anyone more than Hecate Quorn. Besides being massive and menacing to the nth degree, she was endowed with a reverberating contralto which loaned a fearsomely oraculate air to her insistent spate of edicts. Marry for lust and repent in haste, the oldest, saddest lesson in the world, and one my poor friend had almost instantly to learn. Once she'd gripped him in her red remorseless maw, she bullied him incessantly and appeared to dominate him beyond hope of release. Such an old story I need enlarge upon it no more! How many of our old friends have we watched fall prostrate before these daughters of Masrur!

'She demanded that he should at least attempt to teach her to climb, and females of her build are seldom much good at the game, particularly if they are late beginners. She was no exception, and her nerve turned out to be surprisingly more suspect on a steepish slope than her ghastly assurance on the level would have suggested.

Poor Brown plugged away at it, because he feared, if she chucked her hand in, he would never see summer snow again. He did his very desperate best. He hired Fritz Mann, the huskiest and best-tempered of all the Chamonix guides, and between them on one searing and memorable occasion they shoved and pulled and hauled and slid her on feet and rump to creditably near the summit of Mt. Blanc. She loathed the ordeal, but she refused to give in, just because she knew poor Brown was longing to join up with a good party, and have some fun. I need say no more, you have sufficient imagination fully to realize the melancholy and humiliating pass of my sad friend. And, of course, it wasn't only in Haute-Savoie and Valais she made his life hell, it was at least purgatory for the rest of the year; she was eternal punishment one might say. A harsh sentence for a moment's indiscretion!'

'What about those occasional feckless flashes?' I asked; 'had she quenched and overlaid those, too?'

'Permit me to tell this story my own way and pour me out another drink. In the second summer after their marriage the Browns had preceded me by a few days to the Montenvert, which, doubtless you recall, is a hotel overlooking the Mer de Glâce, three thousand feet above Chamonix. When I arrived there late one evening I found the place in a turmoil and Brown, apparently almost out of his mind. Hecate had fallen down a crevasse that morning and, as a matter of fact, her body was never recovered. I took him to my room, gave him a stiff drink, and he blurted out his sorry tale. He had taken her out on the Mer de Glâce for a morning's training, he said, determined to take no risks whatsoever. They had wandered a little way up the glacier, perhaps further than he'd intended. He'd cut some steps for her to practise on, and so forth. Presently he'd encountered a crevasse, crossed by a snow-bridge, which he'd tested and found perfectly reliable. He'd passed over himself, but, when she followed, she'd gone straight through, the rope had snapped—and that was that. They'd lowered a guide, but the hole went down forever and it was quite hopeless. Hecate must have died instantly; that was the only assuaging thought.

"'Should that rope have gone, Arthur?" I asked. "Can I see it?"

'He produced it. It was poor stuff, an Austrian make, which had once been very popular but had been found unreliable and the cause of several accidents. There was also old bruising near the break. It wasn't a reassuring bit of stuff. "I realize," said Brown hurriedly, "I shouldn't have kept that piece. As you know, I'm a stickler for perfection in a rope. But we were just having a little easy work and, as that rope's light and she always found it so hard to manage one, I took it along. I'd no intention of actually having to trust to it. We were just turning back when it happened. I swear to you that bridge seemed absolutely sound."

"'She was a good deal heavier than you, Arthur," I said.

"'I know, but I made every allowance for that."

"'I quite understand," I said. "Well, it's just too bad," or words to that effect. I was rather at a loss for appropriate expressions. He was obviously acting a part. I didn't blame him, he had to. He had to appear heavy with grief when he was feeling, in a sense, as light as mountain air. He got a shade tight that evening, and his efforts to sustain two such conflicting moods would have amused a more cynical and detached observer than myself. Besides, *I* foresaw the troubles ahead.

'The French held an enquiry, of course, and inevitably exonerated him completely, then I took him home to face the music, which, as I'd expected, was strident and loud enough. How far was it justified,

I asked myself. He should, perhaps, not have taken Hecate up so far. Even if that rope hadn't gone, he'd never have been able to pull her up by himself—it would have taken two very strong men to have done that. He could merely have held her there, and she would, I suppose, have died of slow strangulation, unless help had quickly come. Yet there is always risk, however prudently you try to play that game; it is the first of its rules and nothing will ever eliminate it. You must take my word for all this, which is rather outside your sphere of judgment. All the same the condition of that rope—and I wasn't the only one to examine it—didn't help things. Still, all that wouldn't have mattered nearly so much if he'd been a happily married man. I needn't dwell on that. Anyway the dirty rumour followed him home and resounded there,'

'What was your candid opinion, Andrew?' I asked.

'I must ask you,' he replied, 'to believe a rather hard thing, that I had and have no opinion, candid or otherwise. It *could* have been a pure accident. All could have happened exactly as he said it did. I've no valid reason to suppose otherwise. He may have been a bit careless; I might have been so myself. One takes such practice mornings rather lightly. There *is* risk, as I've said, but it's minuscule compared with the real thing. The expert mountaineer develops an exquisitely nice and certain "feel" for degrees of danger, it is the condition precept of his survival—and adjusts his whole personality to changing degrees. He must take the small ones in his stride. The errors of judgment, if any, that Brown committed were petty and excusable. His reason for taking that rope was sensible enough in a way.'

'Yes,' I put in, 'I can more or less understand all that, but you actually knew him well and you're a shrewd judge of character. You were in a privileged position to decide.'

'Was I? A very learned judge once told me he'd find it far easier to decide the guilt or innocence of an absolute stranger than of a close friend; the personal equation confuses the problem and pollutes the understanding. I think he was perfectly right. Anyway I am shrewd enough to know when I am baffled, and I have always felt the balance of probability was peculiarly nicely poised. In a word, I have no opinion.'

'Well, I have,' I proclaimed. 'I think he had a sudden fearful temptation. I don't think it was exactly premeditated, yet always, as it were, at the back of his mind. He realized that bridge would go when she had her weight on it, knew a swift, reckless temptation, and let it rip. I think he'd kept that rotten rope because he'd always felt in a vague half-repressed way, it might, as they say, "come in handy one day."'

Sir Andrew shrugged his shoulders. 'Very subtle, no doubt,' he said, 'and you may be right. But I know I shall never be able to decide. Perhaps it is that personal equation, for I was always fond of him, and he saved my life more than once at the greatest peril to his own; and since his marriage, that ordeal of thumb-screw and rack, I had developed profound sympathy for him. Hecate was far better dead. I greeted his release with a saturnine cheer. We will leave that point.

'Well, he had to face a very bad time. Hecate's relatives were many and influential and they pulled no punches, no stabs in the back, rather. No one, of course, actually cried, "Murder!" in public but such terms as "Darned odd!", "Very happy release!", "Accidents *must* happen!" and so on, were in lively currency.

'Very few people comprehend the first thing about mountaineering, just sultry, celluloid visions of high-altitude-and-octane villains slashing ropes, so this sepsis found receptive blood-streams. I did my best to foster antibodies and rallied my fellow climbers to the defence. But we were hopelessly out-numbered and out-gunned, and it was lucky for poor Brown he had more than sufficient private means to retire from public life to his estate and his farming, and insulate himself to some extent against the slings and arrows which were so freely and cruelly flying about.

'I spent a weekend with him in April and was shocked at his appearance: even life with Hecate had never reduced him to such a pass. His nerves were forever on the jump, he had those glaring insomniac eyes, he was drinking far more and eating far less than was good for him; he looked a driven haunted man.'

'Haunted?' I asked.

'I know what you mean,' he said, 'but I don't think I can be more definite I will say, however, I found the atmosphere of the house unquiet and was very glad to quit it. Anyway, something had to be done.

'"You must start climbing again, Arthur," I said.

'"Never! My nerve's gone!" he replied.

'"Nonsense!" I said. "We'll leave on June third for Chamonix. You must conquer all this and at the very place which tests you most starkly. You will be amongst friends. It will be a superb nerve tonic. This tittle-tattle will inevitably die down—it has started to do so already, I fancy. There is nothing to fear, as you'll discover once you're fit again. Come back to your first, your greatest, your only real love!"

'"What will people say?" he muttered uncertainly.

'"What say they, let them say! Actually I think it'll be very good propaganda; no one'd believe a guilty man would return to the scene of such a crime. My dear Arthur, you're a bit young to die, aren't you! If you stay moping here you'll be in the family vault in a couple of years. I'll get the tickets and we'll dine together at the Alpine Club on June the second at eight p. m. precisely."

'To this he promptly agreed and his fickle spirits rose. So the fourth of June saw us entering the Montenvert, where our reception was cordial enough.

'It took him over a week, far longer than usual, to get back to anything like his old standard, but I'd expected that. On the ninth day I decided it was time for a crucial test of his recovery. It was no use frittering about, he'd got to face the hard thing, something far tougher than the practice grounds.

'After some deliberation I chose the Dent du Géant for the trial run. It was an old friend of ours, and the last time we'd done it, four years before, we'd simply raced to the aluminium Madonna which more or less adorns its summit. The Géant, I will remind you, is a needle, some thirteen thousand feet high, situated towards the southern rim of that great and glorious lake of ice, part French, part Swiss, part Italian, from which rise some of the most renowned peaks in the world, and of those the acknowledged monarchs are the Grandes Jurasses, the Grépon Aiguilles and, of course; the Mont Blanc Massiv itself. It is sacred ground to our fraternity and the very words ring like a silver peal. The Géant culminates in a grotesque colossal tooth or rock, some of which is in a fairly advanced state of decay. These things are relative, of course, it will almost certainly be standing there, somewhat diminished, in five thousand years time. It provides an interesting enough climb, not, in my view, one of the most severe, but sheer and exposed enough. Nowadays, I understand the livelier sections are so festooned with spikes and cords that it resembles the fruit of the union of a porcupine and a puppet. But I have not revisited it for years and, for very sure, I never shall again.

'Brown agreed with my choice, which he declared himself competent to tackle, so off we went late on a promising morning and made our leisurely way up and across the ice to the hut. He seemed in pretty good shape, and once, when a most towering and displeasing sérac fell almost dead on our line, he kept his head, his footing and his life. Yet somehow I didn't quite like the look of him. He didn't improve as the day wore on and to tell the truth, I didn't either.'

Here Sir Andrew paused, lit a cigarette, and continued more slowly. 'You are not familiar with such matters, but I will try and explain the cause of my increasing preoccupation. We were, of course, roped almost all day, and from very early on I began to experience those *intimations*—it is difficult to find the precise, inevitable word— which were increasingly to disturb and perplex me on that tragic expedition. It is extremely hard to make them plain and plausible to you, who have never been hitched to a manila. When merely pursuing a more or less untrammelled course over ice it is our custom to keep the rope neither trailing nor quite taut, but always—I speak as leader—of course, one is very conscious of the presence and pressure of the man behind. Now—how shall I put it? Well, over and over again it seemed to me as if that rope was behaving oddly, as though the pull I experienced was inconsistent with the distance Brown was keeping behind me, as though something else was exercising pressure nearer to me. Do I make myself at all plain?'

'I think so,' I replied. 'You mean, as though there was someone tied to that rope between you and Brown.'

'Nothing like so definite and distinct as that. Imagine if you were driving a car and you continually got the impression the brakes were coming on and off, though you knew they were not.

You would be puzzled and somewhat disconcerted. I'm afraid that analogy isn't very illuminating. It was just that I was conscious of some inexplicable anomaly connected with our roped progress that day. I remember I kept glancing around in search of an explanation. I tried to convince myself it was due to Brown's somewhat inept, sluggish and erratic performance, but I was not altogether successful in this attribution. To make it worse a thick mist came on in the afternoon and this increased our difficulties, delayed us considerably, and intensified my sombre and rather defeatist mood.

'Certain pious, but, in my view, misguided persons, profess to find in the presence, the atmosphere, of these doomed Titans, evidence for a benevolent Providence, and a beneficent cosmic principle. I am not enrolled in their ranks. At best these eminences seem aloof and neutral, at worst, viciously and virulently hostile—I reverse the pathetic fallacy. That is, to a spirited man, half their appeal. Only once in a long while have I been lulled into a sense of their goodwill. And if one must endow them with a Pantheon, I would people it with the fickle and malicious denizens of Olympus and Valhalla, and not the allegedly philanthropic triad of heaven. In no place is the working of a ruthless, blind causality more starkly shown. And never, for some reason, have I felt that oppressive sense of malignity more acutely than during the last few hours of our climb that day, as we forced our groping way through a nightmare world of ice-pillars, many of them as high and ponderous as the Statue of Liberty, destined each one of them, soon to fall with a thunder like the crack of doom. And all the while I was bothered with that rope. Several times, as I glanced round through the murk, I seemed to sense Brown almost at my heels, when he was thirty feet away. Once I actually saw him, as I thought, near enough to touch. It was a displeasing illusion.'

'Were you scared?' I asked.

'I was certainly keyed-up and troubled. I am never scared, I think, when actually on the move. It was just that there was a noxious puzzle I couldn't solve. We were in no great danger, just experiencing the endemic risks inherent in all such places. But I was mainly responsible for the safety of us both and my mode of securing that safety was impaired.'

'I imagine,' I said, 'that the rope establishes, as it were, some psychic bond between those it links.'

'An unexpectedly percipient remark,' replied Sir Andrew. 'That is precisely the case. The rope makes the fate of one the fate of all; and each betrays along its strands his spiritual state; his hopes, anxieties, good-cheer, or lack of confidence. So I could feel Brown's hesitation and poor craftsmanship, as well as this inexplicable interruption of my proper connection with him.

'When we eventually reached the hut I had in no way elucidated the problem. I didn't like the look of Brown; he was far more tired than he should have been and his nerves were sparking again. He put the best face he could on it, as good mountaineers are trained to do, and declared a night's rest would put him right. I hoped for the best.'

'Did you mention your trouble with the rope?'

'I did not,' said Sir Andrew shortly. 'For one thing, it might have been purely subjective. For another, what was there to say? And the first duty of the mountaineer is to keep his fears to himself, unless they are liable to imperil his comrades. Never lower the psychic temperature if it can possibly be avoided. Yet somehow, I cannot define precisely how, I gained the impression he had noticed something and that this was partly the cause of his malaise.

'The hut was full, but not unpleasantly so, with young Italians for the most part, and we secured good sleeping places. Then we fed and lay down. It was a night of evil memory. Brown went to sleep almost at once, to sleep and to dream, and to tell of his dreams. He was, apparently, well, beyond all doubt, dreaming of Hecate and—how shall I put it?—in contact, in debate with her. And what made it far more trying to the listener, he was mimicking her voice with perfect virtuosity. This was at once horrible and ludicrous, the most pestilential and disintegrating combination of all, in my opinion. He was, it seemed, pleading with her to leave him alone, to spare him, and she was ruthlessly refusing. I say "it seemed," because the repulsive surge of words was blurred, and only at times articulate; just sufficient to give, as it were, the sense of the dialogue. But that was more than enough. The sleep-hungry Italians were naturally and vociferously infuriated, and I was compelled to rouse Brown over and over again, but each time he relapsed into that vilely haunted sleep. Once he raised himself and thrust out blindly with his arms. And Hecate's minatory contralto spewed from his throat, while the Italians mocked and cursed. It was a bestial pandemonium.

'The Italians left early, loud in their execrations of us. One of them, his black eyes wide with fear and anger, shook his lantern in my face and exclaimed "Who is this woman!" "What woman?" I replied. He shrugged his shoulders and said: "That is for you to say. I do not think I would climb the Géant with him if I were you! Good luck, Signore, *I think you will need it!*" Then they clattered off, and at four o'clock we followed them.

'I know now I should have taken that Italian's advice and got Brown back by the easiest and quickest route to the hotel, but when I tentatively suggested it, he almost hysterically implored me to carry on. "If I fail this time," he said, "I shall never climb again, I know it! I *must* conquer it!" I was very tired, my judgment and resolution were at a disgracefully low ebb, and I half surrendered. I decided we would go up some of the way to a ledge or platform I remembered, at about the twelve thousand foot level, rest, eat, and turn back.

'We had a tiresome climb up the glacier, Brown in very poor form, and that nuisance on the rope beginning again almost at once. We crossed the big crevasse where the glacier meets the lower rocks and began to ascend. There was still some mist, but it thinned as the sun rose. I led and Brown, making very heavy weather, followed. The difference between his performance this time and that other I have mentioned, was gross and terrifying. I remember doubting if he would ever be a climber again and realizing I had made a shocking error in going on. I had to nurse him with the greatest care and there was always that harassing behaviour of the rope. Only those with expert knowledge of such work could realize the great and deadly difference it made. I could never be quite sure when I had it properly firm on Brown, and he was climbing like a nervous novice. My own standard of the day was, not surprisingly, none too high. I'd had a damned bad, worried night and my mind was fussed and preoccupied. Usually one climbs half-subconsciously, that is the sign-manual of the expert, a rhythmic selection and seizure of holds, with only now and again a fully controlled operation of will and decision. But now I was at full stretch all the time and ever ready for Brown to slip. Over and over again I was forced to belay the rope to some coign of vantage and coax and ease him up, and there was forever that strong interruption between us. The Géant was beating us hands down all the time and I hadn't felt so outclassed since my first season in the Alps. The light became most sinister and garish, the sun striking through the brume, creating a potent and prismed dazzle. So much so that more than once I fancied I saw

Brown's outline duplicated, or rather revealed at different levels. And several times it seemed his head appeared just below me when he was still struggling far down. And then there were our shadows, cast huge on the snow-face across the gulf, vast and distorted by those strange rays.

'That there were *three* such shadows, now stationary, now in motion, was an irresistible illusion. There was mine, there was the lesser one of Brown, and there was another in between us. What was causing it? This fascinating and extraordinary puzzle served somewhat to distract my mind from its heavy and intensifying anxiety. At last, to my vast relief, I glanced up and saw that hospitable little platform not more than sixty feet above me. Once there, the worst would be, I thought, over, for I could lower Brown down more easily than get him up.

'I shouted down to him, "We're nearly there!" but he made no reply. I shouted again and listened carefully. And then I could hear him talking, using alternatively *his* voice and Hecate's.

'I cannot describe to you the kind of ghostly fear which then seized me.

There was I fifteen hundred feet up on a pretty sheer precipice with someone whose mind had clearly gone, on my rope. And I had to get him, first to the ledge, then try and restore him to a condition in which descent might be possible. I could never leave him there; we must survive or die together. First, I must reach that platform. I set myself to it, and for the time being he continued to climb, clumsily and mechanically, and carrying on that insane dialogue, yet *he kept moving!* But for how much longer would that mechanism continue to function and bring him to his holds? I conquered my fear and rallied again that essential detachment of spirit without which we were both certainly doomed.

'So I set myself with the utmost care to reach that ledge. Between me and it was a stretch of the Géant's rottenest rock, which I suddenly remembered well. It is spiked and roped now, I believe. When that gneiss is bad, it is very, very evil indeed. Mercifully, the mist was not freezing or we should have been dead ere then. How I cursed my insensate folly, the one great criminal blunder of my climbing career! This rush of rage may have saved me, for just when I was struggling up that infamous forty-five feet I got a fearful jerk from the rope. I was right out, attacking a short over-hang, exposed a hundred per cent, and how I sustained that jerk I shall never know. I even drove my teeth into the rock. It was one of those super-human efforts only possible to a powerful, fully-trained man at the peak of his physical perfection, when he knows that failure means immediate death. Somehow then he draws out his final erg of strength, and resilience.

'At last I reached the ledge, belayed like lightning, gasped for breath and looked down. As I did so, Brown ceased to climb, screamed, and then a torrent of wild, incoherent words spewed from his mouth. I yelled at him encouragement and assurance, but he paid no heed. And, though he was stationary, clawing to his holds, the rope was still under pressure, working and sounding on the belay. No explanation of that has ever been vouchsafed me. For a moment my glance flickered out across the great gulf on to the dazzling slope opposite; and there were my shadows and Brown's, and another which seemed still on the move and reaching down towards him.

'I could see his body trembling in every muscle and I knew he must go at any second. I shouted down wildly again and again, telling him I had him firm and that he could take his time, but again he paid no heed. I couldn't get him up, I must go down to him. There was just one possible way which, a shade technical, I will not describe to you. Nor is there need or point in doing so, for suddenly Brown relinquished all holds and swung out. As my eye followed him, once more it caught those shadows, and now there were but two, Brown's hideously enlarged. For a moment he hung there screaming and thrashing out with his arms, his whole body in violent motion. And then he began to spin most horribly, faster and faster, and almost it seemed, in the visual chaos of that whirl, as though there were two bodies lashed and struggling in each other's arms. Then somehow, in his writhings he worked free of the rope and fell two thousand feet to his death on the glacier below, leaving my shadow alone gigantic on the snow.

'That is all, and I want no questions, because I know I should have no answers for them and I am off to bed. As for your original question, I've done my best to answer it. But remember this, perchance such questions can never quite be answered.'

THE APPLE TREE

Daphne du Maurier

FIRST PUBLISHED IN *THE APPLE TREE:*
A SHORT NOVEL AND SEVERAL LONG STORIES, 1952

Dame Daphne du Maurier (1907–1989) needs no introduction and her history and bibliography are well documented. 'The Apple Tree', however, gives us a startling insight into her life and in particular, her marriage. In the late 1930s and early 40s du Maurier spent time in Egypt with her husband but with the outbreak of the Second World War she moved to Cornwall with her children, beginning a period in which she felt estranged from her husband. Even with peacetime, du Maurier and her husband were separated during the week and the inevitable tensions this brought influenced her fiction.

'The Apple Tree' is the tale of a widower, who stops short of celebrating his wife's death but can't quite bring himself to mourn. As the months go by he is drawn to two apple trees in his garden—one young and slender, one ominous and threatening. The tension grows as the seasons move towards winter and a horrific and snowy conclusion. Like many of du Maurier's works, the line between supernatural horror and psychological thriller is blurred. —LE

It was three months after she died that he first noticed the apple tree. He had known of its existence, of course, with the others, standing upon the lawn in front of the house, sloping upwards to the field beyond. Never before, though, had he been aware of this particular tree looking in any way different from its fellows, except that it was the third one on the left, a little apart from the rest and leaning more closely to the terrace.

It was a fine clear morning in early spring, and he was shaving by the open window. As he leant out to sniff the air, the lather on his face, the razor in his hand, his eye fell upon the apple tree. It was a trick of light, perhaps, something to do with the sun coming up over the woods, that happened to catch the tree at this particular moment; but the likeness was unmistakable.

He put his razor down on the window-ledge and stared. The tree was scraggy and of a depressing thinness, possessing none of the gnarled solidity of its companions. Its few branches, growing high up on the trunk like narrow shoulders on a tall body, spread themselves in martyred resignation, as though chilled by the fresh morning air. The roll of wire circling the tree, and reaching to about halfway up the trunk from the base, looked like a grey tweed skirt covering lean limbs; while the topmost branch, sticking up into the air above the ones below, yet sagging slightly, could have been a drooping head poked forward in an attitude of weariness.

How often he had seen Midge stand like this, dejected. No matter where it was, whether in the garden, or in the house, or even shopping in the town, she would take upon herself this same stooping posture, suggesting that life treated her hardly, that she had been singled out from her fellows to carry some impossible burden, but in spite of it would endure to the end without complaint. 'Midge, you look worn out, for heaven's sake sit down and take a rest!' But the words would be received with the inevitable shrug of the shoulder, the inevitable sigh, 'Someone has got to keep things going,' and straightening herself she would embark upon the dreary routine of unnecessary tasks she forced herself to do, day in, day out, through the interminable changeless years.

He went on staring at the apple tree. That martyred bent position, the stooping top, the weary branches, the few withered leaves that had not blown away with the wind and rain of the past winter and now shivered in the spring breeze like wispy hair; all of it protested soundlessly to the owner of the garden looking upon it, 'I am like this because of you, because of your neglect.'

He turned away from the window and went on shaving. It would not do to let his imagination run away with him and start building fancies in his mind just when he was settling at long last to freedom. He bathed and dressed and went down to breakfast. Eggs and bacon were waiting for him on the hotplate, and he carried the dish to the single place laid for him at the dining-table. *The Times*, folded smooth and new, was ready for him to read. When Midge was alive he had handed it to her first, from long custom, and when she gave it back to him after breakfast, to take with him to the study, the pages were always in the wrong order and folded crookedly, so that part of the pleasure of reading it was spoilt. The news, too, would be stale to him after she had read the worst of it aloud, which was a morning habit she used to take upon herself, always adding some derogatory remark of her own about what she read. The birth of a daughter to mutual friends would bring a click of the tongue, a little jerk of the head, 'Poor things, another girl,' or if a son, 'A boy can't be much fun to educate these days.' He used to think it psychological, because they themselves were childless, that she should so grudge the entry of new life into the world; but as time passed it became thus with all bright or joyous things, as though there was some fundamental blight upon good cheer.

'It says here that more people went on holiday this year than ever before. Let's hope they enjoyed themselves, that's all.' But no hope lay in her words, only disparagement. Then, having finished breakfast, she would push back her chair and sigh and say, 'Oh well...', leaving the sentence unfinished; but the sigh, the shrug of the shoulders, the slope of her long, thin back as she stooped to clear the dishes from the serving-table—thus sparing work for the daily maid—was all part of her long-term reproach, directed at him, that had marred their existence over a span of years.

Silent, punctilious, he would open the door for her to pass through to the kitchen quarters, and she would labour past him, stooping under the weight of the laden tray that there was no need for her to carry, and presently, through the half-open door, he would hear the swish of the running water from the pantry tap. He would return to his chair and sit down again, the crumpled *Times*, a smear of marmalade upon it, lying against the toast-rack; and once again, with monotonous insistence, the question hammered at his mind, 'What have I done?'

It was not as though she nagged. Nagging wives, like mothers-in-law, were chestnut jokes for music-halls. He could not remember Midge ever losing her temper or quarrelling. It was just that the undercurrent of reproach, mingled with suffering nobly born, spoilt the atmosphere of his home and drove him to a sense of furtiveness and guilt.

Perhaps it would be raining and he, seeking sanctuary within his study, electric fire aglow, his after-breakfast pipe filling the small room with smoke, would settle down before his desk in a pretence of writing letters, but in reality to hide, to feel the snug security of four safe walls that were his alone. Then the door would open and Midge, struggling into a raincoat, her wide-brimmed felt hat pulled low over her brow, would pause and wrinkle her nose in distaste.

'Phew! What a fug.'

He said nothing, but moved slightly in his chair, covering with his arm the novel he had chosen from a shelf in idleness.

'Aren't you going into the town?' she asked him.

'I had not thought of doing so.'

'Oh! Oh, well, it doesn't matter.' She turned away again towards the door.

'Why, is there anything you want done?'

'It's only the fish for lunch. They don't deliver on Wednesdays. Still, I can go myself if you are busy. I only thought...'

She was out of the room without finishing her sentence.

'It's all right, Midge,' he called, 'I'll get the car and go and fetch it presently. No sense in getting wet.'

Thinking she had not heard he went out into the hall. She was standing by the open front door, the mizzling rain driving in upon her. She had a long flat basket over her arm and was drawing on a pair of gardening gloves.

'I'm bound to get wet in any case,' she said, 'so it doesn't make much odds. Look at those flowers, they all need staking. I'll go for the fish when I've finished seeing to them.'

Argument was useless. She had made up her mind. He shut the front door after her and sat down again in the study. Somehow the room no longer felt so snug, and a little later, raising his head to the window, he saw her hurry past, her raincoat not buttoned properly and flapping, little drips of water forming on the brim of her hat and the garden basket filled with limp Michaelmas daisies already dead. His conscience pricking him, he bent down and turned out one bar of the electric fire.

Or yet again it would be spring, it would be summer. Strolling out hatless into the garden, his hands in his pockets, with no other purpose in his mind but to feel the sun upon his back and stare out upon the woods and fields and the slow winding river, he would hear, from the bedrooms above, the high-pitched whine of the Hoover slow down suddenly, gasp and die. Midge called down to him as he stood there on the terrace.

'Were you going to do anything?' she said.

He was not. It was the smell of spring, of early summer, that had driven him out into the garden. It was the delicious knowledge that being retired now, no longer working in the City, time was a thing of no account, he could waste it as he pleased.

'No,' he said, 'not on such a lovely day. Why?'

'Oh, never mind,' she answered, 'it's only that the wretched drain under the kitchen window has gone wrong again. Completely plugged up and choked. No one ever sees to it, that's why. I'll have a go at it myself this afternoon.'

Her face vanished from the window. Once more there was a gasp, a rising groan of sound, and the Hoover warmed to its task again. What foolishness that such an interruption could damp the brightness of the day. Not the demand, nor the task itself—clearing a drain was in its own way a schoolboy piece of folly, playing with

mud—but that wan face of hers looking out upon the sunlit terrace, the hand that went up wearily to push back a strand of falling
hair, and the inevitable sigh before she turned from the window,
the unspoken, 'I wish I had the time to stand and do nothing in
the sun. Oh, well...'

He had ventured to ask once why so much cleaning of the house
was necessary. Why there must be the incessant turning out of
rooms. Why chairs must be lifted to stand upon other chairs, rugs
rolled up and ornaments huddled together on a sheet of newspaper.
And why, in particular, the sides of the upstairs corridor, on which
no one ever trod, must be polished laboriously by hand, Midge
and the daily woman taking it in turns to crawl upon their knees
the whole endless length of it, like slaves of bygone days.

Midge had stared at him, not understanding.

'You'd be the first to complain,' she said, 'if the house was like
a pigsty. You like your comforts.'

So they lived in different worlds, their minds not meeting. Had
it been always so? He did not remember. They had been married
nearly twenty-five years and were two people who, from force of
habit, lived under the same roof.

When he had been in business, it seemed different. He had
not noticed it so much. He came home to eat, to sleep, and to go
up by train again in the morning. But when he retired he became
aware of her forcibly, and day by day his sense of her resentment,
of her disapproval, grew stronger.

Finally, in that last year before she died, he felt himself engulfed
in it, so that he was led into every sort of petty deception to get away
from her, making a pretence of going up to London to have his hair
cut, to see the dentist, to lunch with an old business friend; and in
reality he would be sitting by his club window, anonymous, at peace.

It was mercifully swift, the illness that took her from him. Influenza, followed by pneumonia, and she was dead within a week. He hardly knew how it happened, except that as usual she was over-tired and caught a cold, and would not stay in bed. One evening, coming home by the late train from London, having sneaked into a cinema during the afternoon, finding release amongst the crowd of warm friendly people enjoying themselves—for it was a bitter December day—he found her bent over the furnace in the cellar, poking and thrusting at the lumps of coke.

She looked up at him, white with fatigue, her face drawn.

'Why, Midge, what on earth are you doing?' he said.

'It's the furnace,' she said, 'we've had trouble with it all day, it won't stay alight. We shall have to get the men to see it tomorrow. I really cannot manage this sort of thing myself.'

There was a streak of coal dust on her cheek. She let the stubby poker fall on the cellar floor. She began to cough, and as she did so winced with pain.

'You ought to be in bed,' he said, 'I never heard of such non-sense. What the dickens does it matter about the furnace?'

'I thought you would be home early,' she said, 'and then you might have known how to deal with it. It's been bitter all day, I can't think what you found to do with yourself in London.'

She climbed the cellar stairs slowly, her back bent, and when she reached the top she stood shivering and half closed her eyes.

'If you don't mind terribly,' she said, 'I'll get your supper right away, to have it done with. I don't want anything myself.'

'To hell with my supper,' he said, 'I can forage for myself. You go up to bed. I'll bring you a hot drink.'

'I tell you, I don't want anything,' she said. 'I can fill my hot water bottle myself. I only ask one thing of you. And that is to remember to turn out the lights everywhere, before you come up.' She turned into the hall, her shoulders sagging.

'Surely a glass of hot milk?' he began uncertainly, starting to take off his overcoat; and as he did so the torn half of the ten-and-sixpenny seat at the cinema fell from his pocket on to the floor She saw it. She said nothing. She coughed again and began to drag herself upstairs.

The next morning her temperature was a hundred and three. The doctor came and said she had pneumonia. She asked if she might go to a private ward in the cottage hospital, because having a nurse in the house would make too much work. This was on the Tuesday morning. She went there right away, and they told him on the Friday evening that she was not likely to live through the night. He stood inside the room, after they told him, looking down at her in the high impersonal hospital bed, and his heart was wrung with pity, because surely they had given her too many pillows, she was propped too high, there could be no rest for her that way. He had brought some flowers, but there seemed no purpose now in giving them to the nurse to arrange, because Midge was too ill to look at them. In a sort of delicacy he put them on a table beside the screen, when the nurse was bending down to her.

'Is there anything she needs?' he said. 'I mean, I can easily...' He did not finish the sentence, he left it in the air, hoping the nurse would understand his intention, that he was ready to go off in the car, drive somewhere, fetch what was required.

The nurse shook her head. 'We will telephone you,' she said, 'if there is any change.'

What possible change could there be, he wondered, as he found himself outside the hospital? The white pinched face upon the pillows would not alter now, it belonged to no one.

Midge died in the early hours of Saturday morning.

He was not a religious man, he had no profound belief in immortality, but when the funeral was over, and Midge was buried, it distressed him to think of her poor lonely body lying in that brand-new coffin with the brass handles: it seemed such a churlish thing to permit. Death should be different. It should be like bidding farewell to someone at a station before a long journey, but without the strain. There was something of indecency in this haste to bury underground the thing that but for ill-chance would be a living breathing person. In his distress he fancied he could hear Midge saying with a sigh, 'Oh, well...' as they lowered the coffin into the open grave.

He hoped with fervour that after all there might be a future in some unseen Paradise and that poor Midge, unaware of what they were doing to her mortal remains, walked somewhere in green fields. But who with, he wondered? Her parents had died in India many years ago; she would not have much in common with them now if they met her at the gates of Heaven. He had a sudden picture of her waiting her turn in a queue, rather far back, as was always her fate in queues, with that large shopping bag of woven straw which she took everywhere, and on her face that patient martyred look. As she passed through the turnstile into Paradise she looked at him, reproachfully.

These pictures, of the coffin and the queue, remained with him for about a week, fading a little day by day. Then he forgot her. Freedom was his, and the sunny empty house, the bright crisp winter. The routine he followed belonged to him alone. He never thought of Midge until the morning he looked out upon the apple tree.

Later that day he was taking a stroll round the garden, and he found himself drawn to the tree through curiosity. It had been stupid fancy after all. There was nothing singular about it. An apple tree like any other apple tree. He remembered then that it had always been a poorer tree than its fellows, was in fact more than half dead, and at one time there had been talk of chopping it down, but the talk came to nothing. Well, it would be something for him to do over the weekend. Axing a tree was healthy exercise, and apple wood smelt good. It would be a treat to have it burning on the fire.

Unfortunately wet weather set in for nearly a week after that day, and he was unable to accomplish the task he had set himself. No sense in pottering out of doors this weather, and getting a chill into the bargain. He still noticed the tree from his bedroom window. It began to irritate him, humped there, straggling and thin, under the rain. The weather was not cold, and the rain that fell upon the garden was soft and gentle. None of the other trees wore this aspect of dejection. There was one young tree—only planted a few years back, he recalled quite well—growing to the right of the old one and standing straight and firm, the lithe young branches lifted to the sky, positively looking as if it enjoyed the rain. He peered through the window at it, and smiled. Now why the devil should he suddenly remember that incident, years back, during the war, with the girl who came to work on the land for a few months at the neighbouring farm? He did not suppose he had thought of her in months. Besides, there was nothing to it. At weekends he had helped them at the farm himself—war work of a sort—and she was always there, cheerful and pretty and smiling; she had dark curling hair, crisp and boyish, and a skin like a very young apple.

He looked forward to seeing her, Saturdays and Sundays; it was an antidote to the inevitable news bulletins put on throughout the day by Midge, and to ceaseless war talk. He liked looking at the child—she was scarcely more than that, nineteen or so— in her slim breeches and gay shirts; and when she smiled it was as though she embraced the world.

He never knew how it happened, and it was such a little thing; but one afternoon he was in the shed doing something to the tractor, bending over the engine, and she was beside him, close to his shoulder, and they were laughing together; and he turned round, to take a bit of waste to clean a plug, and suddenly she was in his arms and he was kissing her. It was a happy thing, spontaneous and free, and the girl so warm and jolly, with her fresh young mouth. Then they went on with the work of the tractor, but united now, in a kind of intimacy that brought gaiety to them both, and peace as well. When it was time for the girl to go and feed the pigs he followed her from the shed, his hand on her shoulder, a careless gesture that meant nothing really, a half caress; and as they came out into the yard he saw Midge standing there, staring at them.

'I've got to go in to a Red Cross meeting,' she said. 'I can't get the car to start. I called you. You didn't seem to hear.'

Her face was frozen. She was looking at the girl. At once guilt covered him. The girl said good evening cheerfully to Midge, and crossed the yard to the pigs.

He went with Midge to the car and managed to start it with the handle. Midge thanked him, her voice without expression. He found himself unable to meet her eyes. This, then, was adultery. This was sin. This was the second page in a Sunday newspaper— 'Husband Intimate with Land Girl in Shed. Wife Witnesses Act.' His hands were shaking when he got back to the house and he had to pour himself a drink. Nothing was ever said. Midge never mentioned the matter. Some craven instinct kept him from the farm the next weekend, and then he heard that the girl's mother had been taken ill and she had been called back home.

He never saw her again. Why, he wondered, should he remember her suddenly, on such a day, watching the rain falling on the apple trees? He must certainly make a point of cutting down the old dead tree, if only for the sake of bringing more sunshine to the little sturdy one; it hadn't a fair chance, growing there so close to the other.

On Friday afternoon he went round to the vegetable garden to find Willis, the jobbing gardener, who came three days a week, to pay him his wages. He wanted, too, to look in the toolshed and see if the axe and saw were in good condition. Willis kept everything neat and tidy there—this was Midge's training—and the axe and saw were hanging in their accustomed place upon the wall.

He paid Willis his money, and was turning away when the man suddenly said to him, 'Funny thing, sir, isn't it, about the old apple tree?'

The remark was so unexpected that it came as a shock. He felt himself change colour.

'Apple tree? What apple tree?' he said.

'Why, the one at the far end, near the terrace,' answered Willis. 'Been barren as long as I've worked here, and that's some years now. Never an apple from her, nor as much as a sprig of blossom. We were going to chop her up that cold winter, if you remember, and we never did. Well, she's taken on a new lease now. Haven't you noticed?' The gardener watched him smiling, a knowing look in his eye.

What did the fellow mean? It was not possible that he had been struck also by that fantastic freak resemblance—no, it was out of the question, indecent, blasphemous; besides, he had put it out of his own mind now, he had not thought of it again.

'I've noticed nothing,' he said, on the defensive.

Willis laughed. 'Come round to the terrace, sir,' he said, 'I'll show you.'

They went together to the sloping lawn, and when they came to the apple tree Willis put his hand up and pulled down a branch within reach. It creaked a little as he did so, as though stiff and unyielding, and Willis brushed away some of the dry lichen and revealed the spiky twigs. 'Look there, sir,' he said, 'she's growing buds. Look at them, feel them for yourself. There's life here yet, and plenty of it. Never known such a thing before. See this branch too.' He released the first, and leant up to reach another.

Willis was right. There were buds in plenty, but so small and brown that it seemed to him they scarcely deserved the name, they were more like blemishes upon the twig, dusty, and dry. He put his hands in his pockets. He felt a queer distaste to touch them.

'I don't think they'll amount to much,' he said.

'I don't know, sir,' said Willis, 'I've got hopes. She's stood the winter, and if we get no more bad frosts there's no knowing what we'll see. It would be some joke to watch the old tree blossom. She'll bear fruit yet.' He patted the trunk with his open hand, in a gesture at once familiar and affectionate.

The owner of the apple tree turned away. For some reason he felt irritated with Willis. Anyone would think the damned tree lived. And now his plan to axe the tree, over the weekend, would come to nothing.

'It's taking the light from the young tree,' he said. 'Surely it would be more to the point if we did away with this one, and gave the little one more room?'

He moved across to the young tree and touched a limb. No lichen here. The branches smooth. Buds upon every twig, curling tight. He let go the branch and it sprang away from him, resilient.

'Do away with her, sir,' said Willis, 'while there's still life in her? Oh no, sir, I wouldn't do that. She's doing no harm to the young tree. I'd give the old tree one more chance. If she doesn't bear fruit, we'll have her down next winter.'

'All right, Willis,' he said, and walked swiftly away. Somehow he did not want to discuss the matter any more.

That night, when he went to bed, he opened the window wide as usual and drew back the curtains; he could not bear to wake up in the morning and find the room close. It was full moon, and the light shone down upon the terrace and the lawn above it, ghostly pale and still. No wind blew. A hush upon the place. He leant out, loving the silence. The moon shone full upon the little apple tree, the young one. There was a radiance about it in this light that gave it a fairy-tale quality. Small and lithe and slim, the young tree might have been a dancer, her arms upheld, poised ready on her toes for flight. Such a careless, happy grace about it. Brave young tree. Away to the left stood the other one, half of it in shadow still. Even the moonlight could not give it beauty. What in heaven's name was the matter with the thing that it had to stand there, humped and stooping, instead of looking upwards to the light? It marred the still quiet night, it spoilt the setting. He had been a fool to give way to Willis and agree to spare the tree. Those ridiculous buds would never blossom, and even if they did...

His thoughts wandered, and for the second time that week he found himself remembering the land girl and her joyous smile. He wondered what had happened to her. Married probably, with a young family. Made some chap happy, no doubt. Oh, well... He smiled. Was he going to make use of that expression now? Poor Midge! Then he caught his breath and stood quite still, his hand upon the curtain. The apple tree, the one on the left, was no longer in shadow. The moon shone upon the withered branches, and they looked like skeleton's arms raised in supplication. Frozen arms, stiff and numb with pain. There was no wind, and the other trees were motionless; but there, in those topmost branches, something shivered and stirred, a breeze that came from nowhere and died away again. Suddenly a branch fell from the apple tree to the ground below. It was the near branch, with the small dark buds upon it, which he would not touch. No rustle, no breath of movement came from the other trees. He went on staring at the branch as it lay there on the grass, under the moon. It stretched across the shadow of the young tree close to it, pointing as though in accusation.

For the first time in his life that he could remember he drew the curtains over the window to shut out the light of the moon.

Willis was supposed to keep to the vegetable garden. He had never shown his face much round the front when Midge was alive. That was because Midge attended to the flowers. She even used to mow the grass, pushing the wretched machine up and down the slope, her back bent low over the handles.

It had been one of the tasks she set herself, like keeping the bedrooms swept and polished. Now Midge was no longer there to attend to the front garden and to tell him where he should work, Willis was always coming through to the front. The gardener liked the change. It made him feel responsible.

'I can't understand how that branch came to fall, sir,' he said on the Monday.

'What branch?'

'Why, the branch on the apple tree. The one we were looking at before I left.'

'It was rotten, I suppose. I told you the tree was dead.'

'Nothing rotten about it, sir. Why, look at it. Broke clean off.'

Once again the owner was obliged to follow his man up the slope above the terrace. Willis picked up the branch. The lichen upon it was wet, bedraggled looking, like matted hair.

'You didn't come again to test the branch, over the weekend, and loosen it in some fashion, did you, sir?' asked the gardener.

'I most certainly did not,' replied the owner, irritated. 'As a matter of fact I heard the branch fall, during the night. I was opening the bedroom window at the time.'

'Funny. It was a still night too.'

'These things often happen to old trees. Why you bother about this one I can't imagine. Anyone would think...'

He broke off; he did not know how to finish the sentence.

'Anyone would think that the tree was valuable,' he said.

The gardener shook his head. 'It's not the value,' he said. 'I don't reckon for a moment that this tree is worth any money at all. It's just that after all this time, when we thought her dead, she's alive and kicking, as you might say. Freak of nature, I call it. We'll hope no other branches fall before she blossoms.'

Later, when the owner set off for his afternoon walk, he saw the man cutting away the grass below the tree and placing new wire around the base of the trunk. It was quite ridiculous. He did not pay the fellow a fat wage to tinker about with a half dead tree. He ought to be in the kitchen garden, growing vegetables. It was too much effort, though, to argue with him.

He returned home about half-past five. Tea was a discarded meal since Midge had died, and he was looking forward to his armchair by the fire, his pipe, his whisky-and-soda, and silence.

The fire had not long been lit and the chimney was smoking. There was a queer, rather sickly smell about the living-room. He threw open the windows and went upstairs to change his heavy shoes. When he came down again the smoke still clung about the room and the smell was as strong as ever. Impossible to name it. Sweetish, strange. He called to the woman out in the kitchen.

'There's a funny smell in the house,' he said. 'What is it?'

The woman came out into the hall from the back.

'What sort of a smell, sir?' she said, on the defensive.

'It's in the living-room,' he said. 'The room was full of smoke just now. Have you been burning something?'

Her face cleared. 'It must be the logs,' she said. 'Willis cut them up specially, sir, he said you would like them.'

'What logs are those?'

'He said it was apple wood, sir, from a branch he had sawed up. Apple wood burns well, I've always heard. Some people fancy it very much. I don't notice any smell myself, but I've got a slight cold.'

Together they looked at the fire. Willis had cut the logs small. The woman, thinking to please him, had piled several on top of one another, to make a good fire to last. There was no great blaze. The smoke that came from them was thin and poor. Greenish in colour. Was it possible she did not notice that sickly rancid smell?

'The logs are wet,' he said abruptly. 'Willis should have known better. Look at them. Quite useless on my fire.'

The woman's face took on a set, rather sulky expression. 'I'm very sorry,' she said. 'I didn't notice anything wrong with them when I came to light the fire. They seemed to start well. I've always understood apple wood was very good for burning, and Willis said the same. He told me to be sure and see that you had these on the fire this evening, he had made a special job of cutting them for you. I thought you knew about it and had given orders.'

'Oh, all right,' he answered, abruptly. 'I dare say they'll burn in time. It's not your fault.'

He turned his back on her and poked at the fire, trying to separate the logs. While she remained in the house there was nothing he could do. To remove the damp smouldering logs and throw them somewhere round the back, and then light the fire afresh with dry sticks would arouse comment. He would have to go through the kitchen to the back passage where the kindling wood was kept, and she would stare at him, and come forward and say, 'Let me do it, sir. Has the fire gone out then?' No, he must wait until after supper, when she had cleared away and washed up and gone off for the night. Meanwhile, he would endure the smell of the apple wood as best he could.

He poured out his drink, lit his pipe and stared at the fire. It gave out no heat at all, and with the central heating off in the house the living room struck chill. Now and again a thin wisp of the greenish smoke puffed from the logs, and with it seemed to come that sweet sickly smell, unlike any sort of wood smoke that he knew. That interfering fool of a gardener... Why saw up the logs? He must have known they were damp. Riddled with damp. He leant forward, staring more closely. Was it damp, though, that oozed there in a thin trickle from the pale logs? No, it was sap, unpleasant, slimy.

He seized the poker, and in a fit of irritation thrust it between the logs, trying to stir them to flame, to change that green smoke into a normal blaze. The effort was useless. The logs would not burn. And all the while the trickle of sap ran on to the grate and the sweet smell filled the room, turning his stomach. He took his glass and his book and went and turned on the electric fire in the study and sat in there instead.

It was idiotic. It reminded him of the old days, how he would make a pretence of writing letters, and go and sit in the study because of Midge in the living room. She had a habit of yawning in the evenings, when her day's work was done; a habit of which she was quite unconscious. She would settle herself on the sofa with her knitting, the click-click of the needles going fast and furious; and suddenly they would start, those shattering yawns, rising from the depths of her, a prolonged 'Ah... Ah...Hi-Oh!' followed by the inevitable sigh. Then there would be silence except for the knitting needles, but as he sat behind his book, waiting, he knew that within a few minutes another yawn would come, another sigh.

A hopeless sort of anger used to stir within him, a longing to throw down his book and say, 'Look, if you are so tired, wouldn't it be better if you went to bed?'

Instead, he controlled himself, and after a little while, when he could bear it no longer, he would get up and leave the living-room, and take refuge in the study. Now he was doing the same thing, all over again, because of the apple logs. Because of the damned sickly smell of the smouldering wood.

He went on sitting in his chair by the desk, waiting for supper. It was nearly nine o'clock before the daily woman had cleared up, turned down his bed and gone for the night.

He returned to the living-room, which he had not entered since leaving it earlier in the evening. The fire was out. It had made some effort to burn, because the logs were thinner than they had been before, and had sunk low into the basket grate. The ash was meagre, yet the sickly smell clung to the dying embers. He went out into the kitchen and found an empty scuttle and brought it back into the living room. Then he lifted the logs into it, and the ashes too.

There must have been some damp residue in the scuttle, or the logs were still not dry, because as they settled there they seemed to turn darker than before, with a kind of scum upon them. He carried the scuttle down to the cellar, opened the door of the central heating furnace, and threw the lot inside.

He remembered then, too late, that the central heating had been given up now for two or three weeks, owing to the spring weather, and that unless he relit it now the logs would remain there, untouched, until the following winter. He found paper, matches, and a can of paraffin, and setting the whole alight closed the door of the furnace, and listened to the roar of flames. That would settle it. He waited a moment and then went up the steps, back to the kitchen passage, to lay and relight the fire in the living room. The business took time, he had to find kindling and coal, but with patience he got the new fire started, and finally settled himself down in his armchair before it.

He had been reading perhaps for twenty minutes before he became aware of the banging door. He put down his book and listened. Nothing at first. Then, yes, there it was again. A rattle, a slam of an unfastened door in the kitchen quarters. He got up and went along to shut it. It was the door at the top of the cellar stairs. He could have sworn he had fastened it. The catch must have worked loose in some way. He switched on the light at the head of the stairs, and bent to examine the catch. There seemed nothing wrong with it. He was about to close the door firmly when he noticed the smell again. The sweet sickly smell of smouldering apple wood. It was creeping up from the cellar, finding its way to the passage above.

Suddenly, for no reason, he was seized with a kind of fear, a feeling of panic almost. What if the smell filled the whole house through the night, came up from the kitchen quarters to the floor above, and while he slept found its way into his bedroom, choking him, stifling him, so that he could not breathe? The thought was ridiculous, insane—and yet...

Once more he forced himself to descend the steps into the cellar. No sound came from the furnace, no roar of flames. Wisps of smoke, thin and green, oozed their way from the fastened furnace door; it was this that he had noticed from the passage above.

He went to the furnace and threw open the door. The paper had all burnt away, and the few shavings with them. But the logs, the apple logs, had not burnt at all. They lay there as they had done when he threw them in, one charred limb above another, black and huddled, like the bones of someone darkened and dead by fire. Nausea rose in him. He thrust his handkerchief into his mouth, choking. Then, scarcely knowing what he did, he ran up the steps to find the empty scuttle, and with a shovel and tongs tried to pitch the logs back into it, scraping for them through the narrow door of the furnace. He was retching in his belly all the while. At last the scuttle was filled, and he carried it up the steps and through the kitchen to the back door.

He opened the door. Tonight there was no moon and it was raining. Turning up the collar of his coat he peered about him in the darkness, wondering where he should throw the logs. Too wet and dark to stagger all the way to the kitchen garden and chuck them on the rubbish heap, but in the field behind the garage the grass was thick and long and they might lie there hidden. He crunched his way over the gravel drive, and coming to the fence beside the field threw his burden on to the concealing grass. There they could rot and perish, grow sodden with rain, and in the end become part of the mouldy earth; he did not care. The responsibility was his no longer. They were out of his house, and it did not matter what became of them.

He returned to the house, and this time made sure the cellar door was fast. The air was clear again, the smell had gone.

He went back to the living room to warm himself before the fire, but his hands and feet, wet with the rain, and his stomach, still queasy from the pungent apple smoke, combined together to chill his whole person, and he sat there, shuddering.

He slept badly when he went to bed that night, and awoke in the morning feeling out of sorts. He had a headache, and an ill-tasting tongue. He stayed indoors. His liver was thoroughly upset. To relieve his feelings he spoke sharply to the daily woman.

'I've caught a bad chill,' he said to her, 'trying to get warm last night. So much for apple-wood. The smell of it has affected my inside as well. You can tell Willis, when he comes tomorrow.'

She looked at him in disbelief.

'I'm sure I'm very sorry,' she said. 'I told my sister about the wood last night, when I got home, and that you had not fancied it. She said it was most unusual. Apple-wood is considered quite a luxury to burn, and burns well, what's more.'

'This lot didn't, that's all I know,' he said to her, 'and I never want to see any more of it. As for the smell... I can taste it still, it's completely turned me up.'

Her mouth tightened. 'I'm sorry,' she said. And then, as she left the dining-room, her eye fell on the empty whisky bottle on the sideboard. She hesitated a moment, then put it on her tray.

'You've finished with this, sir?' she said.

Of course he had finished with it. It was obvious. The bottle was empty. He realized the implication, though. She wanted to suggest that the idea of apple-wood smoke upsetting him was all my eye, he had done himself too well. Damned impertinence.

'Yes,' he said, 'you can bring another in its place.'

That would teach her to mind her own business.

He was quite sick for several days, queasy and giddy, and finally rang up the doctor to come and have a look at him. The story of the apple-wood sounded nonsense, when he told it, and the doctor, after examining him, appeared unimpressed.

'Just a chill on the liver,' he said, 'damp feet, and possibly something you've eaten combined. I hardly think wood smoke has much to do with it. You ought to take more exercise, if you're inclined to have a liver. Play golf. I don't know how I should keep fit without my weekend golf' He laughed, packing up his bag. 'I'll make you up some medicine,' he said, 'and once this rain has cleared off I should get out and into the air. It's mild enough, and all we want now is a bit of sunshine to bring everything on. Your garden is farther ahead than mine. Your fruit trees are ready to blossom.' And then, before leaving the room, he added, 'You mustn't forget, you had a bad shock a few months ago. It takes time to get over these things. You're still missing your wife, you know. Best thing is to get out and about and see people. Well, take care of yourself.'

His patient dressed and went downstairs. The fellow meant well, of course, but his visit had been a waste of time. 'You're still missing your wife, you know.' How little the doctor understood. Poor Midge... At least he himself had the honesty to admit that he did not miss her at all, that now she was gone he could breathe, he was free, and that apart from the upset liver he had not felt so well for years.

During the few days he had spent in bed the daily woman had taken the opportunity to spring-clean the living room. An unnecessary piece of work, but he supposed it was part of the legacy Midge had left behind her. The room looked scrubbed and straight and much too tidy. His own personal litter cleared, books and papers neatly stacked. It was an infernal nuisance, really, having anyone to do for him at all. It would not take much for him to sack her and fend for himself as best he could. Only the bother, the tie of cooking and washing up, prevented him. The ideal life, of course, was that led by a man out East, or in the South Seas, who took a native wife. No problem there. Silence, good service, perfect waiting, excellent cooking, no need for conversation; and then, if you wanted something more than that, there she was, young, warm, a companion for the dark hours. No criticism ever, the obedience of an animal to its master, and the light-hearted laughter of a child. Yes, they had wisdom all right, those fellows who broke away from convention. Good luck to them.

He strolled over to the window and looked out up the sloping lawn. The rain was stopping and tomorrow it would be fine; he would be able to get out, as the doctor had suggested. The man was right, too, about the fruit trees. The little one near the steps was in flower already, and a blackbird had perched himself on one of the branches, which swayed slightly under his weight.

The rain-drops glistened and the opening buds were very curled and pink, but when the sun broke through tomorrow they would turn white and soft against the blue of the sky. He must find his old camera, and put a film in it, and photograph the little tree. The others would be in flower, too, during the week. As for the old one, there on the left, it looked as dead as ever; or else the so-called buds were so brown they did not show up from this distance. Perhaps the shedding of the branch had been its finish. And a good job too.

He turned away from the window and set about rearranging the room to his taste, spreading his things about. He liked pottering, opening drawers, taking things out and putting them back again. There was a red pencil in one of the side tables that must have slipped down behind a pile of books and been found during the turn-out. He sharpened it, gave it a sleek fine point. He found a new film in another drawer, and kept it out to put in his camera in the morning. There were a number of papers and old photographs in the drawer, heaped in a jumble, and snapshots too, dozens of them. Midge used to look after these things at one time and put them in albums; then during the war she must have lost interest, or had too many other things to do.

All this junk could really be cleared away. It would have made a fine fire the other night, and might have got even the apple logs to burn. There was little sense in keeping any of it. This appalling photo of Midge, for instance, taken heaven knows how many years ago, not long after their marriage, judging from the style of it. Did she really wear her hair that way? That fluffy mop, much too thick and bushy for her face, which was long and narrow even then. The low neck, pointing to a V, and the dangling earrings, and the smile, too eager, making her mouth seem larger than it was. In the left-hand corner she had written 'To my own darling Buzz, from his loving Midge.' He had completely forgotten his old nickname. It had been dropped years back, and he seemed to remember he had never cared for it: he had found it ridiculous and embarrassing and had chided her for using it in front of people.

He tore the photograph in half and threw it on the fire. He watched it curl up upon itself and burn, and the last to go was that vivid smile. My own darling Buzz... Suddenly he remembered the evening dress in the photograph. It was green, not her colour ever, turning her sallow; and she had bought it for some special occasion, some big dinner party with friends who were celebrating their wedding anniversary. The idea of the dinner had been to invite all those friends and neighbours who had been married roughly around the same time, which was the reason Midge and he had gone.

There was a lot of champagne, and one or two speeches, and much conviviality, laughter, and joking—some of the joking rather broad—and he remembered that when the evening was over, and they were climbing into the car to drive away, his host, with a gust of laughter, said, 'Try paying your addresses in a top hat, old boy, they say it never fails!' He had been aware of Midge beside him, in that green evening frock, sitting very straight and still, and on her face that same smile which she had worn in the photograph just destroyed, eager yet uncertain, doubtful of the meaning of the words that her host, slightly intoxicated, had let fall upon the evening air, yet wishing to seem advanced, anxious to please, and more than either of these things desperately anxious to attract.

When he had put the car away in the garage and gone into the house he had found her waiting there, in the living-room, for no reason at all. Her coat was thrown off to show the evening dress, and the smile, rather uncertain, was on her face.

He yawned, and settling himself down in a chair picked up a book. She waited a little while, then slowly took up her coat and went upstairs. It must have been shortly afterwards that she had that photograph taken. 'My own darling Buzz, from his loving Midge.' He threw a great handful of dry sticks on to the fire. They crackled and split and turned the photograph to ashes. No damp green logs tonight..,

It was fine and warm the following day. The sun shone, and the birds sang. He had a sudden impulse to go to London. It was a day for sauntering along Bond Street, watching the passing crowds. A day for calling in at his tailors, for having a hair-cut, for eating a dozen oysters at his favourite bar. The chill had left him. The pleasant hours stretched before him. He might even look in at a matinee.

The day passed without incident, peaceful, untiring, just as he had planned, making a change from day-by-day country routine. He drove home about seven o'clock, looking forward to his drink and to his dinner. It was so warm he did not need his overcoat, not even now, with the sun gone down. He waved a hand to the farmer, who happened to be passing the gate as he turned into the drive.

'Lovely day,' he shouted.

The man nodded, smiled. 'Can do with plenty of these from now on,' he shouted back. Decent fellow. They had always been very matey since those war days, when he had driven the tractor.

He put away the car and had a drink, and while waiting for supper took a stroll around the garden. What a difference those hours of sunshine had made to everything. Several daffodils were out, narcissi too, and the green hedgerows fresh and sprouting. As for the apple trees, the buds had burst, and they were all of them in flower. He went to his little favourite and touched the blossom. It felt soft to his hand and he gently shook a bough. It was firm, well-set, and would not fall. The scent was scarcely perceptible as yet, but in a day or two, with a little more sun, perhaps a shower or two, it would come from the open flower and softly fill the air, never pungent, never strong, a modest scent. A scent which you would have to find for yourself, as the bees did. Once found it stayed with you, it lingered always, alluring, comforting, and sweet. He patted the little tree, and went down the steps into the house.

Next morning, at breakfast, there came a knock on the dining-room door, and the daily woman said that Willis was outside and wanted to have a word with him. He asked Willis to step in. The gardener looked aggrieved. Was it trouble, then?

'I'm sorry to bother you, sir,' he said, 'but I had a few words with Mr Jackson this morning. He's been complaining.' Jackson was the farmer, who owned the neighbouring fields. 'What's he complaining about?'

'Says I've been throwing wood over the fence into his field, and the young foal out there, with the mare, tripped over it and went lame. I've never thrown wood over the fence in my life, sir. Quite nasty he was, sir. Spoke of the value of the foal, and it might spoil his chances to sell it.'

'I hope you told him, then, it wasn't true.'

'I did, sir. But the point is someone has been throwing wood over the fence. He showed me the very spot. Just behind the garage. I went with Mr Jackson, and there they were. Logs had been tipped there, sir. I thought it best to come to you about it before I spoke in the kitchen, otherwise you know how it is, there would be unpleasantness.'

He felt the gardener's eye upon him. No way out, of course. And it was Willis's fault in the first place.

'No need to say anything in the kitchen, Willis,' he said. 'I threw the logs there myself. You brought them into the house, without my asking you to do so, with the result that they put out my fire, filled the room with smoke, and ruined an evening. I chucked them over the fence in a devil of a temper, and if they have damaged Jackson's foal you can apologize for me, and tell him I'll pay him compensation. All I ask is that you don't bring any more logs like those into the house again.'

'No, sir. I understood they had not been a success. I didn't think, though, that you would go so far as to throw them out.'

'Well, I did. And there's an end to it.'

'Yes, sir.' He made as if to go, but before he left the dining-room he paused and said, 'I can't understand about the logs not burning, all the same. I took a small piece back to the wife, and it burnt lovely in our kitchen, bright as anything.'

'It did not burn here.'

'Anyway, the old tree is making up for one spoilt branch, sir. Have you seen her this morning?'

'No.'

'It's yesterday's sun that has done it, sir, and the warm night. Quite a treat she is, with all the blossom. You should go out and take a look at her directly.'

Willis left the room, and he continued his breakfast.

Presently he went out on to the terrace. At first he did not go up on to the lawn; he made a pretence of seeing to other things, of getting the heavy garden seat out, now that the weather was set fair. And then, fetching a pair of clippers, he did a bit of pruning to the few roses, under the windows. Yet, finally, something drew him to the tree.

It was just as Willis said. Whether it was the sun, the warmth, the mild still night, he could not tell; but the small brown buds had unfolded themselves, had ripened into flower, and now spread themselves above his head into a fantastic cloud of white, moist blossom. It grew thickest at the top of the tree, the flowers so clustered together that they looked like wad upon wad of soggy cotton wool, and all of it, from the topmost branches to those nearer to the ground, had this same pallid colour of sickly white.

It did not resemble a tree at all; it might have been a flapping tent, left out in the rain by campers who had gone away, or else a mop, a giant mop, whose streaky surface had been caught somehow by the sun, and so turned bleached. The blossom was too thick, too great a burden for the long thin trunk, and the moisture clinging to it made it heavier still. Already, as if the effort had been too much, the lower flowers, those nearest the ground, were turning brown; yet there had been no rain.

Well, there it was. Willis had been proved right. The tree had blossomed. But instead of blossoming to life, to beauty, it had somehow, deep in nature, gone awry and turned a freak. A freak which did not know its texture or its shape, but thought to please. Almost as though it said, self-conscious, with a smirk, 'Look. All this is for you.'

Suddenly he heard a step behind him. It was Willis.

'Fine sight, sir, isn't it?'

'Sorry, I don't admire it. The blossom is far too thick.'

The gardener stared at him and said nothing. It struck him that Willis must think him very difficult, very hard, and possibly eccentric. He would go and discuss him in the kitchen with the daily woman.

He forced himself to smile at Willis.

'Look here,' he said, 'I don't mean to damp you. But all this blossom doesn't interest me. I prefer it small and light and colourful, like the little tree. But you take some of it back home, to your wife. Cut as much of it as you like, I don't mind at all. I'd like you to have it.'

He waved his arm, generously. He wanted Willis to go now, and fetch a ladder, and carry the stuff away.

The man shook his head. He looked quite shocked.

'No, thank you, sir, I wouldn't dream of it. It would spoil the tree. I want to wait for the fruit. That's what I'm banking on, the fruit.'

There was no more to be said.

'All right, Willis. Don't bother, then.'

He went back to the terrace. But when he sat down there in the sun, looking up the sloping lawn, he could not see the little tree at all, standing modest and demure above the steps, her soft flowers lifting to the sky. She was dwarfed and hidden by the freak, with its great cloud of sagging petals, already wilting, dingy white, on to the grass beneath. And whichever way he turned his chair, this way or that upon the terrace, it seemed to him that he could not escape the tree, that it stood there above him, reproachful, anxious, desirous of the admiration that he could not give.

That summer he took a longer holiday than he had done for many years—a bare ten days with his old mother in Norfolk, instead of the customary month that he had been used to spend with Midge, and the rest of August and the whole of September in Switzerland and Italy.

He took his car, and so was free to motor from place to place as the mood inclined. He cared little for sight-seeing or excursions, and was not much of a climber. What he liked most was to come upon a little town in the cool of the evening, pick out a small but comfortable hotel, and then stay there, if it pleased him, for two or three days at a time, doing nothing, mooching.

He liked sitting about in the sun all morning, at some café or restaurant, with a glass of wine in front of him, watching the people; so many gay young creatures seemed to travel nowadays. He enjoyed the chatter of conversation around him, as long as he did not have to join in; and now and again a smile would come his way, a word or two of greeting from some guest in the same hotel, but nothing to commit him, merely a sense of being in the swim, of being a man of leisure on his own, abroad.

The difficulty in the old days, on holiday anywhere with Midge, would be her habit of striking up acquaintance with people, some other couple who struck her as looking 'nice' or, as she put it, 'our sort.' It would start with conversation over coffee, and then pass on to mutual planning of shared days, car drives in foursomes—he could not bear it, the holiday would be ruined.

Now, thank heaven, there was no need for this. He did what he liked, in his own time. There was no Midge to say, 'Well, shall we be moving?' when he was still sitting contentedly over his wine, no Midge to plan a visit to some old church that did not interest him.

He put on weight during his holiday, and he did not mind. There was no one to suggest a good long walk to keep fit after the rich food, thus spoiling the pleasant somnolence that comes with coffee and dessert; no one to glance, surprised, at the sudden wearing of a jaunty shirt, a flamboyant tie.

Strolling through the little towns and villages, hatless, smoking a cigar, receiving smiles from the jolly young folk around him, he felt himself a dog. This was the life, no worries, no cares. No 'We have to be back on the fifteenth because of that committee meeting at the hospital'; no 'We can't possibly leave the house shut up for longer than a fortnight, something might happen'. Instead, the bright lights of a little country fair, in a village whose name he did not even bother to find out; the tinkle of music, boys and girls laughing, and he himself, after a bottle of the local wine, bowing to a young thing with a gay handkerchief round her head and sweeping her off to dance under the hot tent. No matter if her steps did not harmonize with his—it was years since he had danced—this was the thing, this was it. He released her when the music stopped, and off she ran, giggling, back to her young friends, laughing at him no doubt. What of it? He had had his fun.

He left Italy when the weather turned, at the end of September, and was back home the first week in October. No problem to it. A telegram to the daily woman, with the probable date of arrival, and that was all. Even a brief holiday with Midge and the return meant complications. Written instructions about groceries, milk and bread, airing of beds, lighting of fires, reminders about the delivery of the morning papers. The whole business turned into a chore.

He turned into the drive on a mellow October evening and there was smoke coming from the chimneys, the front door open, and his pleasant home awaiting him. No rushing through to the back regions to learn of possible plumbing disasters, breakages, water shortages, food difficulties; the daily woman knew better than to bother him with these. Merely, 'Good evening, sir. I hope you had a good holiday. Supper at the usual time?' And then silence. He could have his drink, light his pipe, and relax; the small pile of letters did not matter. No feverish tearing of them open, and then the start of the telephoning, the hearing of those endless one-sided conversations between women friends. 'Well? How are things? Really? My dear... And what did you say to that... She did?... I can't possibly on Wednesday...'

He stretched himself contentedly, stiff after his drive, and gazed comfortably around the cheerful, empty living-room. He was hungry, after his journey up from Dover, and the chop seemed rather meagre after foreign fare. But there it was, it wouldn't hurt him to return to plainer food. A sardine on toast followed the chop, and then he looked about him for dessert.

There was a plate of apples on the sideboard. He fetched them and put them down in front of him on the dining-room table. Poor-looking things. Small and wizened, dullish brown in colour.

He bit into one, but as soon as the taste of it was on his tongue he spat it out. The thing was rotten. He tried another. It was just the same. He looked more closely at the pile of apples. The skins were leathery and rough and hard; you would expect the insides to be sour. On the contrary they were pulpy soft, and the cores were yellow. Filthy tasting things. A stray piece stuck to his tooth and he pulled it out. Stringy, beastly...

He rang the bell, and the woman came through from the kitchen.

'Have we any other dessert?' he said.

'I am afraid not, sir. I remembered how fond you were of apples, and Willis brought in these from the garden. He said they were especially good, and just ripe for eating.'

'Well, he's quite wrong. They're uneatable.'

'I'm very sorry, sir. I wouldn't have put them through had I known. There's a lot more outside, too. Willis brought in a great basketful.'

'All the same sort?'

'Yes, sir. The small brown ones. No other kind, at all.'

'Never mind, it can't be helped. I'll look for myself in the morning.'

He got up from the table and went through to the living-room. He had a glass of port to take away the taste of the apples, but it seemed to make no difference, not even a biscuit with it. The pulpy rotten tang clung to his tongue and the roof of his mouth, and in the end he was obliged to go up to the bathroom and clean his teeth. The maddening thing was that he could have done with a good clean apple, after that rather indifferent supper: something with a smooth clear skin, the inside not too sweet, a little sharp in flavour. He knew the kind. Good biting texture. You had to pick them, of course, at just the right moment.

He dreamt that night he was back again in Italy, dancing under the tent in the little cobbled square. He woke with the tinkling music in his ear, but he could not recall the face of the peasant girl or remember the feel of her, tripping against his feet. He tried to recapture the memory, lying awake, over his morning tea, but it eluded him.

He got up out of bed and went over to the window, to glance at the weather. Fine enough, with a slight nip in the air.

Then he saw the tree. The sight of it came as a shock, it was so unexpected. Now he realized at once where the apples had come from the night before. The tree was laden, bowed down, under her burden of fruit. They clustered, small and brown, on every branch, diminishing in size as they reached the top, so that those on the high boughs, not grown yet to full size, looked like nuts. They weighed heavy on the tree, and because of this it seemed bent and twisted out of shape, the lower branches nearly sweeping the ground; and on the grass, at the foot of the tree, were more and yet more apples, windfalls, the first-grown, pushed off by their clamouring brothers and sisters. The ground was covered with them, many split open and rotting where the wasps had been. Never in his life had he seen a tree so laden with fruit. It was a miracle that it had not fallen under the weight.

He went out before breakfast—curiosity was too great—and stood beside the tree, staring at it. There was no mistake about it, these were the same apples that had been put in the dining-room last night. Hardly bigger than tangerines, and many of them smaller than that, they grew so close together on the branches that to pick one you would be forced to pick a dozen.

There was something monstrous in the sight, something distasteful; yet it was pitiful too that the months had brought this agony upon the tree, for agony it was, there could be no other word for it. The tree was tortured by fruit, groaning under the weight of it, and the frightful part about it was that not one of the fruit was eatable. Every apple was rotten through and through. He trod them underfoot, the windfalls on the grass, there was no escaping them; and in a moment they were mush and slime, clinging about his heels—he had to clean the mess off with wisps of grass.

It would have been far better if the tree had died, stark and bare, before this ever happened. What use was it to him or anyone, this load of rotting fruit, littering up the place, fouling the ground? And the tree itself, humped, as it were, in pain, and yet he could almost swear triumphant, gloating.

Just as in spring, when the mass of fluffy blossom, colourless and sodden, dragged the reluctant eye away from the other trees, so it did now. Impossible to avoid seeing the tree, with its burden of fruit. Every window in the front part of the house looked out upon it. And he knew how it would be. The fruit would cling there until it was picked, staying upon the branches through October and November, and it never would be picked, because nobody could eat it. He could see himself being bothered with the tree throughout the autumn. Whenever he came out on to the terrace there it would be, sagging and loathsome.

It was extraordinary the dislike he had taken to the tree. It was a perpetual reminder of the fact that he... well, he was blessed if he knew what... a perpetual reminder of all the things he most detested, and always had, he could not put a name to them. He decided then and there that Willis should pick the fruit and take it away, sell it, get rid of it, anything, as long as he did not have to eat it, and as long as he was not forced to watch the tree drooping there, day after day, throughout the autumn.

He turned his back upon it and was relieved to see that none of the other trees had so degraded themselves to excess. They carried a fair crop, nothing out of the way, and as he might have known the young tree, to the right of the old one, made a brave little show on its own, with a light load of medium sized, rosy-looking apples, not too dark in colour, but freshly reddened where the sun had ripened them. He would pick one now, and take it in, to eat with breakfast. He made his choice, and the apple fell at the first touch into his hand. It looked so good that he bit into it with appetite. That was it, juicy, sweet-smelling, sharp, the dew upon it still. He did not look back at the old tree. He went indoors, hungry, to breakfast.

It took the gardener nearly a week to strip the tree, and it was plain he did it under protest.

'I don't care what you do with them,' said his employer. 'You can sell them and keep the money, or you can take them home and feed them to your pigs. I can't stand the sight of them, and that's all there is to it. Find a long ladder, and start on the job right away.'

It seemed to him that Willis, from sheer obstinacy, spun out the time. He would watch the man from the windows act as though in slow motion. First the placing of the ladder. Then the laborious climb, and the descent to steady it again. After that the performance of plucking off the fruit, dropping them, one by one, into the basket. Day after day it was the same. Willis was always there on the sloping lawn with his ladder, under the tree, the branches creaking and groaning, and beneath him on the grass baskets, pails, basins, any receptacle that would hold the apples.

At last the job was finished. The ladder was removed, the baskets and pails also, and the tree was stripped bare. He looked out at it, the evening of that day, in satisfaction. No more rotting fruit to offend his eye. Every single apple gone.

Yet the tree, instead of seeming lighter from the loss of its burden, looked, if it were possible, more dejected than ever. The branches still sagged, and the leaves, withering now to the cold autumnal evening, folded upon themselves and shivered. 'Is this my reward?' it seemed to say. 'After all I've done for you?'

As the light faded, the shadow of the tree cast a blight upon the dank night. Winter would soon come. And the short, dull days.

He had never cared much for the fall of the year. In the old days, when he went up to London every day to the office, it had meant that early start by train, on a nippy morning. And then, before three o'clock in the afternoon, the clerks were turning on the lights, and as often as not there would be fog in the air, murky and dismal, and a slow chugging journey home, daily bread-ers like himself sitting five abreast in a carriage, some of them with colds in their heads. Then the long evening followed, with Midge opposite him before the living-room fire, and he listening, or feigning to listen, to the account of her days and the things that had gone wrong.

If she had not shouldered any actual household disaster, she would pick upon some current event to cast a gloom. 'I see fares are going up again, what about your season ticket?', or 'This business in South Africa looks nasty, quite a long bit about it on the six o'clock news', or yet again 'Three more cases of polio over at the isolation hospital. I don't know, I'm sure, what the medical world thinks it's doing...'

Now, at least, he was spared the rôle of listener, but the memory of those long evenings was with him still, and when the lights were lit and the curtains were drawn he would be reminded of the click-click of the needles, the aimless chatter, and the 'Heigh-ho' of the yawns. He began to drop in, sometimes before supper, sometimes afterwards, at the Green Man, the old public house a quarter of a mile away on the main road. Nobody bothered him there. He would sit in a corner, having said good evening to genial Mrs Hill, the proprietress, and then, with a cigarette and a whisky and soda, watch the local inhabitants stroll in to have a pint, to throw a dart, to gossip.

In a sense it made a continuation of his summer holiday. It bore resemblance, admittedly slight, to the care-free atmosphere of the cafes and the restaurants; and there was a kind of warmth about the bright smoke-filled bar, crowded with working men who did not bother him, which he found pleasant, comforting. These visits cut into the length of the dark winter evenings, making them more tolerable.

A cold in the head, caught in mid-December, put a stop to this for more than a week. He was obliged to keep to the house. And it was odd, he thought to himself, how much he missed the Green Man, and how sick to death he became of sitting about in the living-room or in the study, with nothing to do but read or listen to the wireless. The cold and the boredom made him morose and irritable, and the enforced inactivity turned his liver sluggish. He needed exercise. Whatever the weather, he decided towards the end of yet another cold grim day, he would go out tomorrow. The sky had been heavy from mid-afternoon and threatened snow, but no matter, he could not stand the house for a further twenty-four hours without a break.

The final edge to his irritation came with the fruit tart at supper. He was in that final stage of a bad cold when the taste is not yet fully returned, appetite is poor, but there is a certain emptiness within that needs ministration of a particular kind. A bird might have done it. Half a partridge, roasted to perfection, followed by a cheese soufflé. As well ask for the moon. The daily woman, not gifted with imagination, produced plaice, of all fish the most tasteless, the most dry. When she had borne the remains of this away—he had left most of it upon his plate—she returned with a tart, and because hunger was far from being satisfied he helped himself to it liberally.

One taste was enough. Choking, spluttering, he spat out the contents of his spoon upon the plate. He got up and rang the bell.

The woman appeared, a query on her face, at the unexpected summons.

'What the devil is this stuff?'

'Jam tart, sir.'

'What sort of jam?'

'Apple jam, sir. Made from my own bottling.'

He threw down his napkin on the table.

'I guessed as much. You've been using some of those apples that I complained to you about months ago. I told you and Willis quite distinctly that I would not have any of those apples in the house.'

The woman's face became tight and drawn.

'You said, sir, not to cook the apples, or to bring them in for dessert. You said nothing about not making jam. I thought they would taste all right as jam. And I made some myself, to try. It was perfectly all right. So I made several bottles of jam from the apples Willis gave me. We always made jam here, madam and myself.'

'Well, I'm sorry for your trouble, but I can't eat it. Those apples disagreed with me in the autumn, and whether they are made into jam or whatever you like they will do so again. Take the tart away, and don't let me see it, or the jam, again. I'll have some coffee in the living-room.'

He went out of the room, trembling. It was fantastic that such a small incident should make him feel so angry. God! What fools people were. She knew, Willis knew, that he disliked the apples, loathed the taste and the smell of them, but in their cheese-paring way they decided that it would save money if he was given home-made jam, jam made from the apples he particularly detested.

He swallowed down a stiff whisky and lit a cigarette.

In a moment or two she appeared with the coffee. She did not retire immediately on putting down the tray.

'Could I have a word with you, sir?'

'What is it?'

'I think it would be for the best if I gave in my notice.'

Now this, on top of the other. What a day, what an evening. 'What reason? Because I can't eat apple-tart?'

'It's not just that, sir. Somehow I feel things are very different from what they were. I have meant to speak several times.'

'I don't give much trouble, do I?'

'No, sir. Only in the old days, when madam was alive, I felt my work was appreciated. Now it's as though it didn't matter one way or the other. Nothing's ever said, and although I try to do my best I can't be sure. I think I'd be happier if I went where there was a lady again who took notice of what I did.'

'You are the best judge of that, of course. I'm sorry if you haven't liked it here lately.'

'You were away so much too, sir, this summer. When madam was alive it was never for more than a fortnight. Everything seems so changed. I don't know where I am, or Willis either.'

'So Willis is fed-up too?'

'That's not for me to say, of course. I know he was upset about the apples, but that's some time ago. Perhaps he'll be speaking to you himself.'

'Perhaps he will. I had no idea I was causing so much concern to you both. All right, that's quite enough. Good-night.'

She went out of the room. He stared moodily about him. Good riddance to them both, if that was how they felt. Things aren't the same. Everything so changed. Damned nonsense. As for Willis being upset about the apples, what infernal impudence. Hadn't he a right to do what he liked with his own tree? To hell with his cold and with the weather. He couldn't stand sitting about in front of the fire thinking about Willis and the cook. He would go down to the Green Man and forget the whole thing.

He put on his overcoat and muffler and his old cap and walked briskly down the road, and in twenty minutes he was sitting in his usual corner in the Green Man, with Mrs Hill pouring out his whisky and expressing her delight to see him back. One or two of the habitués smiled at him, asked after his health.

'Had a cold, sir? Same everywhere. Everyone's got one.'

'That's right.'

'Well, it's the time of year, isn't it?'

'Got to expect it. It's when it's on the chest it's nasty.'

'No worse than being stuffed up, like, in the head.'

'That's right. One's as bad as the other. Nothing to it.'

Likeable fellows. Friendly. Not harping at one, not bothering.

'Another whisky, please.'

'There you are, sir. Do you good. Keep out the cold.'

Mrs Hill beamed behind the bar. Large, comfortable old soul. Through a haze of smoke he heard the chatter, the deep laughter, the click of the darts, the jocular roar at a bull's eye.

'... and if it comes on to snow, I don't know how we shall manage,' Mrs Hill was saying, 'them being so late delivering the coal. If we had a load of logs it would help us out, but what do you think they're asking? Two pounds a load. I mean to say...'

He leant forward and his voice sounded far away, even to himself.

'I'll let you have some logs,' he said.

Mrs Hill turned round. She had not been talking to him.

'Excuse me?' she said.

'I'll let you have some logs,' he repeated. 'Got an old tree, up at home, needed sawing down for months. Do it for you tomorrow.'

He nodded, smiling.

'Oh no, sir. I couldn't think of putting you to the trouble. The coal will turn up, never fear.'

'No trouble at all. A pleasure. Like to do it for you, the exercise, you know, do me good. Putting on weight. You count on me.'

He got down from his seat and reached, rather carefully, for his coat.

'It's apple-wood,' he said. 'Do you mind apple-wood?'

'Why no,' she answered, 'any wood will do. But can you spare it, sir?'

He nodded, mysteriously. It was a bargain, it was a secret.

'I'll bring it down to you in my trailer tomorrow night,' he said.

'Careful, sir,' she said, 'mind the step...'

He walked home, through the cold crisp night, smiling to himself. He did not remember undressing or getting into bed, but when he woke the next morning the first thought that came to his mind was the promise he had made about the tree.

It was not one of Willis's days, he realized with satisfaction. There would be no interfering with his plan. The sky was heavy and snow had fallen in the night. More to come. But as yet nothing to worry about, nothing to hamper him.

He went through to the kitchen garden, after breakfast, to the tool shed. He took down the saw, the wedges and the axe. He might need all of them. He ran his thumb along the edges. They would do. As he shouldered his tools and walked back to the front garden he laughed to himself, thinking that he must resemble an executioner of old days, setting forth to behead some wretched victim in the Tower.

He laid his tools down beneath the apple-tree. It would be an act of mercy, really. Never had he seen anything so wretched, so utterly woebegone, as the apple-tree. There couldn't be any life left in it. Not a leaf remained. Twisted, ugly, bent, it ruined the appearance of the lawn. Once it was out of the way the whole setting of the garden would change.

A snowflake fell on to his hand, then another. He glanced down past the terrace to the dining-room window. He could see the woman laying his lunch. He went down the steps and into the house. 'Look,' he said, 'if you like to leave my lunch ready in the oven, I think I'll fend for myself today. I may be busy, and I don't want to be pinned down for time. Also it's going to snow. You had better go off early today and get home, in case it becomes really bad. I can manage perfectly well. And I prefer it.'

Perhaps she thought his decision came through offence at her giving notice the night before. Whatever she thought, he did not mind. He wanted to be alone. He wanted no face peering from the window.

She went off at about twelve-thirty, and as soon as she had gone he went to the oven and got his lunch. He meant to get it over, so that he could give up the whole short afternoon to the felling of the tree.

No more snow had fallen, apart from a few flakes that did not lie. He took off his coat, rolled up his sleeves, and seized the saw. With his left hand he ripped away the wire at the base of the tree. Then he placed the saw about a foot from the bottom and began to work it, backwards, forwards.

For the first dozen strokes all went smoothly. The saw bit into the wood, the teeth took hold. Then after a few moments the saw began to bind. He had been afraid of that.

He tried to work it free, but the opening that he had made was not yet large enough, and the tree gripped upon the saw and held it fast. He drove in the first wedge, with no result. He drove in the second, and the opening gaped a little wider, but still not wide enough to release the saw.

He pulled and tugged at the saw, to no avail. He began to lose his temper. He took up his axe and started hacking at the tree, pieces of the trunk flying outwards, Scattering on the grass.

That was more like it. That was the answer.

Up and down went the heavy axe, Splitting and tearing at the tree. Off came the pealing bark, the great white strips of under-wood, raw and stringy. Hack at it, blast at it, gouge at the tough tissue, throw the axe away, claw at the rubbery flesh with the bare hands. Not far enough yet, go on, go on.

There goes the saw, and the wedge, released. Now up with the axe again. Down there, heavy, where the stringy threads cling so steadfast. Now she's groaning, now she's splitting, now she's rocking and swaying, hanging there upon one bleeding strip. Boot her, then. That's it, kick her, kick her again, one final blow, she's over, she's falling... she's down... damn her, blast her... she's down, Splitting the air with sound, and all her branches spread about her on the ground.

He stood back, wiping the sweat from his forehead, from his chin. The wreckage surrounded him on either side, and below him, at his feet, gaped the torn, white, jagged stump of the axed tree.

It began snowing.

His first task, after felling the apple-tree, was to hack off the branches and the smaller boughs, and so to grade the wood in stacks, which made it easier to drag away.

The small stuff, bundled and roped, would do for kindling; Mrs Hill would no doubt be glad of that as well. He brought the car, with the trailer attached, to the garden gate, hard by the terrace. This chopping up of the branches was simple work; much of it could be done with a hook. The fatigue came with bending and tying the bundles, and then heaving them down past the terrace and through the gate up on to the trailer. The thicker branches he disposed of with the axe, then split them into three or four lengths, which he could also rope and drag, one by one, to the trailer.

He was fighting all the while against time. The light, what there was of it, would be gone by half-past four, and the snow went on falling. The ground was already covered, and when he paused for a moment in his work, and wiped the sweat away from his face, the thin frozen flakes fell upon his lips and made their way, insidious and soft, down his collar to his neck and body. If he lifted his eyes to the sky he was blinded at once. The flakes came thicker, faster, swirling about his head, and it was as though the heaven had turned itself into a canopy of snow, ever descending, coming nearer, closer, stifling the earth. The snow fell upon the torn boughs and the hacked branches, hampering his work. If he rested but an instant to draw breath and renew his strength, it seemed to throw a protective cover, soft and white, over the pile of wood.

He could not wear gloves. If he did so he had no grip upon his hook or his axe, nor could he tie the rope and drag the branches. His fingers were numb with cold, soon they would be too stiff to bend. He had a pain now, under the heart, from the strain of dragging the stuff on to the trailer; and the work never seemed to lessen. Whenever he returned to the fallen tree the pile of wood would appear as high as ever, long boughs, short boughs, a heap of kindling there, nearly covered with the snow, which he had forgotten: all must be roped and fastened and carried or pulled away.

It was after half-past four, and almost dark, when he had disposed of all the branches, and nothing now remained but to drag the trunk, already hacked into three lengths, over the terrace to the waiting trailer.

He was very nearly at the point of exhaustion. Only his will to be rid of the tree kept him to the task. His breath came slowly, painfully, and all the while the snow fell into his mouth and into his eyes and he could barely see.

He took his rope and slid it under the cold slippery trunk, knotting it fiercely. How hard and unyielding was the naked wood, and the bark was rough, hurting his numb hands.

'That's the end of you,' he muttered, 'that's your finish.'

Staggering to his feet he bore the weight of the heavy trunk over his shoulder, and began to drag it slowly down over the slope to the terrace and to the garden gate. It followed him, bump... bump... down the Steps of the terrace. Heavy and lifeless, the last bare limbs of the apple-tree dragged in his wake through the wet snow.

It was over. His task was done. He stood panting, one hand upon the trailer. Now nothing more remained but to take the stuff down to the Green Man before the snow made the drive impossible. He had chains for the car, he had thought of that already.

He went into the house to change the clothes that were clinging to him and to have a drink. Never mind about his fire, never mind about drawing curtains, seeing what there might be for supper, all the chores the daily woman usually did—that would come later. He must have his drink and get the wood away.

His mind was numb and weary, like his hands and his whole body. For a moment he thought of leaving the job until the following day, flopping down into the armchair, and closing his eyes. No, it would not do. Tomorrow there would be more snow, tomorrow the drive would be two or three feet deep. He knew the signs. And there would be the trailer, stuck outside the garden gate, with the pile of wood inside it, frozen white. He must make the effort and do the job tonight.

He finished his drink, changed, and went out to Start the car. It was still snowing, but now that darkness had fallen a colder, cleaner feeling had come into the air, and it was freezing. The dizzy, swirling flakes came more slowly now, with precision.

The engine started and he began to drive downhill, the trailer in tow. He drove slowly, and very carefully, because of the heavy load. And it was an added strain, after the hard work of the afternoon, peering through the falling snow, wiping the windscreen. Never had the lights of the Green Man shone more cheerfully as he pulled up into the little yard.

He blinked as he stood within the doorway, smiling to himself.

'Well, I've brought your wood,' he said.

Mrs Hill stared at him from behind the bar, one or two fellows turned and looked at him, and a hush fell upon the dart-players.

'You never...' began Mrs Hill, but he jerked his head at the door and laughed at her.

'Go and see,' he said, 'but don't ask me to unload it tonight.'

He moved to his favourite corner, chuckling to himself, and there they all were, exclaiming and talking and laughing by the door, and he was quite a hero, the fellows crowding round with questions, and Mrs Hill pouring out his whisky and thanking him and laughing and shaking her head. 'You'll drink on the house tonight,' she said.

'Not a bit of it,' he said, 'this is my party. Rounds one and two to me. Come on, you chaps.'

It was festive, warm, jolly, and good-luck to them all, he kept saying, good luck to Mrs Hill, and to himself, and to the whole world. When was Christmas? Next week, the week after? Well, here's to it, and a merry Christmas. Never mind the snow, never mind the weather. For the first time he was one of them, not isolated in his corner. For the first time he drank with them, he laughed with them, he even threw a dart with them, and there they all were in that warm stuffy smoke-filled bar, and he felt they liked him, he belonged, he was no longer 'the gentleman' from the house up the road.

The hours passed, and some of them went home, and others took their place, and he was still sitting there, hazy, comfortable, the warmth and the smoke blending together. Nothing of what he heard or saw made very much sense but somehow it did not seem to matter, for there was jolly, fat, easy-going Mrs Hill to minister to his needs, her face glowing at him over the bar.

Another face swung into his view, that of one of the labourers from the farm, with whom, in the old war days, he had shared the driving of the tractor. He leant forward, touching the fellow on the shoulder.

'What happened to the little girl?' he said.

The man lowered his tankard. 'Beg pardon, sir?' he said.

'You remember. The little land girl. She used to milk the cows, feed the pigs, up at the farm. Pretty girl, dark curly hair, always smiling.'

Mrs Hill turned round from serving another customer.

'Does the gentleman mean May, I wonder?' she asked.

'Yes, that's it, that was the name, young May,' he said.

'Why, didn't you ever hear about it, sir?' said Mrs Hill, filling up his glass. 'We were all very much shocked at the time, everyone was talking of it, weren't they, Fred?'

'That's right, Mrs Hill.'

The man wiped his mouth with the back of his hand.

'Killed,' he said, 'thrown from the back of some chap's motor-bike. Going to be married very shortly. About four years ago, now. Dreadful thing, eh? Nice kid too.'

'We all sent a wreath, from just around,' said Mrs Hill. 'Her mother wrote back, very touched, and sent a cutting from the local paper, didn't she, Fred? Quite a big funeral they had, ever so many floral tributes. Poor May. We were all fond of May.'

'That's right,' said Fred.

'And fancy you never hearing about it, sir!' said Mrs Hill.

'No,' he said, 'no, nobody ever told me. I'm sorry about it. Very sorry.'

He stared in front of him at his half-filled glass.

The conversation went on around him but he was no longer part of the company. He was on his own again, silent, in his corner. Dead. That poor, pretty girl was dead. Thrown off a motor-bike. Been dead for three or four years. Some careless, bloody fellow, taking a corner too fast, the girl behind him, clinging on to his belt, laughing probably in his ear, and then crash... finish. No more curling hair, blowing about her face, no more laughter.

May, that was the name; he remembered clearly now. He could see her smiling over her shoulder, when they called to her. 'Coming,' she sang out, and put a clattering pail down in the yard and went off, whistling, with big clumping boots. He had put his arm about her and kissed her for one brief, fleeting moment. May, the land girl, with the laughing eyes.

'Going, sir?' said Mrs Hill.

'Yes. Yes, I think I'll be going now.'

He stumbled to the entrance and opened the door. It had frozen hard during the past hour and it was no longer snowing. The heavy pall had gone from the sky and the stars shone.

'Want a hand with the car, sir?' said someone.

'No, thank you,' he said, 'I can manage.'

He unhitched the trailer and let it fall. Some of the wood lurched forward heavily. That would do tomorrow. Tomorrow, if he felt like it, he would come down again and help to unload the wood. Not tonight. He had done enough. Now he was really tired; now he was spent.

It took him some time to start the car, and before he was half-way up the side-road leading to his house he realized that he had made a mistake to bring it at all. The snow was heavy all about him, and the track he had made earlier in the evening was now covered. The car lurched and slithered, and suddenly the right wheel dipped and the whole body plunged sideways. He had got into a drift.

He climbed out and looked about him. The car was deep in the drift, impossible to move without two or three men to help him, and even then, if he went for assistance, what hope was there of trying to continue further, with the snow just as thick ahead? Better leave it. Try again in the morning, when he was fresh. No sense in hanging about now, spending half the night pushing and shoving at the car, all to no purpose. No harm would come to it, here on the side-road; nobody else would be coming this way tonight.

He started walking up the road towards his own drive. It was bad luck that he had got the car into the drift. In the centre of the road the going was not bad and the snow did not come above his ankles. He thrust his hands deep in the pockets of his overcoat and ploughed on, up the hill, the countryside a great white waste on either side of him.

He remembered that he had sent the daily woman home at midday and that the house would strike cheerless and cold on his return. The fire would have gone out, and in all probability the furnace too. The windows, uncurtained, would stare bleakly down at him, letting in the night. Supper to get into the bargain. Well, it was his own fault. No one to blame but himself. This was the moment when there should be someone waiting, someone to come running through from the living-room to the hall, opening the front-door, flooding the hall with light. 'Are you all right, darling? I was getting anxious.'

He paused for breath at the top of the hill and saw his home, shrouded by trees, at the end of the short drive. It looked dark and forbidding, without a light in any window. There was more friendliness in the open, under the bright stars, standing on the crisp white snow, than in the sombre house.

He had left the side-gate open, and he went through that way to the terrace, shutting the gate behind him. What a hush had fallen upon the garden—there was no sound at all. It was as though some spirit had come and put a spell upon the place, leaving it white and still.

He walked softly over the snow towards the apple-trees.

Now the young one stood alone, above the steps, dwarfed no longer; and with her branches spread, glistening white, she belonged to the spirit world, a world of fantasy and ghosts. He wanted to stand beside the little tree and touch the branches, to make certain she was still alive, that the snow had not harmed her, so that in the spring she would blossom once again.

She was almost within his reach when he stumbled and fell, his foot twisted underneath him, caught in some obstacle hidden by the snow. He tried to move his foot but it was jammed, and he knew suddenly, by the sharpness of the pain biting his ankle, that what had trapped him was the jagged split stump of the old apple-tree he had felled that afternoon.

He leant forward on his elbows, in an attempt to drag himself along the ground, but such was his position, in falling, that his leg was bent backwards, away from his foot, and every effort that he made only succeeded in imprisoning the foot still more firmly in the grip of the trunk. He felt for the ground, under the snow, but wherever he felt his hands touched the small broken twigs from the apple-tree that had scattered there, when the tree fell, and then were covered by the falling snow. He shouted for help, knowing in his heart no one could hear.

'Let me go,' he shouted, 'let me go,' as though the thing that held him there in its mercy had the power to release him, and as he shouted tears of frustration and of fear ran down his face. He would have to lie there all night, held fast in the clutch of the old apple-tree. There was no hope, no escape, until they came to find him in the morning, and supposing it was then too late, that when they came he was dead, lying stiffly in the frozen snow?

Once more he struggled to release his foot, swearing and sobbing as he did so. It was no use. He could not move. Exhausted, he laid his head upon his arms, and wept. He sank deeper, ever deeper into the snow, and when a stray piece of brushwood, cold and wet, touched his lips, it was like a hand, hesitant and timid, feeling its way towards him in the darkness.

THE LEAF-SWEEPER

Muriel Spark

FIRST PUBLISHED IN *THE LONDON MYSTERY
MAGAZINE* NUMBER 31, 1956

Dame Muriel Sarah Spark (née Camberg; 1918–2006) was an
acclaimed writer and is known for novels including *The Prime of
Miss Jean Brodie* (1961), *The Driver's Seat* (1970) and *A Far Cry from
Kensington* (1988). Born in Edinburgh, she later lived in Zimbabwe
(then Southern Rhodesia), Camberwell in South London, and in
New York City before settling in Italy. Her handful of ghost stories
were written mostly in the late 1950s. She had converted to Roman
Catholicism in 1954 and later said that she believed this gave her
the confidence she needed to start writing novels (her first, *The
Comforters*, was published in 1957). Her contemporary Penelope
Fitzgerald wrote that Spark 'had pointed out that it wasn't until
she became a Roman Catholic... that she was able to see human
existence as a whole, as a novelist needs to do'.

'The Leaf-sweeper' is an unusual weird tale, featuring themes of
identity and mental health, told with a surrealist edge. It's possible
that Spark was inspired by the hallucinations she suffered when
overdosing on amphetamine-based slimming pills a couple of years
earlier, and the depression which followed during her recovery.

—TK

Behind the town hall there is a wooded parkland which, towards the end of November, begins to draw a thin blue cloud right into itself; and as a rule the park floats in this haze until mid-February. I pass every day, and see Johnnie Geddes in the heart of this mist, sweeping up the leaves. Now and again he stops, and jerking his long head erect, looks indignantly at the pile of leaves, as if it ought not to be there; then he sweeps on. This business of leaf-sweeping he learnt during the years he spent in the asylum; it was the job they always gave him to do; and when he was discharged the town council gave him the leaves to sweep. But the indignant movement of the head comes naturally to him, for this has been one of his habits since he was the most promising and buoyant and vociferous graduate of his year. He looks much older than he is, for it is not quite twenty years ago that Johnnie founded the Society for the Abolition of Christmas.

Johnnie was living with his aunt then. I was at school, and in the Christmas holidays Miss Geddes gave me her nephew's pamphlet, *How to Grow Rich at Christmas*. It sounded very likely, but it turned out that you grow rich at Christmas by doing away with Christmas, and so pondered Johnnie's pamphlet no further.

But it was only his first attempt. He had, within the next three years, founded his society of Abolitionists. His new book, *Abolish*

Christmas or We Die, was in great demand at the public library, and my turn for it came at last. Johnnie was really convincing, this time, and most people were completely won over until after they had closed the book. I got an old copy for sixpence the other day, and despite the lapse of time it still proves conclusively that Christmas is a national crime. Johnnie demonstrates that every human unit in the kingdom faces inevitable starvation within a period inversely proportional to that in which one in every six industrial-productivity units, if you see what he means, stops producing toys to fill the stockings of the educational-intake units. He cites appalling statistics to show that 1.024 per cent of the time squandered each Christmas in reckless shopping and thoughtless churchgoing brings the nation closer to its doom by five years. A few readers protested, but Johnnie was able to demolish their muddled arguments, and meanwhile the Society for the Abolition of Christmas increased. But Johnnie was troubled. Not only did Christmas rage throughout the kingdom as usual that year, but he had private information that many of the Society's members had broken the Oath of Abstention.

He decided, then, to strike at the very roots of Christmas. Johnnie gave up his job on the Drainage Supply Board; he gave up all his prospects, and, financed by a few supporters, retreated for two years to study the roots of Christmas. Then, all jubilant, Johnnie produced his next and last book, in which he established, either that Christmas was an invention of the Early Fathers to propitiate the pagans, or it was invented by the pagans to placate the Early Fathers, I forget which. Against the advice of his friends, Johnnie entitled it *Christmas and Christianity*. It sold eighteen copies. Johnnie never really recovered from this; and it happened, about that time, that the girl he was engaged to, an ardent Abolitionist, sent him a pullover she had knitted, for Christmas; he sent it back, enclosing a copy of the Society's rules, and she sent back the ring. But in any case, during Johnnie's absence, the Society had been undermined by a moderate faction. These moderates finally became more moderate, and the whole thing broke up.

Soon after this, I left the district, and it was some years before I saw Johnnie again. One Sunday afternoon in summer, I was idling among the crowds who were gathered to hear the speakers at Hyde Park. One little crowd surrounded a man who bore a banner marked 'Crusade against Christmas'; his voice was frightening; it carried an unusually long way. This was Johnnie. A man in the crowd told me Johnnie was there every Sunday, very violent about Christmas, and that he would soon be taken up for insulting language. As I saw in the papers, he was soon taken up for insulting language. And a few months later I heard that poor Johnnie was in a mental home, because he had Christmas on the brain and couldn't stop shouting about it.

After that I forgot all about him until three years ago, in December, I went to live near the town where Johnnie had spent his youth. On the afternoon of Christmas Eve I was walking with a friend, noticing what had changed in my absence, and what hadn't. We passed a long, large house, once famous for its armoury, and I saw that the iron gates were wide open.

'They used to be kept shut,' I said.

'That's an asylum now,' said my friend; 'They let the mild cases work in the grounds, and leave the gates open to give them a feeling of freedom.

'But,' said my friend, 'they lock everything inside. Door after door. The lift as well; they keep it locked.'

While my friend was chattering, I stood in the gateway and

looked in. Just beyond the gate was a great bare elm tree. There I saw a man in brown corduroys, sweeping up the leaves. Poor soul, he was shouting about Christmas.

'That's Johnnie Geddes,' I said. 'Has he been here all these years?'

'Yes,' said my friend as we walked on. 'I believe he gets worse at this time of year.'

'Does his aunt see him?'

'Yes. And she sees nobody else.'

We were, in fact, approaching the house where Miss Geddes lived. I suggested we call on her. I had known her well.

'No fear,' said my friend.

I decided to go in, all the same, and my friend walked on to the town.

Miss Geddes had changed, more than the landscape. She had been a solemn, calm woman, and now she moved about quickly, and gave short agitated smiles. She took me to her sitting-room, and as she opened the door she called to someone inside.

'Johnnie, see who's come to see us!'

A man, dressed in a dark suit, was standing on a chair, fixing holly behind a picture. He jumped down.

'Happy Christmas,' he said. 'A Happy and a Merry Christmas indeed. I do hope,' he said, 'you're going to stay for tea, as we've got a delightful Christmas cake, and at this season of goodwill I would be cheered indeed if you could see how charmingly it's decorated; it has "Happy Christmas" in red icing, and then there's a robin and...'

'Johnnie,' said Miss Geddes, 'you're forgetting the carols.'

'The carols,' he said. He lifted a gramophone record from a pile and put it on. It was *The Holly and the Ivy*.

'It's *The Holly and the Ivy*,' said Miss Geddes. 'Can't we have something else? We had that all morning.'

'It is sublime,' he said, beaming from his chair, and holding up his hand for silence.

While Miss Geddes went to fetch the tea, and he sat absorbed in his carol, I watched him. He was so like Johnnie, that if I hadn't seen poor Johnnie a few moments before, sweeping up the asylum leaves, I would have thought he really was Johnnie. Miss Geddes returned with the tray, and while he rose to put on another record, he said something that startled me.

'I saw you in the crowd that Sunday when I was speaking at Hyde Park.'

'What a memory you have!' said Miss Geddes.

'It must be ten years ago,' he said.

'My nephew has altered his opinion of Christmas,' she explained. 'He always comes home for Christmas now, and don't we have a jolly time, Johnnie?'

'Rather!' he said. 'Oh, let me cut the cake.'

He was very excited about the cake. With a flourish he dug a large knife into the side. The knife slipped, and I saw it run deep into his finger. Miss Geddes did not move. He wrenched his cut finger away, and went on slicing the cake.

'Isn't it bleeding?' I said.

He held up his hand. I could see the deep cut, but there was no blood. Deliberately, and perhaps desperately, I turned to Miss Geddes.

'That house up the road,' I said, 'I see it's a mental home now. I passed it this afternoon.'

'Johnnie,' said Miss Geddes, as one who knows the game is up, 'go and fetch the mince-pies.'

He went, whistling a carol.

'You passed the asylum,' said Miss Geddes wearily.

'Yes,' I said.

'And you saw Johnnie sweeping up the leaves.'

'Yes.'

We could still hear the whistling of the carol.

'Who is *he*?' I said.

'That's Johnnie's ghost,' she said. 'He comes home every Christmas.

'But,' she said, 'I don't like him. I can't bear him any longer, and I'm going away tomorrow. I don't want Johnnie's ghost, I want Johnnie in flesh and blood.'

I shuddered, thinking of the cut finger that could not bleed. And I left, before Johnnie's ghost returned with the mince-pies.

Next day, as I had arranged to join a family who lived in the town, I started walking over about noon. Because of the light mist, I didn't see at first who it was approaching. It was a man, waving his arm to me. It turned out to be Johnnie's ghost.

'Happy Christmas. What do you think,' said Johnnie's ghost, 'my aunt has gone to London. Fancy, on Christmas Day, and I thought she was at church, and here I am without anyone to spend a jolly Christmas with and, of course, I forgive her, as it's the season of goodwill, but I'm glad to see you, because now I can come with you, wherever it is you're going and we can all have a Happy...'

'Go away,' I said, and walked on.

It sounds hard. But perhaps you don't know how repulsive and loathsome is the ghost of a living man. The ghosts of the dead may be all right, but the ghost of mad Johnnie gave me the creeps.

'Clear off,' I said.

He continued walking beside me. 'As it's the time of goodwill, I make allowances for your tone,' he said. 'But I'm coming.'

We had reached the asylum gates, and there, in the grounds, I saw Johnnie sweeping the leaves. I suppose it was his way of going on strike, working on Christmas Day. He was making a noise about Christmas.

On a sudden impulse I said to Johnnie's ghost, 'You want company?'

'Certainly,' he replied. 'It's the season of...'

'Then you shall have it,' I said.

I stood in the gateway. 'Oh, Johnnie,' I called.

He looked up.

'I've brought your ghost to see you, Johnnie.'

'Well, well,' said Johnnie, advancing to meet his ghost, 'Just imagine it!'

'Happy Christmas,' said Johnnie's ghost.

'Oh, really?' said Johnnie.

I left them to it. And when I looked back, wondering if they would come to blows, I saw that Johnnie's ghost was sweeping the leaves as well. They seemed to be arguing at the same time. But it was still misty, and really, I can't say whether, when I looked a second time, there were two men or one man sweeping the leaves.

Johnnie began to improve in the New Year. At least, he stopped shouting about Christmas, and then he never mentioned it at all; in a few months, when he had almost stopped saying anything, they discharged him.

The town council gave him the leaves of the park to sweep. He seldom speaks, and recognizes nobody. I see him every day at the late end of the year, working within the mist. Sometimes, if there is a sudden gust, he jerks his head up to watch a few leaves falling behind him, as if amazed that they are undeniably there, although, by rights, the falling of leaves should be stopped.

THE VISITING STAR

Robert Aickman

FIRST PUBLISHED IN *POWERS OF DARKNESS:*
MACABRE STORIES (1966)

Robert Fordyce Aickman (1914–1981) is best known as both a writer of what he called 'strange stories' and as a campaigner for the preservation of England's canal system. He was the grandson of Richard Marsh, whose horror novel *The Beetle* outsold Bram Stoker's *Dracula* in 1897, the year they were both published. The Oxford Dictionary of National Biography describes the rather odd basis of Aickman's early life:

'Richard Marsh met William Arthur Aickman in the gentlemen's lavatory of a grand hotel in Edwardian Eastbourne, and was soon to encourage his marriage to his younger daughter, thirty years William Arthur Aickman's junior. The marriage, and Aickman's childhood, was predictably unhappy.'

In 1951, whilst working as a literary agent in Bloomsbury, Aickman penned a collection of ghost tales called *We are for the Dark* (together with the novelist Elizabeth Jane Howard). He went on to become a prolific writer of the genre, publishing eleven collections of his own stories. They are characterized by an extremely unsettling nightmarish weirdness. This is one of very few Christmas-themed tales he produced, and it draws on his strong interest in and enthusiasm for the theatre.   —TK

The first time that Colvin, who had never been a frequent theatre-goer, ever heard of the great actress Arabella Rokeby was when he was walking past the Hippodrome one night and Malnik, the Manager of the Tabard Players, invited him into his office.

Had Colvin not been awarded a grant, remarkably insufficient for present prices, upon which to compose, collate, and generally scratch together a book upon the once thriving British industries of lead and plumbago mining, he would probably never have set eyes upon this bleak town. Tea was over (today it had been pilchard salad and chips); and Colvin had set out from the Emancipation Hotel, where he boarded, upon his regular evening walk. In fifteen or twenty minutes he would be beyond the gas-lights, the granite setts, the nimbus of the pits. (Lead and plumbago mining had long been replaced by coal as the town's main industry.) There had been no one else for tea and Mrs Royd had made it clear that the trouble he was causing had not passed unnoticed.

Outside it was blowing as well as raining, so that Palmerston Street was almost deserted. The Hippodrome (called, when built, the Grand Opera House) stood at the corner of Palmerston Street and Aberdeen Place. Vast, ornate, the product of an unfulfilled aspiration that the town would increase in size and devotion to the Muses, it had been for years unused and forgotten. About it like rags, when Colvin first beheld it, had hung scraps of posters: 'Harem Nights. Gay! Bright! ! Alluring ! ! !' But a few weeks ago the Hippodrome had reopened to admit the Tabard Players ('In Association with the Arts Council'); and, it was hoped, their audiences. The Tabard Players offered soberer joys: a new and respectable play each week, usually a light comedy or West End crook drama; but, on one occasion, *Everyman*. Malnik, their Manager, a youngish bald man, was an authority on the British Drama of the Nineteenth Century, upon which he had written an immense book, bursting with carefully verified detail. Colvin had met him one night in the Saloon Bar of the Emancipation Hotel; and, though neither knew anything of the other's subject, they had exchanged cultural life-belts in the ocean of apathy and incomprehensible interests which surrounded them. Malnik was lodging with the sad-faced Rector, who let rooms.

Tonight, having seen the curtain up on Act I, Malnik had come outside for a breath of the wind. There was something he wanted to impart; and, as he regarded the drizzling and indifferent town, Colvin obligingly came into sight. In a moment, he was inside Malnik's roomy but crumbling office.

'Look,' said Malnik.

He shuffled a heap of papers on his desk and handed Colvin a photograph. It was yellow, and torn at the edges. The subject was a wild-eyed young man with much dark curly hair and a blobby face. He was wearing a high stiff collar, and a bow like Chopin's.

'John Nethers,' said Malnik. Then, when no light of rapture flashed from Colvin's face, he said 'Author of *Cornelia*.'

'Sorry,' said Colvin, shaking his head.

'John Nethers was the son of a chemist in this town. Some books say a miner, but that's wrong. A chemist. He killed himself at twenty-two. But before that I've traced that he'd written at least six plays. *Cornelia*, which is the best of them, is one of the great plays of the nineteenth century.'

'Why did he kill himself?'

'It's in his eyes. You can see it. *Cornelia* was produced in London with Arabella Rokeby. But never here. Never in the author's own town. I've been into the whole thing closely. Now we're going to do *Cornelia* for Christmas.'

'Won't you lose money?' asked Colvin.

'We're losing money all the time, old man. Of course we are. We may as well do something we shall be remembered by.'

Colvin nodded. He was beginning to see that Malnik's life was a single-minded struggle for the British Drama of the Nineteenth Century and all that went with it.

'Besides I'm going to do *As You Like It* also. As a fill-up.' Malnik stooped and spoke close to Colvin's ear as he sat in a bursting leather armchair, the size of a Judge's seat. 'You see, Arabella Rokeby's *coming*.'

'But how long is it since—'

'Better not be too specific about that. They say it doesn't matter with Arabella Rokeby. She can get away with it. Probably in fact she can't. Not altogether. But all the same, think of it. Arabella Rokeby in *Cornelia*. In my theatre.'

Colvin thought of it.

'Have you ever seen her?'

'No, I haven't. Of course she doesn't play regularly nowadays. Only special engagements. But in this business one has to take a chance sometimes. And golly what a chance!'

'And she's willing to come? I mean at Christmas,' Colvin added, not wishing to seem rude.

Malnik did seem slightly unsure. 'I have a contract,' he said. Then he added: 'She'll love it when she gets here. After all: *Cornelia!* And she must know that the nineteenth-century theatre is my subject.' He had seemed to be reassuring himself, but now he was glowing.

'But *As You Like It?*' said Colvin, who had played Touchstone at his preparatory school. 'Surely she can't manage Rosalind?'

'It was her great part. Happily you can play Rosalind at any age. Wish I could get old Ludlow to play Jaques. But he won't.' Ludlow was the company's veteran.

'Why not?'

'He played with Rokeby in the old days. I believe he's afraid she'll see he isn't the Grand Old Man he should be. He's a good chap, but proud. Of course he may have other reasons. You never know with Ludlow.'

The curtain was down on Act I.

Colvin took his leave and resumed his walk.

Shortly thereafter Colvin read about the Nethers Gala in the local evening paper ('this forgotten poet', as the writer helpfully phrased it), and found confirmation that Miss Rokeby was indeed to grace it ('the former London star'). In the same issue of the paper appeared an editorial to the effect that wide-spread disappointment would be caused by the news that the Hippodrome would not be offering a pantomime at Christmas in accordance with the custom of the town and district.

'She can't 'ardly stop 'ere, Mr Colvin,' said Mrs Royd, when Colvin, thinking to provide forewarning, showed her the news, as she lent a hand behind the saloon bar. 'This isn't the Cumberland. She'd get across the staff.'

'I believe she's quite elderly,' said Colvin soothingly.

'If she's elderly, she'll want special attention, and that's often just as bad.'

'After all, where she goes is mainly a problem for her, and perhaps Mr Malnik.'

'Well, there's nowhere else in town for her to stop, is there?' retorted Mrs Royd with fire. 'Not nowadays. She'll just 'ave to make do. We did for theatricals in the old days. Midgets once. Whole troupe of 'em.'

'I'm sure you'll make her very comfortable.'

'Can't see what she wants to come at all for, really. Not at Christmas.'

'Miss Rokeby needs no *reason* for her actions. What she does is sufficient in itself. You'll understand that, dear lady, when you meet her.' The speaker was a very small man, apparently of advanced years, white-haired, and with a brown sharp face, like a Levantine. The bar was full, and Colvin had not previously noticed him, although he was conspicuous enough, as he wore an overcoat with a fur collar and a scarf with a large black pin in the centre. 'I wonder if *I* could beg a room for a few nights,' he went on. 'I assure you I'm no trouble at all.'

'There's only Number Twelve A. It's not very comfortable,' replied Mrs Royd sharply.

'Of course you must leave room for Miss Rokeby.'

'Nine's for her. Though I haven't had a word from her.'

'I think she'll need two rooms. She has a companion.'

'I can clear out Greta's old room upstairs. If she's a friend of yours, you might ask her to let me know when she's coming.'

'Not a friend,' said the old man, smiling. 'But I follow her career.'

Mrs Royd brought a big red book from under the bar.

'What name, please?'

'Mr Superbus,' said the little old man. He had yellow, expressionless eyes.

'Will you register?'

Mr Superbus produced a gold pen, long and fat. His writing was so curvilinear that it seemed purely decorative, like a design for ornamental ironwork. Colvin noticed that he paused slightly at the 'Permanent Address' column, and then simply wrote (although it was difficult to be sure) what appeared to be 'North Africa'.

'Will you come this way?' said Mrs Royd, staring suspiciously at the newcomer's scrollwork in the visitor's book. Then, even more suspiciously, she added: 'What about luggage?'

Mr Superbus nodded gravely. 'I placed two bags outside.'

'Let's hope they're still there. They're rough in this town, you know.'

'I'm sure they're still there,' said Mr Superbus.

As he spoke the door opened suddenly and a customer almost fell into the bar. 'Sorry, Mrs Royd,' he said with a mildness which in the circumstances belied Mrs Royd's words. 'There's something on the step.'

'My fault, I'm afraid,' said Mr Superbus. 'I wonder—have you a porter?'

'The porter works evenings at the Hippodrome nowadays. Scene-shifting and that.'

'Perhaps I could help?' said Colvin.

On the step outside were what appeared to be two very large suitcases. When he tried to lift one of them, he understood what Mr Superbus had meant. It was remarkably heavy. He held back the bar door, letting in a cloud of cold air. 'Give me a hand, someone,' he said.

The customer who had almost fallen volunteered, and a short procession, led by Mrs Royd, set off along the little dark passage to Number Twelve A. Colvin was disconcerted when he realized that Twelve A was the room at the end of the passage, which had no number on its door and had never, he thought, been occupied since his arrival; the room, in fact, next to his.

'Better leave these on the floor,' said Colvin, dismissing the rickety luggage-stand.

'Thank you,' said Mr Superbus, transferring a coin to the man who had almost fallen. He did it like a conjuror unpalming something.

'I'll send Greta to make up the bed,' said Mrs Royd. 'Tea's at six.'

'At six?' said Mr Superbus, gently raising an eyebrow. 'Tea?' Then, when Mrs Royd and the man had gone, he clutched Colvin very hard on the upper part of his left arm. 'Tell me,' enquired Mr Superbus, 'are you in love with Miss Rokeby? I overheard you defending her against the impertinence of our hostess.'

Colvin considered for a moment.

'Why not admit it?' said Mr Superbus, gently raising the other eyebrow. He was still clutching Colvin's arm much too hard.

'I've never set eyes on Miss Rokeby.'

Mr Superbus let go. 'Young people nowadays have no imagination,' he said with a whinny, like a wild goat.

Colvin was not surprised when Mr Superbus did not appear for tea (pressed beef and chips that evening).

After tea Colvin, instead of going for a walk, wrote to his mother. But there was little to tell her, so that at the end of the letter he mentioned the arrival of Mr Superbus. 'There's a sort of sweet blossomy smell about him like a meadow,' he ended. 'I think he must use scent.'

When the letter was finished, Colvin started trying to construct tables of output from the lead and plumbago mines a century ago. The partitions between the bedrooms were thin, and he began to wonder about Mr Superbus's nocturnal habits.

He wondered from time to time until the time came for sleep; and wondered a bit also as he dressed the next morning and went to the bathroom to shave. For during the whole of this time no sound whatever had been heard from Number Twelve A, despite the thinness of the plywood partition; a circumstance which Colvin already thought curious when, during breakfast, he overheard Greta talking to Mrs Royd in the kitchen. 'I'm ever so sorry, Mrs Royd. I forgot about it with the crowd in the bar.' To which Mrs Royd simply replied: 'I wonder what 'e done about it. 'E could 'ardly do without sheets or blankets, and this December. Why didn't 'e *ask*?' And when Greta said, 'I suppose nothing ain't happened to him?' Colvin put down his porridge spoon and unobtrusively joined the party which went out to find out.

Mrs Royd knocked several times upon the door of Number Twelve A, but there was no answer. When they opened the door, the bed was bare as Colvin had seen it the evening before, and there was no sign at all of Mr Superbus except that his two big cases lay on the floor, one beside the other.

'What's he want to leave the window open like that for?' enquired Mrs Royd. She shut it with a crash. 'Someone will fall over those cases in the middle of the floor.'

Colvin bent down to slide the heavy cases under the bed. But the pair of them now moved at a touch.

Colvin picked one case up and shook it slightly. It emitted a muffled flapping sound, like a bat in a box. Colvin nearly spoke, but stopped himself, and stowed the cases, end on, under the unmade bed in silence.

'Make up the room, Greta,' said Mrs Royd. 'It's no use just standing about.' Colvin gathered that it was not altogether unknown for visitors to the Emancipation Hotel to be missing from their rooms all night.

But there was a further little mystery. Later that day in the bar, Colvin was accosted by the man who had helped to carry Mr Superbus's luggage.

'Look at that.' He displayed, rather furtively, something which lay in his hand.

It was a sovereign.

'He gave it me last night.'

'Can I see it?' It had been struck in Queen Victoria's reign, but gleamed like new.

'What d'you make of that?' asked the man.

'Not much,' replied Colvin, returning the pretty piece. 'But now I come to think of it, *you* can make about forty-five shillings.'

When this incident took place, Colvin was on his way to spend three or four nights in another town where lead and plumbago mining had formerly been carried on, and where he needed to consult an invaluable collection of old records which had been presented to the Public Library at the time the principal mining company went bankrupt.

On his return, he walked up the hill from the station through a thick mist, laden with coal dust and sticky smoke, and apparently in no way diminished by a bitter little wind, which chilled while hardly troubling to blow. There had been snow, and little archipelagos of slush remained on the pavements, through which the immense boots of the miners crashed noisily. The male population wore heavy mufflers and were unusually silent. Many of the women wore shawls over their heads in the manner of their grandmothers.

Mrs Royd was not in the bar, and Colvin hurried through it to his old room, where he put on a thick sweater before descending to tea. The only company consisted in two commercial travellers, sitting at the same table and eating through a heap of bread and margarine but saying nothing. Colvin wondered what had happened to Mr Superbus.

Greta entered as usual with a pot of strong tea and a plate of bread and margarine.

'Good evening, Mr Colvin. Enjoy your trip?'

'Yes, thank you, Greta. What's for tea?'

'Haddock and chips.' She drew a deep breath. 'Miss Rokeby's come... I don't think she'll care for haddock and chips do you, Mr Colvin?' Colvin looked up in surprise. He saw that Greta was trembling. Then he noticed that she was wearing a thin black dress, instead of her customary casual attire.

Colvin smiled up at her. 'I think you'd better put on something warm. It's getting colder every minute.'

But at that moment the door opened and Miss Rokeby entered.

Greta stood quite still, shivering all over, and simply staring at her. Everything about Greta made it clear that this was Miss Rokeby. Otherwise the situation was of a kind which brought to Colvin's mind the cliché about there being some mistake.

The woman who had come in was very small and slight. She had a triangular gazelle-like face, with very large dark eyes, and a mouth which went right across the lower tip of the triangle, making of her chin another, smaller triangle. She was dressed entirely in black, with a high-necked black silk sweater, and wore long black earrings. Her short dark hair was dressed like that of a faun; and her thin white hands hung straight by her side in a posture resembling some Indian statuettes which Colvin recalled but could not place.

Greta walked towards her, and drew back a chair. She placed Miss Rokeby with her back to Colvin.

'Thank you. What can I eat?' Colvin was undecided whether Miss Rokeby's voice was high or low: it was like a bell beneath the ocean.

Greta was blushing. She stood, not looking at Miss Rokeby, but at the other side of the room, shivering and reddening. Then tears began to pour down her cheeks in a cataract. She dragged at a chair, made an unintelligible sound, and ran into the kitchen

Miss Rokeby half turned in her seat, and stared after Greta. Colvin thought she looked quite as upset as Greta. Certainly she was very white. She might almost have been eighteen...

'Please don't mind. It's nerves, I think.' Colvin realized that his own voice was far from steady, and that he was beginning to blush also, he hoped only slightly.

Miss Rokeby had risen to her feet and was holding on to the back of her chair.

'I didn't say anything which could frighten her.'

It was necessary to come to the point, Colvin thought.

'Greta thinks the menu unworthy of the distinguished company.'

'What?' She turned and looked at Colvin. Then she smiled. 'Is that it?' She sat down again. 'What is it? Fish and chips?'

'Haddock. Yes.' Colvin smiled back, now full of confidence.

'Well. There it is.' Miss Rokeby made the prospect of haddock sound charming and gay. One of the commercial travellers offered to pour the other a fourth cup of tea. The odd little crisis was over.

247

But when Greta returned, her face seemed set and a trifle hostile. She had put on an ugly custard-coloured cardigan.

'It's haddock and chips.'

Miss Rokeby merely inclined her head, still smiling charmingly.

Before Colvin had finished, Miss Rokeby, with whom further conversation had been made difficult by the fact that she had been seated with her back to him, and by the torpid watchfulness of the commercial travellers, rose, bade him, 'Good evening', and left.

Colvin had not meant to go out again that evening, but curiosity continued to rise in him, and in the end he decided to clear his thoughts by a short walk, taking in the Hippodrome. Outside it had become even colder, the fog was thicker, the streets emptier.

Colvin found that the entrance to the Hippodrome had been transformed. From frieze to floor, the walls were covered with large photographs. The photographs were not framed, but merely mounted on big sheets of pasteboard. They seemed to be all the same size. Colvin saw at once that they were all portraits of Miss Rokeby.

The entrance hall was filled with fog, but the lighting within had been greatly reinforced since Colvin's last visit. Tonight the effect was mistily dazzling. Colvin began to examine the photographs. They depicted Miss Rokeby in the widest variety of costumes and make-up, although in no case was the name given of the play or character. In some Colvin could not see how he recognized her at all. In all she was alone. The number of the photographs, their uniformity of presentation, the bright swimming lights, the emptiness of the place (for the Box Office had shut) combined to make Colvin feel that he was dreaming. He put his hands before his eyes, inflamed by the glare and the fog. When he looked again, it was as if all the Miss Rokebys had been so placed that their gaze converged upon the spot where he stood. He closed his eyes tightly and began to feel his way to the door and the dimness of the street outside. Then there was a flutter of applause behind him; the evening's audience began to straggle out, grumbling at the weather; and Malnik was saying 'Hullo, old man. Nice to see you.'

Colvin gesticulated uncertainly. 'Did she bring them all with her?'

'Not a bit of it, old man. Millie found them when she opened up.'

'Where did she find them?'

'Just lying on the floor. In two whacking great parcels. Rokeby's agent, I suppose, though she appeared not to have one. Blest if I know, really, I myself could hardly shift one of the parcels, let alone two.'

Colvin felt rather frightened for a moment; but he only said: 'How do you like her?'

'Tell you when she arrives.'

'She's arrived.'

Malnik stared.

'Come back with me and see for yourself.'

Malnik seized Colvin's elbow. 'What's she look like?'

'Might be any age.'

All the time Malnik was bidding good night to patrons, trying to appease their indignation at being brought out on such a night.

Suddenly the lights went, leaving only a pilot. It illumined a photograph of Miss Rokeby holding a skull.

'Let's go,' said Malnik. 'Lock up, Frank, will you?'

'You'll need a coat,' said Colvin.

'Lend me your coat, Frank.'

*

On the short cold walk to the Emancipation Hotel, Malnik said little. Colvin supposed that he was planning the encounter before him. Colvin did ask him whether he had ever heard of a Mr Superbus, but he hadn't.

Mrs Royd was, it seemed, in a thoroughly bad temper. To Colvin it appeared that she had been drinking; and that she was one whom drink soured rather than mellowed. 'I've got no one to send,' she snapped. 'You can go up yourself, if you like. Mr Colvin knows the way.' There was a roaring fire in the bar, which after the cold outside seemed very overheated.

Outside Number Nine, Colvin paused before knocking. Immediately he was glad he had done so, because inside were voices speaking very softly. All the evening he had been remembering Mr Superbus's reference to a 'companion'.

In dumb-show he tried to convey the situation to Malnik, who peered at his efforts with a professional's dismissal of the amateur. Then Malnik produced a pocket-book, wrote in it, and tore out the page, which he thrust under Miss Rokeby's door. Having done this, he prepared to return with Colvin to the bar, and await a reply. Before they had taken three steps, however, the door was open, and Miss Rokeby was inviting them in.

To Colvin she said, 'We've met already', though without enquiring his name.

Colvin felt gratified; and at least equally pleased when he saw that the fourth person in the room was a tall, frail-looking girl with long fair hair drawn back into a tight bun. It was not the sort of companion he had surmised.

'This is Myrrha. We're never apart.'

Myrrha smiled slightly, said nothing, and sat down again. Colvin thought she looked positively wasted. Doubtless by reason of the cold, she wore heavy tweeds, which went oddly with her air of fragility.

'How well do you know the play?' asked Malnik at the earliest possible moment.

'Well enough not to play in it.' Colvin saw Malnik turn grey. 'Since you've got me here, I'll play Rosalind. The rest was lies. Do you know,' she went on, addressing Colvin, 'that this man tried to trick me? You're not in the theatre, are you?'

Colvin, feeling embarrassed, smiled and shook his head.

'*Cornelia* is a masterpiece,' said Malnik furiously. 'Nethers was a genius.'

Miss Rokeby simply said 'Was' very softly, and seated herself on the arms of Myrrha's armchair, the only one in the room. It was set before the old-fashioned gas-fire.

'It's announced. Everyone's waiting for it. People are coming from London. They're even coming from Cambridge.' Myrrha turned away her head from Malnik's wrath.

'I was told—Another English Classic. Not an out-pouring by little Jack Nethers. I won't do it.'

'*As You Like It* is only a fill-up. What more is it ever? *Cornelia* is the whole point of the Gala. Nethers was *born* in this town. Don't you understand?'

Malnik was so much in earnest that Colvin felt sorry for him. But even Colvin doubted whether Malnik's was the best way to deal with Miss Rokeby.

'Please play for me. Please.'

'Rosalind only.' Miss Rokeby was swinging her legs. They were young and lovely. There was more than one thing about this interview which Colvin did not care for.

'We'll talk it over in my office tomorrow.' Colvin identified this as a customary admission of defeat.

'This is a horrid place, isn't it?' said Miss Rokeby conversationally to Colvin.

'I'm used to it,' said Colvin, smiling. 'Mrs Royd has her softer side.'

'She's put poor Myrrha in a cupboard.'

Colvin remembered about Greta's old room upstairs.

'Perhaps she'd like to change rooms with me? I've been away and haven't even unpacked. It would be easy.'

'How kind you are! To that silly little girl! To me! And now to Myrrha! May I see?'

'Of course.'

Colvin took her into the passage. It seemed obvious that Myrrha would come also, but she did not. Apparently she left it to Miss Rokeby to dispose of her. Malnik sulked behind also.

Colvin opened the door of his room and switched on the light. Lying on his bed and looking very foolish was his copy of Bull's *Graphite and Its Uses*. He glanced round for Miss Rokeby. Then for the second time that evening, he felt frightened.

Miss Rokeby was standing in the ill-lit passage, just outside his doorway. It was unpleasantly apparent that she was terrified. Formerly pale, she was now quite white. Her hands were clenched, and she was breathing unnaturally deeply. Her big eyes were half shut, and to Colvin it seemed that it was something she *smelt* which was frightening her. This impression was so strong that he sniffed the chilly air himself once or twice, unavailingly. Then he stepped forward, and his arms were around Miss Rokeby, who was palpably about to faint. Immediately Miss Rokeby was in his arms, such emotion swept through him as he had never before known. For what seemed a long moment, he was lost in the wonder of it. Then he was recalled by something which frightened him more than anything else, though for less reason. There was a sharp sound from Number Twelve A. Mr Superbus must have returned.

Colvin supported Miss Rokeby back to Number Nine. Upon catching sight of her, Myrrha gave a small but jarring cry, and helped her on to the bed.

'It's my heart,' said Miss Rokeby. 'My absurd heart.'

Malnik now looked more black than grey. 'Shall we send for a doctor?' he enquired, hardly troubling to mask the sarcasm.

Miss Rokeby shook her head once. It was the sibling gesture to her nod.

'Please don't trouble about moving,' she said to Colvin.

Colvin, full of confusion, looked at Myrrha, who was being resourceful with smelling-salts.

'Good night,' said Miss Rokeby, softly but firmly. And as Colvin followed Malnik out of the room, she touched his hand.

Colvin passed the night almost without sleep, which was another new experience for him. A conflict of feelings about Miss Rokeby, all of them strong, was one reason for insomnia: another was the sequence of sounds from Number Twelve A. Mr Superbus seemed to spend the night in moving things about and talking to himself. At first it sounded as if he were rearranging all the furniture in his room. Then there was a period, which seemed to Colvin timeless, during which the only noise was of low and unintelligible mutterings, by no means continuous, but broken by periods of silence and then resumed as before just as Colvin was beginning to hope that all was over. Colvin wondered whether Mr Superbus was saying his prayers. Ultimately the banging about recommenced.

Presumably Mr Superbus was still dissatisfied with the arrangement of the furniture; or perhaps was returning it to its original dispositions. Then Colvin heard the sash-window thrown sharply open. He remembered the sound from the occasion when Mrs Royd had sharply shut it. After that silence continued. In the end Colvin turned on the light and looked at his watch. It had stopped.

At breakfast, Colvin asked when Mr Superbus was expected down. 'He doesn't come down,' replied Greta. 'They say he has all his meals out.'

Colvin understood that rehearsals began that day, but Malnik had always demurred at outsiders being present. Now, moreover, he felt that Colvin had seen him at an unfavourable moment, so that his cordiality was much abated. The next two weeks, in fact, were to Colvin heavy with anti-climax. He saw Miss Rokeby only at the evening meal, which, however, she was undeniably in process of converting from tea to dinner, by expending charm, will-power, and cash. Colvin participated in this improvement, as did even such few of the endless commercial travellers as wished to do so; and from time to time Miss Rokeby exchanged a few pleasant, generalities with him, though she did not ask him to sit at her table, nor did he, being a shy man, dare to invite her. Myrrha never appeared at all; and when on one occasion Colvin referred to her interrogatively, Miss Rokeby simply said, 'She pines, poor lamb,' and plainly wished to say nothing more. Colvin remembered Myrrha's wasted appearance, and concluded that she must be an invalid. He wondered if he should again offer to change rooms. After that single disturbed night, he had heard no more of Mr Superbus. But from Mrs Royd he had gathered that Mr Superbus had settled for several weeks in advance. Indeed, for the first time in years the Emancipation Hotel was doing good business.

It continued as cold as ever during all the time Miss Rokeby remained in the town, with repeated little snow storms every time the streets began to clear. The miners would stamp as they entered the bar until they seemed likely to go through to the cellar beneath; and all the commercial travellers caught colds. The two local papers, morning and evening, continued their efforts to set people against Malnik's now diminished Gala. When *Cornelia* was no longer offered, the two editors pointed out (erroneously, Colvin felt) that even now it was not too late for a pantomime: but Malnik seemed to have succeeded in persuading Miss Rokeby to reinforce *As You Like It* with a piece entitled *A Scrap of Paper* which Colvin had never heard of, but which an elderly local citizen whom the papers always consulted upon matters theatrical described as 'very old-fashioned', Malnik caused further comment by proposing to open on Christmas Eve, when the unfailing tradition had been Boxing Night.

The final week of rehearsal was marred by an exceedingly distressing incident. It happened on the Tuesday. Coming in that morning from a cold visit to the Technical Institute Library, Colvin found in the stuffy little saloon bar a number of the Tabard Players. The Players usually patronized an establishment nearer to the Hippodrome; and the fact that the present occasion was out of the ordinary was emphasized by the demeanour of the group, who were clustered together and talking in low, serious voices. Colvin knew none of the players at all well, but the group looked so distraught that, partly from curiosity and partly from compassion, he ventured to enquire of one of them, a middle-aged actor named Shillitoe to whom Malnik had introduced him, what was the matter. After a short silence, the group seemed collectively to decide upon accepting Colvin among them, and all began to enlighten him in short strained bursts of over-eloquence. Some of the references were not wholly clear to Colvin, but the substance of the story was simple.

Colvin gathered that when the Tabard Players took possession of the Hippodrome, Malnik had been warned that the 'grid' above the stage was undependable, and that scenery should not be 'flown' from it. This restriction had caused grumbling, but had been complied with until, during a rehearsal of *A Scrap of Paper*, the producer had rebelled and asked Malnik for authority to use the grid. Malnik had agreed; and two stage-hands began gingerly to pull on some of the dusty lines which disappeared into the almost complete darkness far above. Before long one of them had cried out that there was 'something up there already'. At these words, Colvin was told, everyone in the theatre fell silent. The stage-hand went on paying out line, but the stage was so ample and the grid so high that an appreciable time passed before the object came slowly into view.

The narrators stopped, and there was a silence which Colvin felt must have been like the silence in the theatre. Then Shillitoe resumed: 'It was poor old Ludlow's body. He'd hanged himself right up under the grid. Eighty feet above the floor of the stage. Some time ago, too. He wasn't in the Christmas plays, you know. Or in this week's play. We all thought he'd gone home.'

Colvin learnt that the producer had fainted right away; and, upon tactful enquiry, that Miss Rokeby had fortunately not been called for that particular rehearsal.

On the first two Sundays after her arrival, Miss Rokeby had been no more in evidence than on any other day; but on the morning of the third Sunday Colvin was taking one of his resolute lonely walks across the windy fells which surrounded the town when he saw her walking ahead of him through the snow. The snow lay only an inch or two deep upon the hillside ledge along which the path ran; and Colvin had been wondering for some time about the small footsteps which preceded him. It was the first time he had seen Miss Rokeby outside the Emancipation Hotel, but he had no doubt that it was she he saw, and his heart turned over at the sight. He hesitated; then walked faster, and soon had overtaken her. As he drew near, she stopped, turned, and faced him. Then, when she saw who it was, she seemed unsurprised. She wore a fur coat with a collar which reached almost to the tip of her nose; a fur hat; and elegant boots which laced to the knee.

'I'm glad to have a companion,' she said gravely, sending Colvin's thought to her other odd companion. 'I suppose you know all these paths well?'

'I come up here often to look for lead-workings. I'm writing a dull book on lead and plumbago mining.'

'I don't see any mines up here.' She looked around with an air of grave bewilderment.

'Lead mines aren't like coal mines. They're simply passages in hillsides.'

'What do you do when you find them?'

'I mark them on a large-scale map. Sometimes I go down them.'

'Don't the miners object?'

'There are no miners.'

A shadow crossed her face.

'I mean, not any longer. We don't mine lead any more.'

'Don't we? Why not?'

'That's a complicated story.'

She nodded. 'Will you take me down a mine?'

'I don't think you'd like it. The passages are usually both narrow and low. One of the reasons why the industry's come to an end is that people would no longer work in them. Besides, now the mines are disused, they're often dangerous.'

She laughed. It was the first time he had ever heard her do so. 'Come on.' She took hold of his arm. 'Or aren't there any mines on this particular hillside?' She looked as concerned as a child.

'There's one about a hundred feet above our heads. But there's nothing to see. Only darkness.'

'Only *darkness*,' cried Miss Rokeby. She implied that no reasonable person could want more. 'But you don't go down all these passages only to see darkness?'

'I take a flashlight.'

'Have you got it now?'

'Yes.' Colvin never went to the fells without it.

'Then that will look after *you*. Where's the mine? Conduct me.'

They began to scramble together up the steep snow-covered slope. Colvin knew all the workings round here; and soon they were in the entry.

'You see,' said Colvin. 'There's not even room to stand, and a fat person couldn't get in at all. You'll ruin your coat.'

'I'm not a fat person.' There was a small excited patch in each of her cheeks. 'But you'd better go first.'

Colvin knew that this particular working consisted simply in a long passage, following the vein of lead. He had been to the end of it more than once. He turned on his flashlight. 'I assure you, there's nothing to see,' he said. And in he went.

Colvin perceived that Miss Rokeby seemed indeed to pass along the adit without even stooping or damaging her fur hat. She insisted on going as far as possible, although near the end Colvin made a quite strenuous effort to persuade her to let them return.

'What's that?' enquired Miss Rokeby when they had none the less reached the extremity of the passage.

'It's a big fault in the limestone. A sort of cave. The miners chucked their débris down it.'

'Is it deep?'

'Some of these faults are supposed to be bottomless.'

She took the light from his hand, and, squatting down on the brink of the hole, flashed it round the depths below.

'Careful,' cried Colvin. 'You're on loose shale. It could easily slip.' He tried to drag her back. The only result was that she dropped the flashlight, which went tumbling down the great hole like a meteor, until after many seconds they heard a faint crash. They were in complete darkness.

'I'm sorry,' said Miss Rokeby's voice. 'But you did push me.'

Trying not to fall down the hole, Colvin began to grope his way back. Suddenly he had thought of Malnik, and the irresponsibility of the proceedings upon which he was engaged appalled him. He begged Miss Rokeby to go slowly, test every step, and mind her head; but her unconcern seemed complete. Colvin tripped and toiled along for an endless period of time, with Miss Rokeby always close behind him, calm, sure of foot, and unflagging. As far into the earth as this, it was both warm and stuffy. Colvin began to fear that bad air might overcome them, forced as they were to creep so laboriously and interminably. He broke out in heavy perspiration.

Suddenly he knew that he would have to stop. He could not even pretend that it was out of consideration for Miss Rokeby. He subsided upon the floor of the passage and she seated herself near him, oblivious of her costly clothes. The blackness was still complete.

'Don't feel unworthy,' said Miss Rokeby softly. 'And don't feel frightened. There's no need. We shall get out.'

Curiously enough, the more she said, the worse Colvin felt. The strange antecedents to this misadventure were with him; and, even more so, Miss Rokeby's whole fantastic background. He had to force his spine against the stone wall of the passage if he were not to give way to panic utterly and leap up screaming. Normal speech was impossible.

'Is it me you are frightened of?' asked Miss Rokeby, with dreadful percipience.

Colvin was less than ever able to speak.

'Would you like to know more about me?'

Colvin was shaking his head in the dark.

'If you'll promise not to tell anyone else.'

But, in fact, she was like a child, unable to contain her secret.

'I'm sure you won't tell anyone else... It's my helper. He's the queer one. Not me.'

Now that the truth was spoken Colvin felt a little better. 'Yes,' he said in a low, shaken voice, 'I know.'

'Oh, you know... I don't see him or—' she paused—'or encounter him, often for years at a time. Years.'

'But you encountered him the other night?'

He could feel her shudder. 'Yes... You've seen him?'

'Very briefly... How did you... encounter him first?'

'It was years ago. Have you any idea how many years?'

'I think so.'

Then she said something which Colvin never really understood; not even later, in his dreams of her. 'You know I'm not here at all, really. Myrrha's me. That's why she's called Myrrha. That's how I act.'

'How?' said Colvin. There was little else to say.

'My helper took my own personality out of me. Like taking a nerve out of a tooth. Myrrha's my personality.'

'Do you mean your soul?' asked Colvin.

'Artists don't have souls,' said Miss Rokeby. 'Personality's the word... I'm anybody's personality. Or everybody's. And when I lost my personality, I stopped growing older. Of course I have to look after Myrrha, because if anything happened to Myrrha—well, you do see,' she continued.

'But Myrrha looks as young as you do.'

'That's what she *looks*.'

Colvin remembered Myrrha's wasted face.

'But how can you live without a personality? Besides,' added Colvin, 'you seem to me to have a very strong personality.'

'I have a mask for every occasion.'

It was only the utter blackness, Colvin felt, which made this impossible conversation possible.

'What do you do in exchange? I suppose you must repay your helper in some way?'

'I suppose I must... I've never found out what way it is.'

'What else does your helper do for you?'

'He smooths my path. Rids me of people who want to hurt me. He rid me of little Jack Nethers. Jack was mad, you know. You can see it even in his photograph.'

'Did he rid you of this wretched man Ludlow?'

'I don't know. You see, I can't remember Ludlow. I think he often rids me of people that I don't know want to hurt me.'

Colvin considered.

'Can you be rid of him?'

'I've never really tried.'

'Don't you *want* to be rid of him?'

'I don't know. He frightens me terribly whenever I come near him, but otherwise... I don't know... But for him I should never have been down a lead mine.'

'How many people know all this?' asked Colvin after a pause.

'Not many. I only told you because I wanted you to stop being frightened.'

As she spoke the passage was filled with a strange sound. Then they were illumined with icy December sunshine. Colvin perceived that they were almost at the entry to the working, and supposed that the portal must have been temporarily blocked by a miniature avalanche of melting snow. Even now there was, in fact, only a comparatively small hole, through which they would have to scramble.

'I told you we'd get out,' said Miss Rokeby. 'Other people haven't believed a word I said. But now *you'll* believe me.'

Not the least strange thing was the matter-of-fact manner in which, all the way back, Miss Rokeby questioned Colvin about his researches into lead and plumbago mining, with occasionally, on the perimeter of their talk, flattering enquiries about himself; although equally strange, Colvin considered, was the matter-of-fact manner in which he answered her. Before they were back in the town he was wondering how much of what she had said in the darkness of the mine had been meant only figuratively; and after that he wondered whether Miss Rokeby had not used the circumstances to initiate an imaginative and ingenious boutade. After all, he reflected, she was an actress. Colvin's hypothesis was, if anything, confirmed when at their parting she held his hand for a moment and said: 'Remember! *No one.*'

But he resolved to question Mrs Royd in a business-like way about Mr Superbus. An opportunity arose when he encountered her after luncheon (at which Miss Rokeby had not made an appearance), reading *The People* before the fire in the saloon bar. The bar had just closed, and it was, Mrs Royd explained, the only warm spot in the house. In fact it was, as usual, hot as a kiln.

'Couldn't say, I'm sure,' replied Mrs Royd to Colvin's firm enquiry, and implying that it was neither her business nor his. 'Anyway, 'e's gone. Went last Tuesday. Didn't you notice, with 'im sleeping next to you?'

After the death of poor Ludlow (the almost inevitable verdict was suicide while of unsound mind), it was as if the papers felt embarrassed about continuing to carp at Malnik's plans; and by the opening night the editors seemed ready to extend the Christmas spirit even to Shakespeare. Colvin had planned to spend Christmas with his mother; but when he learned that Malnik's first night was to be on Christmas Eve, had been unable to resist deferring his departure until after it, despite the perils of a long and intricate railway journey on Christmas Day. With Miss Rokeby, however, he now felt entirely unsure of himself.

On Christmas Eve the town seemed full of merriment. Colvin was surprised at the frankness of the general rejoicing. The shops, as is usual in industrial districts, had long been off-setting the general drabness with drifts of Christmas cards and whirlpools of tinsel. Now every home seemed to be decorated and all the shops to be proclaiming bonus distributions and bumper share-outs. Even the queues, which were a prominent feature of these celebrations, looked more sanguine, Colvin noticed, when he stood in one of them for about half an hour in order to send Miss Rokeby some flowers, as he felt the occasion demanded. By the time he set out for the Hippodrome, the more domestically-minded citizens were everywhere quietly toiling at preparations for the morrow's revels; but a wilder minority, rebellious or homeless, were inaugurating such a carouse at the Emancipation Hotel as really to startle the comparatively retiring Colvin. He suspected that some of the bibbers must be Irish.

Sleet was slowly descending as Colvin stepped out of the sweltering bar in order to walk to the Hippodrome. A spot of it sailed gently into the back of his neck, chilling him in a moment. But notwithstanding the weather, notwithstanding the claims of the season and the former attitude of the Press, there was a crowd outside the Hippodrome such as Colvin had never previously seen there. To his great surprise, some of the audience were in evening dress; many of them had expensive cars, and one party, it appeared, had come in a closed carriage with two flashing black horses. There was such a concourse at the doors that Colvin had to stand a long time in the slowly falling sleet before he was able to join the throng which forced its way, like icing on to a cake, between the countless glittering photographs of beautiful Miss Rokeby. The average age of the audience, Colvin observed, seemed very advanced, and especially of that section of it which was in evening dress. Elderly white-haired men with large noses and carnations in their buttonholes spoke in elegant Edwardian voices to the witch-like ladies on their arms, most of whom wore hot-house gardenias.

Inside, however, the huge and golden Hippodrome looked as it was intended to look when it was still named the Grand Opera House. From his gangway seat in the stalls Colvin looked backwards and upwards at the gilded satyrs and bacchantes who wantoned on the dress-circle balustrade; and at the venerable and orchidaceous figures who peered above them. The small orchestra was frenziedly playing selections from *L'Étoile du Nord*. In the gallery distant figures, unable to find seats, were standing watchfully. Even the many boxes, little used and dusty, were filling up. Colvin could only speculate how this gratifying assembly had been collected. But then he was on his feet for the National Anthem, and the faded crimson and gold curtain, made deceivingly splendid by the footlights, was about to rise.

The play began, and then: 'Dear Celia, I show more mirth than I am mistress of, and would you yet I were merrier? Unless you could teach me to forget a banished father, you must not learn me how to remember any extraordinary pleasure.'

Colvin realized that in his heart he had expected Miss Rokeby to be good, to be moving, to be lovely; but the revelation he now had was something he could never have expected because he could never have imagined it; and before the conclusion of Rosalind's first scene in boy's attire in the Forest, he was wholly and terribly bewitched.

No one coughed, no one rustled, no one moved. To Colvin, it seemed as if Miss Rokeby's magic had strangely enchanted the normally journeyman Tabard Players into miracles of judgment. Plainly her spell was on the audience also; so that when the lights came up for the interval, Colvin found that his eyes were streaming, and felt not chagrin, but pride.

The interval was an uproar. Even the bells of fire-engines pounding through the wintry night outside could hardly be heard above the din. People spoke freely to unknown neighbours, groping to express forgotten emotions. 'What a prelude to Christmas!' everyone said. Malnik was proved right in one thing.

During the second half, Colvin, failing of interest in Sir Oliver Martext's scene, let his eyes wander round the auditorium. He noticed that the nearest dress-circle box, previously unoccupied, appeared to be unoccupied no longer. A hand, which, being only just above him, he could see was gnarled and hirsute, was tightly gripping the box's red velvet curtain. Later in the scene between Silvius and Phebe (Miss Rokeby having come and gone meanwhile), the hand was still there, and still gripping tightly; as it was (after Rosalind's big scene with Orlando) during the Forester's song. At the beginning of Act V, there was a rush of feet down the gangway, and someone was crouching by Colvin's seat. It was Greta. 'Mr Colvin! There's been a fire. Miss Rokeby's friend jumped out of the window. She's terribly hurt. Will you tell Miss Rokeby?'

'The play's nearly over,' said Colvin. 'Wait for me at the back.' Greta withdrew, whimpering.

After Rosalind's Epilogue the tumult was millennial. Miss Rokeby, in Rosalind's white dress, stood for many seconds not bowing but quite still and unsmiling, with her hands by her sides as Colvin had first seen her. Then as the curtain rose and revealed the rest of the company, she began slowly to walk backwards upstage. Door-keepers and even stage-hands, spruced up for the purpose, began to bring armfuls upon armfuls of flowers, until there was a heap, a mountain of them in the centre of the stage, so high that it concealed Miss Rokeby's figure from the audience. Suddenly a bouquet flew through the air from the dress-circle box. It landed at the very front of the heap. It was a hideous dusty laurel wreath, adorned with an immense and somewhat tasteless purple bow. The audience were yelling for Miss Rokeby like Dionysians; and the company, flagging from unaccustomed emotional expenditure, and plainly much scared, were looking for her; but in the end the stage-manager had to lower the Safety Curtain and give orders that the house be cleared.

*

Back at the Emancipation Hotel, Colvin, although he had little title, asked to see the body.

'You wouldn't ever recognize her,' said Mrs Royd. Colvin did not pursue the matter.

The snow, falling ever more thickly, had now hearsed the town in silence.

'She didn't 'ave to do it,' wailed on Mrs Royd. 'The brigade had the flames under control. And tomorrow Christmas Day!'

A FALL OF SNOW

James Turner

FIRST PUBLISHED IN *STAIRCASE TO THE SEA* (1974)

James Ernest Turner was born in Foots Cray in Kent in 1909. After attending the University of Oxford he trained as a gardener and in 1947 leased a piece of land in Norfolk to work as a smallholding. The land in question was the site of the former Borley Rectory, dubbed 'the most haunted house in England', and the location of multiple reported ghost sightings and instances of poltergeist activity. Whilst living there, Turner and his wife Lucie saw and heard several unexplained phenomena, and Turner was involved in excavations at the site of Borley Church which uncovered bones buried under the altar.

Turner had some success in the early 1940s as a poet and published a number of novels throughout the 1950s and 60s. He also wrote a book about Borley, and edited *The Fourth Ghost Book* (part of a series established by Lady Cynthia Asquith in the 1920s). 'A Fall of Snow' was published in his short story collection *Staircase to the Sea* the year before his death in 1975. Despite its publication long after the golden age of the ghost story in the late nineteenth and early twentieth century, it has a feel of this earlier time and is extremely effective. —TK

It happens every year about Christmas time. I have only to go into a shop to buy my Christmas cards and there is bound to be one of boys tobogganing in deep snow. Rather old-fashioned, I suppose, though whether there are fashions in snowfalls I don't know. Nevertheless, to me, these cards bring it all back. There is generally a farmhouse in the background, an open gate with a robin in his crimson winter coat, great swags of snow on the hedgerows. In the centre of the picture these two boys are flying downhill, waving their hands, their faces like red apples. Of course, it is an idealized sort of Dickensian picture for of one thing I'm certain. The boys careering downhill in the picture would never have had the time to wave, they would have been clinging too tightly to the toboggan.

Further it is an ideal Christmas picture, at least for my part of the country, Cornwall, where we rarely get enough snow to make a snow man, let alone toboggan. There had only been one year, since I've lived in Cornwall, when the snow was so thick that I was able actually to go on to the beach, in the bay near my home, and make a snowball and throw it into the sea. It was 1963, that very bad winter, and what I did must, I feel, be some sort of a record. So that these kind of Christmassy pictures are pleasant enough to send to a friend, but scarcely real.

Yet what I remember when I see such a card is that it did, once, happen to me; it did once become very real indeed. And the two boys in that faraway 'real' picture are David, my cousin, and myself. Of course, it is not so much the picture of two boys tobogganing that causes me, even today, to shiver slightly. It is the nature of fear itself. For fear is a very odd thing. I mean that now, today, when I am so much older, I'm not in the least afraid of snow. It's merely a nuisance which has to be cleared away from the front door. It means cold weather which I can't abide. Yet I'm still afraid of what happened, so long ago, in that snowfall, in East Anglia.

But, then, that Christmas of 1922, when my uncle invited me to spend the holiday at his home near Orford, in Suffolk, snow was very much a novelty to me. It is difficult to explain exactly, most childhood fears are when you look back at them from middle age. But, when I remember that fear each year, I can only explain it by saying that something was waiting for me behind the snowstorm. Was it, I have often wondered, because I was fifteen and young for my age? Was it because snow was so great a novelty to me, whereas to David who lived all the year in East Anglia and therefore knew the land well, as well as being used to snow, nothing happened.

It really began when I arrived at my uncle's house. I had gone straight from school instead of going back to Cornwall, since my parents had gone to New York on business. It seemed odd, at first, to be going to Liverpool Street station rather than to Paddington. When I left Sussex the sun was shining, but the sky gradually clouded over and by the time I had crossed London and the train left Liverpool Street, a light fall of snow covered the station roof. I was thrilled. If snow did come in any quantity this was going to be a Christmas to remember.

My uncle's car was waiting for me at Ipswich. I felt very grand being whisked through the town and into the lanes, through Woodbridge and past the lonely farmhouses towards Orford.

Although this was Christmas week no one else but me and the chauffeur seemed to be about in that desolate landscape until we passed the old and secret wood of Staverton, where St Edmund is reputed to have been martyred by the Danes. Then a couple, a man and a woman, emerged from beneath those gnarled and twisted oak and holly trees, with great bunches of red berries in their arms. It was a further sign of a good Christmas.

As the car sped on I looked back. They were walking in the centre of the road after us. I had the uncanny feeling, in the warmth of the car, that neither of them was real. And then they were gone in a turn of the road. So far, however, no snow had fallen here. But the lights from the house—every window seemed to be illuminated—fell on the gravel drive. The lawns were glittering with frost.

My aunt, however, knew what was coming. She welcomed me in the hall, beside the stuffed bear with uplifted arms and paws on which lay a silver tray for visiting cards. Her first words gave me hope.

'Nicky, dear, it's lovely to see you. David will be pleased. And I really believe we shall have snow for Christmas Day. You've brought it with you. How clever you are! Now you must come at once and get really warm. You must be frozen.'

I hardly remembered my uncle's house. It's true I had been in it once before but that was in summer. Then, of course, I had run all over the farms helping, as I thought, with the animals; I had gone off with David often enough to the sea at Orford and Bawdsey and I knew of the merman who had, years ago, come out of the sea and stayed awhile at Orford itself. He had been rather a pet with the inhabitants until, one night, he had slipped away again across the marshes to the shore. It was said that the fact that the local vicar made him go to church, and that he could not bear the long sermons he was forced to listen to any longer, decided him to leave. From my own experience of church, I did not blame him. David and I had, also, explored the old castle keep and the numerous Martello towers along the coast.

What I did remember, however, was that the farmhouse was a tall and impressive Queen Anne house; that it had many rooms from the huge drawing room, the study, the dining-room, to the bedrooms and attics. The maidservants—you have to remember that this was in the 'old-fashioned' days of 1922, when servants were still kept,—lived in these attics and went down the back stairs to the kitchen and sculleries, pantries and dairies.

That first time I had been ten years old. Even so I was conscious of the warmth and comfort of real wealth, even if farming was in a bad state, especially in East Anglia, though it was to get even worse later. The point was that my uncle did not depend on his farms for his income. That came from his business enterprises. I did not know, then, what they were. Truth to tell I didn't care. All I knew was that it, Scarletts it was called, with its endless acres, its workmen and farmers, was to me a wonderful playground. And that David was a wonderful companion, making up new adventures each day and telling the most absurd lies each night as we lay in bed in his bedroom on the first floor overlooking the woods back into the heart of Suffolk.

This evening, four nights before Christmas 1922, what I remembered of the house was quite changed. The interior was alight with welcome. Whatever was to happen outside, in the house there was safety and gaiety. The staircase was festooned with branches of green holly and ivy, paper-chains and Chinese lanterns alternated with bunches of mistletoe and the sideboard groaned under the weight of fruit and nuts. Furthermore the house seemed full of servants. It didn't take much intelligence to sense all the other good things, plum puddings, mince pies, York hams, that Mrs Horsely, the cook, had up her sleeve for Christmas Day itself.

While I was warming myself before the huge log fire in the drawing room my uncle came in. He was a short man, thick-set, rather Dickensian. He was smoking a cigar and his first remark was what I should have expected of him. He always spoke in a ponderous manner, weighing his words as if everything he said was of the utmost importance. Now, of course, when I look back at him, it is easy to see him at the head of a boardroom table, or deciding the fate of the companies under his command. But then he was a person I should not have cared to cross.

After I had stood up and thanked him for asking me to come to stay he shook hands with me in a formal manner and went on, 'I regret, Nicholas,' (he would never have dreamed of calling me Nicky), 'I regret very much the holly this year has few, I might almost say, no berries. And Christmas, you'll agree, depends largely for its full effect on red holly berries.'

Actually I would have thought, and did even then, that it was brandy which really made Christmas for him. Neither did I dare to tell him that I had seen two people emerge from Staverton Forest, so near his property, with berried holly in their hands. He might have sacked one of his employees for not knowing the right place to go.

'And snow, uncle,' I exclaimed, catching sight of my cousin, David, coming down the stairs. 'It was snowing a little in London. Surely it will come this way soon?'

'Your aunt,' my uncle said, 'who knows all about winds and weather, seems to think it will. She is making preparations for it, too.' And with that he walked out of the room and, no doubt thinking that he had done all that could be expected of him towards a nephew of fifteen, shut himself into his study.

I suppose it was just after eleven that we went to bed that first night. I was to sleep in David's room. We were hardly undressed when he said excitedly, 'You on, Nick?' I had no idea what he was talking about but I was not going to show myself a coward in front of him.

'Yes, of course. But what do you mean?'

'You haven't been here at Christmas before, have you? Well, we're going to raid the servants. The young ones at least.' He was laughing and rolling up one long football stocking into a ball and thrusting it into the foot of another, making a fairly soft, primitive club.

'But you might hurt someone with that,' I said.

'Nonsense, Nick,' he threw the 'club' across the bed to me, 'it will only give them a fright. Couldn't hurt them.' He smiled in what I thought was a rather nasty manner and brought his wadded stocking down with a thump on the bed. 'We do this every year,' he went on, 'What's more, they'll be expecting us. And there's generally some chap from school staying. None of 'em could come this year, though.' I felt his contempt for me as a substitute. He banged the waddy, as he called it, down on the bed again. He laughed once more, 'We'll have to be careful we don't get hurt ourselves.'

Although it seemed silly to me I followed him on to the dark landing. He flashed a torch, ran up the attic stairs silently and stood outside the second door on the right of the corridor.

'We don't have to worry about old Horsely, the cook. She's snoring her head off at the end of the corridor. Anyway she never wakes up.' He turned to me and whispered, 'We'll burst

in and run straight across the room, lashing out with our wad-
dies and, then, out again, like a whirlwind. Don't waste any time
once we're inside.' I stood shivering outside the door in pyjamas
and dressing gown, excited at the adventure and wrought up by
David's mood.

As he burst open the door the light went on. Far from us just
running across the room, delivering a few well-aimed blows, and out
again, we were taken entirely by surprise. The maids were waiting
for us. But so great was our impetus that we were amongst the three
of them before we could stop. The noise of laughter and David's
war-whoops must have been terrific. I felt my club wrenched from
my hand. I was tripped and fell across the bed. The lights suddenly
went out and I felt myself firmly held down. I had no idea what had
happened to David or what was to happen to me.

All I now really remember, because it was the first time it had
happened to me, was that when the lights went up again, Helen,
one of the housemaids, was holding me down and laughing at me.
I was vaguely aware of my uncle shouting at us from below to be
quiet. I tried to get up from Helen's bed. But I was too firmly held.
Indeed, this was David's error of tactics. He forgot that all the maids
had to do was to get hold of our arms and we would be helpless
to wield our weapons.

'Oh, no, master Nicholas,' Helen was saying as I heard my uncle
roar again. 'You've lost the battle and you'll have to pay. Like this.'
I felt her hot lips on mine. She kissed me three times before she
released me, sweet, gentle kisses. 'Now go,' she said, taking away
the lovely warmth of her arms. 'And happy Christmas to you.'

I remember I ran out of their bedroom, between the other
two beds, with all of them laughing, my face burning. The whole
episode—it shows you the kind of escapade David got up to—had

hardly taken more than ten minutes. Nevertheless, even now, I cannot forget Helen's face that night and the warmth of her kisses. Perhaps I would have forgotten if the snow had not come.

And while we were asleep it did come. No one heard it, no one was kept awake by its coming. But when I looked out of the bedroom window before dressing to go down to breakfast, there it was. The miracle, which had begun at Liverpool Street station, was now clear to us all. I was caught up in the wonder of it and hardly heard David call out, 'Hurry up, Nick, and get dressed. Father's driving us over to Orlik's Farm to get the turkey and I bet we'll be able to toboggan. It's colossally thick.'

I did dress quickly. No doubt the smell of bacon and eggs coming up from the dining room would have hurried me anyway. I sat down between David and my aunt, and Helen brought me a plate of beautiful breakfast. She was smiling at me as if we shared a secret. I suppose, in a rather schoolboy manner, I had fallen in love with her.

The snow was still a wonder when we got into the car. The very suddenness of its coming, as it were, over the fields and woods behind the house; the amazing difference its coming made to everything; the joy of living inside a house and being able to run out into a world of icing sugar, made its arrival the supreme Christmas present. To me this landscape of gleaming white increased the mysteriousness of the countryside. It did more. Now that I was actually out in it, it frightened me.

For it was while my uncle was interviewing Andrews, his tenant at Orlik's Farm, and examining the fallen roof of one of the barns that David and I first got out into this whiteness. I was suddenly lost. I see that now. That this vast expanse of white had torn away the edges of my familiar world. Where before I knew my way about, now everything, the fields, the trees, the church, even the cottages on my uncle's estate, was strange and terrifying. Every landmark was changed.

David had, of course, already formed one of his mad schemes. The snow did not frighten him, he saw nothing at all strange in it, only a phenomenon laid on for his special benefit, only a natural event against which to pit his strength. He had the idea of pulling out, into the untrodden snow, the top half of a pigsty door and converting it into a toboggan. I went to help him lift it to where the field began to slope downwards to the valley below. Nothing could have made me tell him of my fears. In fact, I was rather proud that he considered me capable of helping him. The battle we had lost the night before was never mentioned.

'You sit in front, Nick,' he said, throwing himself, in a professional manner, full length at the back, 'I'll steer. I'm an expert at it.'

Even as I did what he told me I recalled how, last night, as we stood outside the maid's door, his confidence had led him into error.

Our craft, imbued all at once with a life of its own, sprang across the snow silently and with gathering speed. For one crazy moment it turned and twisted like a top, until, either under its own weight or David's feet, it righted its course. We shot downhill at what seemed to me a terrific speed. We were alone, cruising on a white sea, a vast opalescent ocean with land before us in the shape of a gate-opening between two ends of a hedge. Cold air was tearing into my lungs. My whole body was ecstatic with the cold and the fright of speed. I frantically grasped the iron ring used to open the door, when it was in place. In a mad dream of pleasure and terror I heard David's voice giving the command, as it were, from the bridge. 'I'm going to steer through the gate. Don't move. Hold on and keep your feet in.'

The sun, low over the approaching hedge, was burning with one great eye at me. The frail craft that we were adrift upon tore across the snow and, with an immense surge of power, drilled its way through the hedge-opening, through the massive banks of hedge-snow. Shooting up the far hill it came to a stop. It was then that I felt the pain in my leg and the terror in my mind. Of the two the terror was the worst.

I bit back a cry. David was already off the wooden door and preparing to drag it back up the hill for a second ride. He looked at me, where I was still lying in the snow.

'Hey,' he said, contemptuously, 'Get up, Nick. Help me pull this thing to the top again. I'll show you something even better.'

I was astonished that he could be so calm, that he made no reference to what I had seen, for, surely, he must have seen it, too. 'I can't, David,' I said, 'I'm afraid I can't. It's my leg. Something happened when we shot through the gate.'

For one brief moment I saw the look of anger on his face and, then, either from the sight of so much blood on the snow, or because of the sharpness of the pain, I fainted. I gather, because David told me afterwards, that I called out to him. 'Get help for Helen. She's by the gate.'

I don't remember being taken back to my uncle's house. David told me that they, my uncle and Andrews from the farm, carried me to the car. And it turned out that I had not broken my leg after all. There must have been an iron spike on the gate, concealed by the snow, and it had ripped a long deep wound in my calf as we shot through. It bled profusely. My aunt's doctor came and put in twelve stitches. But when I awoke in bed, in one of the guest rooms, not in David's, warm and protected, it was not the accident to my leg which worried me. It was what had happened to Helen.

She was lying against the hedge as we rushed through, a widening pool of blood issuing from her head and matting her hair. Her eyes were staring, as if she were appealing to me for help. She was wearing a thin summer dress. In the short time I saw her I was not only horrified by her accident but also by the fact that she was out in this cold weather with no coat on. She must have been walking across the field (though why, when she would have more than her share of work back at the house, with everyone so busy?), and slipped in some way and hit her head on the same iron projection which had ripped open the calf of my leg. She, like me, would have fainted from loss of blood. But now here, in bed, I knew with a certainty I could not deny, that Helen was dead, that help did not come in time to save her.

I had expected something horrible to happen. I was convinced that this 'miracle' of snow which had so excited me when I could look at it from the house or the car, was malevolent. The unnaturalness of it, to one who was not used to it, was frightening. It, the snow, did not want me out in it. I was uneasy the moment I went into it with David. Unlike him I was not master of every situation. Nor was I able, as he was, to create situations which I could command. He would never have felt that something was hidden in this all-obscuring white blanket, suffocating, waiting to rush out at him in the same way that an open door at the head of a dark staircase may conceal something ready to spring out at your approach.

I can explain it in no other way but, from the second the toboggan began to rush downhill, I saw the features of this threat rushing up to meet me as I was rushing to meet it. And then there was no stopping. And, indeed, I had been right, for here I lay in bed when I should have been enjoying the final preparations for Christmas. And Helen was dead.

I was, too, acutely embarrassed at being such a nuisance. I almost wept at the thought that, by my ineffectiveness or stupidity as David would have called it, I was spoiling Christmas for every one else. I did not know that my aunt paid me several visits before I came out of the anaesthetic, but she was beside me when I did.

'Is it very painful, Nicky, dear?' she asked, 'Because if so, the doctor says that you can have a pill to ease it.'

'No, Aunt Amy.' I was propped on pillows and, I daresay, I looked white and wan. I put out my hand and touched hers as if, by so doing, I could grasp her protection. For this was the whole point of what had happened. The pain in my leg did not matter. I wasn't going to let her think that I couldn't stand it. 'But, please,' I asked, 'did they get to Helen in time? Was she still alive?'

My aunt smiled. She must have thought that I was still wandering under the effects of the anaesthetic.

'Helen, dear, there's nothing wrong with Helen. At least I hope not, we depend on her a great deal at a time like this. She's a good girl.'

'But she was there in the snow. I saw her. She'd had an accident. She'd hit her head.'

'Where, dear?'

'By the gate. Just as we rushed through. It was horrible. She was lying there in a pool of blood. Did uncle manage to save her?'

I suppose what I was saying must have sounded melodramatic to my aunt. She smiled again and pulled the sheets up to my chin.

'Nicky, you're not to worry about such things. You've been dreaming. A nasty dream, I agree, but when one hurts oneself and loses a lot of blood as you have, and then had an anaesthetic, you do have funny dreams.' She got up from the bed. 'All you have to do is to get strong again so that we can have you with us on Christmas Day.'

'But, Aunt, I did see her, I did. And she was hurt.'

'Well we can soon prove it was all a dream, my dear. Besides, weren't you and David up in the maids' room last night? You made a great deal of noise and I'm not sure that I approve of it at all.'

I suddenly remembered how Helen had held me, then, and the warmth of her arms. And now she was dead. I could not hold back my tears. It was obvious that my aunt thought me too weak to be told the truth. 'I'll send her up with a cup of cocoa,' she said, 'That'll do you good. You see.'

As she shut the door I don't think I expected to see Helen come in, a kind of resuscitated corpse. In my still fuddled state I thought my aunt, too, was playing a macabre joke on me. It must have been ten minutes later that I heard the knock on the bedroom door. I shrank back into the bed-clothes in fear.

Helen came in carrying a tray. I must have stared at her in my fright.

'Master Nicholas,' she laughed, 'whatever's the matter? You look as if you'd seen a ghost.' She put the tray down beside my bed as I gasped out. 'Is it really you, Helen?'

'Of course it is, Master Nicholas. Here, take my hand. You'll soon find out.'

I did take her hand. It was warm and strong. She was laughing as she had laughed the night before. 'There,' she said, 'I'm flesh and blood, aren't I?'

'But, but...' I stammered out, realizing that what my aunt had said was true. It *was* all a dream. I had not seen Helen in the snow covered with blood, dead. She was very much alive.

'But nothing,' she said, 'You hurry up and get that leg well again or Christmas will be spoiled. And, hey, let go my hand, I've work to do, you know. Can't lie about in bed all day like some I know.'

'Helen,' I asked, 'Helen, it was last night David and I played that silly joke, wasn't it?'

'It was. Very silly, too, since we knew all about it and expected you.'

'And you did kiss me, didn't you? Three times?'

'Well, Master Nicholas, that was all a bit of fun really, wasn't it?' I noticed that she was blushing.

'Then,' I begged, leaning towards her, 'Kiss me once again. It's important to me.'

She patted my hand gently. 'Whatever next?' She laughed, 'Just suppose your aunt was to come in while we were at it?'

'She won't,' I said, 'and even if she did I think she'd understand.'

'Well,' she laughed again, knowing nothing of my reasons for asking her to kiss me, 'if it will make you better quickly then, here.' She leaned over and kissed me as warmly as she had the night before. When she had gone I closed my eyes. So, after all, it was only hallucination.

What still worried me, however, was the strangeness of the occurrence and why I should have 'dreamed' that I saw something in the snow that wasn't there, a semblance of Helen dead. Because my life, up to then, had been completely normal. I was a normal boy who often trembled in mock fear of the supernatural. Because, for all my aunt said, for all Helen's kiss, I was not deceived. I knew that I had seen her in the snow as the iron cut into my leg.

Like any other boy I expected ghost stories at Christmas, that was the time for them. What I had not expected, and now feared, was that such things should actually become real, could come out of some secret place and threaten every thread of normal life. I was convinced, as I sipped the cocoa Helen had brought me, that for a moment in the snow out there, I had touched the rim of another, hidden world which had nothing to do with such things as school life, holidays, friendships. I was beginning to see, in a very immature way, that there were other realities beneath the life I lived so unthinkingly. I hardly heard my aunt say, when she came to visit me again, 'You know what, Nicky, the snow isn't going to last long. I'm so sorry. The wind has changed back to the south.'

Far from missing any festivities I became what my uncle, in his ponderous way, called 'the centre of interest.' He even went so far as to suggest that I was a bit of a hero and David himself was almost—but not quite—put in the shade.

As I fell asleep the night before, when my aunt left me with her weather predictions, the house was full of noise. I heard my uncle go to the front door and invite inside the company of waits who were doing their best with 'Noel'. David told me that his father had brewed a special bowl of punch for them. Two female cousins had arrived and already a dance for New Year's Eve was being talked about.

In the excitement of presents, the Christmas tree, the huge turkey which my uncle carved with so much skill, I forgot what had happened two days ago. When Helen and the other maids were ushered in by Mrs Horsley, to drink the health of the company, I no longer worried about what I thought I had seen. Time, as always on Christmas Day when I was young, passed so swiftly that I hardly noticed it. Almost before I realized it my aunt was ordering me back to bed. My uncle and David carried me up stairs. I fell asleep at once. It shows what a normal kind of boy I was, for it never occurred to me that I should have any further bad dreams.

When I woke I lay for some minutes listening. Something was beating against the window panes. I was conscious, too, that something was missing and yet, at the same time, I was filled with an amazing, overwhelming happiness. I looked at the chest of drawers where the presents I had been given were spread out like a shop window. But the explanation of my happiness was not there. It was some greater miracle. I got up and, with great care, put my injured leg to the floor. I could walk haltingly, clutching the edge of the table. I drew myself to the window.

I caught my breath at the sight which met my eyes for, magically it seemed, the snow had disappeared and the noise I had heard was rain. A warm wind was blowing and everything, the stables, the church, the chimney pots of the cottages, the trees themselves, was clearly outlined under the dawn-light. My aunt had been right. As if someone had pulled off a white dustsheet from a roomful of furniture, the countryside was again visible. Now there was nowhere for anything to lurk, no spot so obscured by snow that it could hold a threat. Once again the world was familiar and safe.

I pulled up the window and leaned out into the warm rain which you sometimes get in late December. I watched a curl of smoke rise from a cottage chimney. Someone had lighted a fire. Christmas, when nothing really bad could happen, had even defeated the snow itself.

By the middle of January I was back in Cornwall.

*

I spent the next two Christmases with my parents who had returned
from the States. In fact, one Christmas Day it was so warm that I
bathed in Treyanon Bay, just below our house. I hardly remembered
the contrast from the Christmas of 1922.

Now it was the summer term of 1924. I was beginning to enjoy
school and had recently been made a prefect. Probably, as I was
seventeen and already thinking of following David to Oxford, not
before time. I think it was a Thursday in the middle of July when
Thompson, the head of my house and a great friend, called out to
me as we passed in the long study corridor, 'See your uncle's got
his name in the *Telegraph*.'

'What do you mean?'

'Well,' he laughed and walked on, 'Seems that he's been killing
off his maids.'

I ran to the papers which were always laid out on a table in the
Common Room. There it was on the front page. I recognized the
picture at once. I had seen it before, though then snow covered
that particular field. And although the photograph did not show
much of her face, I knew, at once, that it was Helen. I recognized
the summer dress she was wearing as she lay beside the gate. In
death she was that small, woebegone figure I had seen, in the snow,
over two years ago. 'The body of Helen Simpson,' I read, unable to
repress my shivering, holding on to the table tightly, so vivid were
the pictures of what I had once seen in the snow,

> a maidservant in the household of Sir Thomas May, the finan-
> cier, was found at about eleven o'clock yesterday morning,
> beside a gate at Orlik's Farm, owned by Sir Thomas, by his
> tenant, Mr James Andrews.

A farm hand, assumed to be her lover, has been arrested and charged with her murder. The police are anxious to interview a boy of about fifteen whom Mr Andrews says ran off as he approached the body of the girl.